A DARING ENCOUNTER

"I had thought, Miss Somers," Ruxart said, tight-lipped, "that you had chosen not to dance this evening."

"Indeed, my lord, such was my intention. But as Mr. Fletcher overcame my every objection . . ."

"I had not realized my cousin could be so determined," he cut in with faint derision. "Come, Miss Somers, I believe the next dance shall be mine."

Beneath the gleaming mirrors, they paused and faced one another. His gloved hand clasped hers and the room dissolved into a kaleidoscope of colors. A startling tremor of desire passed between them as he took her in his arms and twirled her into a blur of time and essence. Jane saw nothing but the dark passion burning in his eyes; she heard nothing but the erratic leaping of her heartbeat; she felt nothing but the heated touch of his hand resting on her waist.

The music faded to stillness. Ruxart stood motionless, staring at her. Then, abruptly, he turned and strode away.

Wager on Love

BY PRUDENCE MARTIN

ZEBRA BOOKS
KENSINGTON PUBLISHING CORP.

ZEBRA BOOKS

are published by

Kensington Publishing Corp.
475 Park Avenue South
New York, N.Y. 10016

First printing: April 1985

Printed in the United States of America

For Martin, with love

Chapter One

The sporty curricle ripped neatly through the arched gateway of Kerrington Keep and pulled to an abrupt halt amidst a fine spray of gravel.

Pursing his lips in an admiring whistle, a thin groom jumped from the back of the vehicle and ran to hold the heads of two splendidly matched grays. The driver to whom this wordless compliment had been addressed threw down the ribbons and leapt nimbly to the ground. From the curly beaverskin hat perched jauntily atop his black hair to the gleaming Hessians on his feet, the gentleman looked every inch the Corinthian as he mounted the imposing marble steps up to the Keep's grand entrance two at a time.

A collection of servants lined to greet the darkly handsome man who strode briskly into the drafty Great Hall, dropping his kid gloves, many-caped greatcoat and beaver hat each into the hands of a different footman. At the end of this row of liveried men stood a solemn figure of indeterminate age who had stood thus to meet him for as long as the Viscount Ruxart could remember.

"Welcome, my lord," said that venerable with a creaky bow.

"Hullo, Leaming," responded the viscount. "Does the old curmudgeon await me?"

There was a flash of a twinkle in the old servant's eye which was reflected in his lordship's. "Yes, my lord. The earl desires to see you immediately in his library."

Though he well knew the way, Ruxart followed the ancient up the wide stairway to wait restively in a polished, panelled hall while Leaming announced his presence to the Earl of Kerrington. Left to kick his heels, the viscount gazed fondly about him, appreciating the effect of the classical archways cut into the wall, each giving rest to a fine statuette. Those acquainted with Nicholas Armytage would have been amazed at the warmth shining in those large ebony eyes, for the gleam beneath the heavy lids was usually coolly cynical. But within the walls of the Keep, Ruxart generally shed the sardonic mask he wore among the *ton*.

Kerrington Keep had become Ruxart's home when his parents had been tragically killed nearly twenty years before. Their coach had overturned in a severe summer storm the year of his eighth birthday; all that remained of them in his memories were dim images of a vivacious, handsome pair. A feminine scent and tinkling laugh came to mind as he stood waiting and Ruxart nearly heard his mother's soft voice saying, "Not now, darling! You'll smudge my gown! Run along with Nurse." He could almost feel those delicate white hands pushing him firmly away as they had so often done, and his jaw clenched.

The frown lingered as Leaming returned to escort him into the lion's den. Seated in a heavy wingback chair before a blazing fire, an elderly man perused a long, much-crossed letter. He did not acknowledge his grandson's presence, but left the tall young man standing. Only the tense flexing of his cheek muscles showed the viscount's annoyance with this ploy.

At last Kerrington waved the viscount to a matching chair opposite. "I must account myself fortunate, indeed," began the earl on a crackling drawl, "for though my grandson does not choose to honor me with frequent visits, I never fail to hear of him. His activities keep half the London tongues clacking!" He tapped the parchment of the letter with one long, thin fingertip. "I trust Mrs. Manderley was not too disconsolate to lose your company," he finished dryly.

The viscount lifted one straight black brow. "Surely you did not summon me from London to lecture me about my mistress!"

"Nor did I summon you here to be impertinent, Ruxart!" returned the old man in the hard tone that never failed to silence the younger lord. After a lengthy pause during which the earl stared keenly at his grandson, he asked conversationally, "When do you anticipate your meeting with Manderley?"

"Sir?"

"I do not fancy Manderley will long tolerate your indiscreet handling of his wife."

"I shall not kill him, sir," said Ruxart in a voice of disinterest, "if that is your worry."

Kerrington studied the viscount's face gravely, misliking the lines of dissipation beginning to mar the youthful set of his wide mouth and creasing the corners of his large black eyes. The jaw was still firm in the squared face, but the pallor washing over it caused the earl to retort more intensely than he had intended. "Manderley is a fair shot, and it is not inconceivable that *he* should kill *you*!"

The youth shrugged, boredom shuddering his face as he gazed down into the flickering fire.

"And, of course, if you do not manage to end your life over one of your many light-skirts, you will no doubt manage to do it in the reckless manner in which you drive. Still going hell for leather with those grays of yours?"

"The finest pair of high-goers in England cannot be driven like some commonplace cattle, sir."

"I would have you take more care, Nicholas!"

9

The use of his given name brought Ruxart's head up. A crease marked his brow as he examined his grandfather's thin, lined face beneath the powdery white hair. He saw the old man's vivid blue eyes filled with concern, yet hardened with the same determination Nicholas had known since he was in short coats. It was this strong and loving man who had first set him upon a horse, given him his first snuffbox, eased him to bed after his first bout of drinking. With a gentle warmth that was but seldom heard from him, Ruxart said, "You need not worry, sir. I assure you I shall take care."

The elder lord set his lips in a thin line. "An Armytage has governed Kerrington since the Conquest and I desire to see the title secured before I meet my maker, Ruxart—or before some jealous husband sends you to yours! It's time for you to marry and beget Kerrington an heir!"

"My Aunt Frances—" began Ruxart.

"Paugh! I won't have any of Fanny's brood taking over the Keep! How my own daughter could produce such a pack of fools is more than I can fathom!" The earl leaned toward his grandson and said firmly, "You've watched society's belles pass by year after year and turned your back upon them all. I tell you, it is time—nay, past time—for you to marry. Pick one and be done with it!"

"Dare I point out, sir, that I am not yet thirty?"

"You'll take a wife this season, Ruxart!" snapped the earl.

"And if I do not, sir?" asked the viscount slowly.

"I should very much dislike having to select one for you," came the harsh answer, "but should I be put to that effort, I would not hesitate to publish the banns as well."

An amused spark lit Ruxart's dark eyes as he inquired in an interested tone, "Have you a bride in mind? Or will just any woman do?"

His grandfather reflected upon the dancing flames for a moment. "Barnhurst's youngest might do very well," he mused.

"Lucinda Barnhurst!" exclaimed Ruxart in disbelief. "My

god, sir, she's at least ten stone and she squints besides! You cannot be serious!"

"Serious is precisely what I am, Nicholas," the earl returned decisively. "I shan't be alive much longer and I mean to see the Armytage line continued before I go."

Ruxart came to bend over his grandfather's thin, bluish hand. "You shall most likely outlive us all, sir. But since you wish for it, I shall pick out a chit to marry as soon as may be."

The earl's hand curled tightly about his grandson's wrist. "You would do well to have care, Nicky! If a silly fool like Fanny can be so aware of your liaison with the Manderley woman, you can be damned certain her husband ain't in the dark! Give her up, my boy!"

"So you *did* bring me here to lecture me about my mistress!" said Ruxart with a laugh as he extracted his wrist. He strode quickly from the room before the earl could respond with the set-down he deserved. As the door closed behind the recklessly charming viscount, Kerrington returned his attention to his daughter's letter. With a cackle of laughter, he tossed it into the flames before him.

It was as well that the earl did not witness his grandson's return to London, for Ruxart set his grays going at a punishing pace. Having been in service long enough to recognize the set line of his lordship's jaw, the young groom kept mutely in his place. If Jem wondered just what the old earl could have done to put that cold frown into the viscount's eyes, he was far too well-trained to show it.

Upon reaching his townhome in Half Moon Street, Ruxart retired to his study where he flipped through a sizable stack of correspondence while sipping from a curved snifter of fine brandy. It was a man's room, darkly panelled and liberally decorated with leather and brass. Bookcases stuffed with leathered volumes of all sizes and colors lined three walls before which stood a massive cherry-wood desk.

Ruxart threw a number of gilt-edged invites down atop this desk, tossed off the end of the brandy, and flung himself in the burgundy leather chair facing the desk. Once seated, he did not hesitate, but dashed off an abrupt note. *Penelope*, it read, *I must cry off. R.*

His grandfather's imperious warning had only spurred the inevitable, for Ruxart was already bored with Penelope's tantrums and constant demands on his time. It had been commented of the viscount that he discarded women the way other men did cloaks, and it was with nearly as little concern that he now dismissed Penelope Manderley from his life.

After he had sanded and sealed the brief missive, he sat for a time in a brown study, his heavy brows pushed together and his lips set in a grim line. Although he felt one woman to be much like another, he was having difficulty contemplating marriage with any of the eligible females he knew. Having promised the earl to do so, however, Ruxart was set upon making one of them an offer, no matter how disagreeable the thought of it seemed.

With an impatient shrug, he rang for a servant. As the door opened he instructed flatly, "Have this delivered immediately, Goswick. And send another bottle up to me." Goswick waited until the viscount had quit the room to give his head a shake. He soon confirmed to the servants' hall what had already been suspected, that his lordship was indeed in one of his wild moods tonight.

Shortly thereafter, Ruxart was standing in full evening dress arguing with his valet. "I do not wish to look like some damned fop, Oundle!" he said coldly.

"But, my lord, just one small diamond placed just so," persisted the diminutive servant, "would make all the difference!" He was reaching up toward Ruxart's frilled shirt when the door opened and a footman announced, "Mr. St. Juste, my lord."

Armand St. Juste had adopted Brummell's dictum of dressing only in somber colors, to the extreme that he only wore shades of black and white. The style accentuated the gold of his blond hair and the ghostly fairness of his skin. His green eyes, long, thin nose and bloodless lips were featured in a narrow face accounted by most to be handsome, but his nature was thought to be so cold and distant that he had formed few attachments. He always wore a square ruby ring upon one niveous hand, and when most bored, lowered his gaze to the ring in such a manner as to depress anyone's intentions of wearying him further. The *ton* believed him to be wildly dangerous, particularly in association with the rash Viscount Ruxart, but they forgave him because he was worth quite twenty thousand pounds a year.

He strolled casually in, observing the glitter in Ruxart's eye and the open bottle standing on the dressing table as he did so. He leaned wearily on the marble edge of this table, stretching out his long legs before him. His air of lethargy did not deceive Nicholas, who knew St. Juste to be as restlessly discontent as he was himself. Ruxart now pushed Oundle's hand away and presented his friend with a rare genuine smile that transformed his harsh handsomeness into a boyish charm. "B'god, I'm glad you're back!" he declared. "London has been a dead bore without you!"

"My dear Nick," drawled St. Juste, "*everywhere* is a dead bore without me. Even now I am certain someone in the wilds of Dorset or possibly Northumberland is saying, 'Ah, if only St. Juste were here to make life worth living.'"

Ruxart laughed. "I don't doubt it in the least, Armand."

"I have heard you and the Manderley have been stirring up the *ton* in my absence. Is it true that when she cropped her hair she sent you the shorn locks?"

"Quite true—bound into the shape of a heart, no less," replied the viscount as he wandered aimlessly about his room. "I fear, however, I shall have to disappoint the *ton* in future. I have broken with the passionate Pen."

"Oh?" inquired St. Juste with the tilt of one blond brow.

"Her dramatics bored me. God, *all* women bore me!"

13

"Must you continuously pace about the room?" asked Armand on a fretful note. "You are quite wearing me out, Ruxart."

The younger man flashed a twisted smile and threw himself onto an armless chair. His companion slowly raised his ribboned quizzing glass and scrutinized the dark lord from head to toe. "I fear, I very much fear, Nicholas," he complained pettishly, "that I simply cannot be seen anywhere with someone whose neckcloth is tied so abominably."

"I don't give a fig for fashion, St. Juste!"

"That is only too apparent, dear boy. Oundle, please remove that thing from his lordship's neck and bring me a fresh muslin."

The valet stepped from the shadows to take the crumpled cloth from Ruxart's hand as his lordship untied it, then disappeared silently from the room. He had long been used to Mr. St. Juste's dictates where his master's dress was concerned and far from resenting the interference, actually welcomed the fact that he could influence the viscount into presenting a more fashionable appearance.

"You had best tell me what has put you into such a pet, Ruxart," said Armand as the valet left the room. "I cannot endure an entire evening having you wear me out with this tiresome energy of yours."

"My grandfather has decided it's time for me to wed," explained Ruxart shortly. "And I promised him to do so as quickly as possible. The damnation of it is that I cannot think of one woman of my acquaintance for whom I would even remotely wish to offer!"

St. Juste studied the lines on the square face before him. He saw there what few others had ever seen, for at the moment the unhappiness was clearly etched into his lordship's features.

"But where is your hunting spirit?" he asked lightly. "The matter seems simple enough to me—we must go on the hunt for a suitable bride for the Viscount Ruxart."

Nicholas put his head back and laughed with full enjoyment. "Armand, you astound me," he said at last. "I should have realized that only you would be capable of finding me a proper wife. By all means, then, let us find me a bride—tonight! Where do we conduct the hunt?"

"Lady Castleberry's ball, of course. All the young belles will be there displaying their wares."

Oundle returned to hand St. Juste a freshly starched square of muslin which the beau whipped adroitly round Ruxart's neck and skillfully tied in the manner which he himself had developed, known as "The Saint."

"You shall be much envied, Nick, for though many have attempted The Saint, only I have achieved the intricate knot," said St. Juste as he stepped back to admire the effect of his handiwork.

"Indeed you will, my lord," concurred Oundle. "Do you think a diamond, perhaps, Mr. St. Juste?"

"I am much honored," murmured Ruxart gravely. "But no diamonds, Oundle. Do I make myself clear?"

"Quite, my lord," answered that little man unhappily as he bowed out of the room.

"I believe it is time we set out to discover which lucky lady is to have the honor of becoming the Viscountess Ruxart," said St. Juste.

"I entrust the matter to you with complete confidence," responded his friend as they descended the stairs.

Chapter Two

The appearance of Viscount Ruxart and Armand St. Juste at Lady Castleberry's ball caused even more than their usual stir as the news of their arrival rippled through the excited belles and their gasping mamas.

"I had no idea they'd returned to town," whispered one turbaned matron to another.

"My dear Mrs. Trendall, surely you realized," responded her companion behind her fan, "that those two make it a habit to always be where you least expect them."

Thrilled to have London's two most sought-after bachelors grace her evening, thus assuring the rating of her ball as a success, Lady Castleberry waited breathlessly for them to reach her. "I am so pleased," she gushed as the pair came forward, "to have you attend my small gathering."

Her small gathering consisted of some two hundred of the town's beau monde squeezed into her drawing room, numerous small salons and her columned ballroom. Several people had opted for a few rubbers of whist in the salons, but Ruxart and St. Juste went purposefully into the marbled ballroom. There, beneath the bright glow of hundreds of candles, they were entertained by an orchestra at the far end of the room and surrounded by elegantly dressed guests passing the latest *on dits* and drinking vast amounts of flowing champagne.

"I perceive," intoned Armand as they stood surveying the scene, "that my instincts were, as usual, correct. Every fresh miss of the season is here."

"Well, to quote the earl, pick one and be done with it," said Nicholas impatiently, his dark eyes sweeping the room.

"Dear boy, you cannot rush an artist," protested St. Juste.

They moved leisurely through the rooms, nodding to acquaintances and skillfully depressing the attentions of overzealous mamas and social climbers while intently studying and eliminating various damsels from the rank of viscountess. They were seriously regarding a slender fair beauty whom Ruxart had termed delectable when that unfortunate miss laughed.

"I cannot feel," remarked St. Juste, "that you can possibly wish for a wife whose laugh sounds like a jungle screech."

"No, I must admit, even my dogs bark more gently," agreed the viscount. As he turned his gaze from the blonde, he suddenly said with a hint of disgust, "Oh, Lord, here comes my cousin John."

"What, the preacher-faced one?" inquired Armand, raising his quizzing glass.

"He's a good enough fellow, but he's so damned solemn and pure, he makes Cromwell look like a hardened libertine!"

The young man coming toward them did indeed look solemn, but there was a friendly shine to his hazel eyes that bespoke a kind nature. Physically, the two cousins were as dissimilar as their modes of life. John was of moderate height rather than tall, and though he was dark like Nicholas, his face was more oval than square and his eyes did not turn down in the lazy manner of Ruxart's. His nose was narrow where his cousin's was broad and no one would ever

18

describe his straight lips as sensual. John Fletcher was, moreover, of a calm temperament utterly foreign to Nicholas Armytage.

As he reached his cousin, John stretched out a hand. "You did not rusticate long, Nick. Did Grandfather give you a proper set-down? My mother was certain he would."

"I fear I must once again disappoint my Aunt Frances," replied Ruxart. "I believe you are not acquainted with my friend, Armand St. Juste? My cousin, John Fletcher."

Fletcher bowed correctly, but the friendly light went out of his eyes. Mr. St. Juste was, in his opinion, a disturbing influence on one whose tendencies were already far too wild. Ruxart's reckless escapades had long been a source of embarrassment to the Fletcher side of the family, whose members were forever counseling the young viscount to more sedate pursuits, thus spurring Ruxart on to some of his worst scrapes. With a coldness that quite amused Armand, Fletcher turned away from him to inquire of his cousin, "Why did you not stay longer at Kerrington? I'm certain Grandfather would have liked your company and it would do you no harm to ruralize for a bit."

Ruxart gritted his teeth at this, prompted by his resentment of such advice to reply, "As a matter of fact, it is on the earl's directive that I am here. He wishes me to take a wife—something I fear I cannot do by remaining at the Keep." He leaned toward St. Juste, who was scanning the crowds through his beribboned glass. "Have you seen any prospects yet, Armand? If we spend all night looking for my bride, we'll not have time for a game of piquet at White's."

"What is this?" Fletcher looked from one to the other with a grave frown.

"St. Juste is being so obliging as to find me a likely chit," offered Ruxart as bait. He was rewarded, for his cousin's mouth dropped open and his eyes widened in dismay.

"You cannot be serious!" he protested. "Marriage is not a matter for such levity."

19

The viscount shrugged and said with a wide yawn, "Why not? One petticoat is much like another. It makes no odds to me which of 'em shares my name."

"Nicholas, if this is your idea of a joke—" began John.

"Unless I mistake," cut in St. Juste with a drawl, "a thing which I am not prone to do, that little beauty will utterly destroy the current fashion for blondes."

The two followed St. Juste's gaze and saw a lovely vision in white satin and lace sitting delicately on a gilt chair across the room.

Miss Helen Somers was a petite brunette of breathtaking beauty. Had she been named for Helen of Troy it would have been no less than her due. Beneath a crown of glossy chestnut curls was a finely structured oval face in which two dainty brows were arched over sparkling blue eyes and a small straight nose was centered above a pair of red heart-shaped lips. These features came delightfully together in her creamy face to such effect that all three men were, for a lengthy pause, awe-struck. Her figure, too, was such as must please even the most discriminating, being small, graceful and proportioned exactly.

"She appears a suitable viscountess," said Ruxart finally. "I commend you, Armand. Your taste, as always, is impeccable."

St. Juste continued to eye the lovely girl as she laughed with a cheerful blonde seated next to her. "What do you wager, Ruxart?" he asked at length.

"A hundred guineas that she's mine within a fortnight," answered Ruxart promptly.

"Are you that uncertain of your charm? I should say five hundred would be nearer the mark," said his friend as he dropped his glass and faced him, amusement stamping his face with a faint tinge of color.

"My God!" exclaimed Fletcher in horror. "You cannot place a wager upon Miss Somers as if she were some horse!"

"Observe, St. Juste, how the fates smile upon your choice.

20

My good cousin knows the beauty. Introduce us, John!"

"No," said that worthy flatly. "I will not be made a party to this improper charade."

Ruxart studied his cousin with an amused glint. "My dear St. Juste," he began sweetly, "did I ever tell you of the time I called upon Harriette Wilson in her private boudoir only to find my cousin—"

"Ruxart!" broke in John hastily. "You cannot wish to tell that tale!"

"On the contrary, cousin, I shall enjoy relating that little incident to everyone here—including, I perceive, your dear mama. Unless, that is, you introduce me to Miss Somers."

"But that's infamous!"

Nicholas laughed outright at this, then turned to St. Juste. "Five hundred it is, Armand. To be doubled if I have her within the week." The terms were accepted with a half-bow and Ruxart directed a curt command to his cousin. "John, lead us on to the future Viscountess Ruxart."

"I must protest this entire disgraceful proceeding. Your behavior is scandalous."

"I do hope so," drawled the viscount, giving his cousin a gentle nudge toward the beauty.

The trio crossed the room in silence, arriving at their destination as the strains of the waltz being played came to an end. Pushing through a knot of gentlemen surrounding the gilt chair containing their object, Fletcher bowed to an older lady seated on the left. "Good evening, Mrs. Willoughby."

She responded with a surprisingly youthful smile. "Good evening, Mr. Fletcher. I've seen your mother here, but have not yet had a chance to speak with her. All is well with you?"

"Yes, ma'am. May I present my cousin, Viscount Ruxart, and a friend, Mr. St. Juste?" said John stiffly as the pair moved forward. "They have been looking forward to meeting you. Gentlemen, Mrs. Willoughby, a dear friend of my mother's."

An amused, knowing glint came into her eye. She nodded at each in turn, saying, "How do you do? I should like to make you known to my daughter, Miss Caroline Willoughby—" she indicated the giggling blonde on the beauty's other side—"and my niece, Miss Helen Somers."

The dark goddess looked up, her lovely lips forming a silent circle as she saw the two handsome men—the one so very dark, the other so very fair—standing before her.

"I am happy to meet you," she murmured in a musical voice.

"Not near so happy as I," said Ruxart with a perfect bow. "May I dare hope you will honor me with a dance?"

She hesitated, glancing toward her aunt. When that lady tipped her head in a brief nod, Miss Somers rose gracefully and said softly, "Of course, my lord. It is I who am honored."

With practiced ease, Ruxart extracted Miss Somers from her ring of admiring beaux and led her into the set then forming. They began the country dance in silence, but presently, as the steps brought them together, the viscount remarked, "I must remember to say my prayers this evening."

"My lord?" questioned Miss Somers, her puzzled smile displaying two delightful dimples at the corners of her pretty mouth.

"I must certainly thank the Fates that led me here to meet you tonight," he replied with his most charming smile. "I begin to appreciate young Montague's feelings upon meeting Juliet."

Miss Helen blushed. She could not be unaware of her beauty, but she was not used to such outright flattery and had, indeed, always felt herself unworthy of such compliments as her loveliness brought forth. Watching the light mantle of color rise over her cheeks, Ruxart coolly calculated his next remark.

"I wonder that I have not seen you before, Miss Somers."

"I've not been in London long," she responded, thankful

to have the subject changed. "Indeed, this is my first ball, though I've been several times to the Assembly Rooms in Norwich."

"You are from Norfolk, then?"

"Yes, my lord. Our home is in Sloley near Norwich."

"It is a great pity," he said softly, "that I've never before had occasion to visit Sloley near Norwich."

The speaking look beneath the heavy lids unnerved her and she colored prettily as she stammered a brief reply. As he continued to rake her over lazily with his dark eyes, she managed to observe, "Lady Castleberry must be vastly admired, for there are ever so many people here."

"It is my belief that is because they all knew what I did not . . . that you were to be here tonight."

She paused, then made a fresh attempt. "Your cousin, Mr. Fletcher, has been very kind. He escorted Caro—Miss Willoughby—and me to Astley's yesterday."

"I trust that in future, Miss Somers, you will have no need to look to my cousin for escort."

When the dance took her away from the viscount, Miss Helen felt a wave of relief. His fulsome compliments, delivered as they were with an easy charm that never dispelled the mockery from his black eyes, had quite overset her. She was a simple, direct girl, not used to the light manners of the *ton*. She had never before encountered the art of dalliance as practiced by society and was unsure how to respond to Ruxart's flirtatious comments.

He resumed, when they again drew close, by stating, "The bucks in Norfolk must be flatter than the Broads there to have let you out of the vicinity."

She had by now determined to ignore such flattery, so Helen let this go by, asking him instead where it was he came from.

"My family home is in Kent," he answered. "Kerrington Keep," he added, looking as if he expected her to know of it.

Helen saw that some reaction was expected of her, but not

knowing what, stammered, "Is . . . is it a nice town?"

A startled look briefly crossed his features, then Ruxart laughed, showing a sincerity which his manner had previously lacked. She thought perhaps she may have been mistaken in her first impression of him as a remote and forbidding man.

"The Keep is my grandfather's estate, my dear," he explained with a smile. "I'm inclined to think of it as somewhat nice."

"I am sorry!" she apologized, then instantly wished she had not. Despite his continued smile, the disturbing chill returned to his eyes. Though she racked her brain for something to say, Helen could think of nothing. They continued to dance without conversing, but his stare put her so out of countenance that she missed a step and felt even more miserable.

The fact that the lovely young miss dancing with the Viscount Ruxart had entertained him so well was not missed by the ever-watchful members of the *ton*. Speculation began to spread as tongues wagged throughout the room.

Armand St. Juste was among those who stood watching the pair, his thin lips curled up in amusement as he did so. His satisfaction was not shared by the younger man standing rigidly beside him.

"You should not encourage him in this outrage," said Fletcher in a furious undertone, unable to refrain any longer from speaking. "You must see that Nicholas cannot marry Miss Somers!"

"Are you suggesting," inquired St. Juste with cool contempt, "that Miss Somers would not suit? Is she the daughter of some country cit?"

"No! Of course not! But to select a wife as if one were at Tattersall's is offensive to any person of sensibility."

"But, my dear sir, you mistake! Ruxart would never choose his horses with so much haste!" objected St. Juste before bowing and moving languidly off.

Fletcher's face clearly showed his shock and it was some little while before he felt himself composed enough to attend to the activity around him. He sought out his mother, but by the time he reached her side, John had decided to keep his own counsel on this matter for the time being. He resolved instead to call upon his cousin on the morrow to talk Nick out of this mad scheme.

St. Juste reappeared as the viscount returned Miss Helen to her aunt's care. Her cheeks were mantled with a soft rose, heightening the appeal of her blue eyes and deeply red lips, and Armand silently congratulated himself on his unerring taste. He stepped forward. "I claim this next dance, Miss Somers."

This time Miss Helen did not look to her aunt for approval, but lightly laid her fingers upon St. Juste's velvet sleeve. She did cast a glance over her shoulder as they moved away and thus saw the viscount settling himself beside Elizabeth Willoughby.

Mindful of her mistakes during the previous dance and still feeling disconcerted from her encounter with Ruxart, Helen at first paid more attention to her steps than to her partner. St. Juste did not press her in any way; after a bit, she peered up shyly at him through her thick lashes in such an enchanting manner, Armand experienced an unaccustomed desire to please. His habitual coolness evaporated and he smiled warmly down at her.

"Have you been enjoying London, Miss Somers?" he asked in a friendly tone that elicited an open response.

"Oh, yes. There is so much to see and do that I've been quite in a whirl since I arrived. Although, of course, it would be even more enjoyable if Jane or Clarence were here to share in all the pleasures."

"You have brothers and sisters, then?"

"Yes, two of each, all of them older than I."

25

"And are your sisters as lovely as you?" he questioned, much enjoying the honeyed tones of her voice.

"Well, *I* think so," she answered stoutly, leaving him in no doubt that they were not. "And Jane is quite wonderful—she can take care of anything!"

This last was said with so much fervor that Miss Helen looked totally and charmingly animated.

"And Clarence?" prompted St. Juste, diverted.

"He's a scholar, you see, and would much enjoy all the museums and sights. Have you seen the Egyptian Hall in Piccadilly?"

St. Juste suppressed a shudder to reply evenly, "No, I've not yet had that particular pleasure."

"Well, I could not help but think of Clarence while there," she said with a solemnity that brought an expression of delight to Armand's narrow face.

They continued to converse in much the same vein, with St. Juste quietly drawing Miss Helen out so that she was thoroughly at ease with the normally unapproachable man.

While he watched the couple upon the dance floor, Ruxart was maintaining an easy flow of talk with Mrs. Willoughby.

"Oh, indeed," she was saying in response to his lordship's admission of surprise that Miss Somers came from Norfolk. "I could not but be grateful that Helen doesn't have any of the Broads inflections in her speech, though, of course, it would not have greatly mattered. She is as lovely in her manners as she is in her looks." She raised a hand to brush back a few strands of flaxen hair dusted lightly with gray.

"And her father?" queried Ruxart.

"Mr. Somers passed away a number of years ago—not too long before my own husband, in fact—and her brother William is the head of the family now." She would have expanded on this, but the music stopped and Caroline sailed up with her partner in tow. Ruxart came to his feet as St. Juste escorted Helen to her seat.

Sometime after midnight, Ruxart and St. Juste took their leave of their hostess. By the time they departed, all two hundred of Lady Castleberry's guests were aware that the Viscount Ruxart had embarked on a new flirtation, for he had remained by the side of Miss Helen Somers throughout the evening. Though he had danced with no one else, he had actually led the country beauty out twice; his unusual attentiveness had not gone unremarked and was recounted several times all over London before dawn broke through.

While on the way to White's, St. Juste inquired in an indifferent tone, "What do you think of the future viscountess?"

"Blushing virgins aren't much to my taste," yawned Ruxart, "but I suppose she will do well enough." As his friend was seated in the shadowed corner of the carriage, Nick did not see the spasm of annoyance which crossed Armand's face and he continued blithely. "At any rate, she's a damn sight easier to take than Lucinda Barnhurst."

"Lucinda Barnhurst!" ejaculated St. Juste.

"My reaction exactly. She was my grandfather's threat as a fiancée."

"Ah, that explains it."

"Explains what?"

"All the brandy you were diving into earlier."

The viscount's laughter filled the carriage, while the moment of displeasure that had piqued St. Juste completely dissipated. As he calmed, Ruxart said, "I shall send one of my men to Norfolk in the morning to make certain she's not some damned millowner's daughter or anything as undesirable. I learned from her aunt that her father is dead and her brother is head of the family."

"Clarence?"

"No, his name is William. Who is Clarence?"

"A brother, according to Miss Somers, of scholarly pursuits. I was also given to understand she has two sisters. It seems, dear boy, you are about to be saddled with a family of considerable size," laughed St. Juste.

"Your guineas in my pocket shall compensate me to a large degree," retorted Ruxart as the coach came to a halt before the impressive edifice of the exclusive men's club known as White's. "Yes, it shall be most satisfying to win this wager."

Chapter Three

Helen Somers awoke late the following morning to the cacophony that was London's traffic outside her window. She sleepily noted the cheery display of sunlight upon the papered pattern of the walls, wondering for a few moments just where she was. She still had difficulty in comprehending the fact that she was not at home, that this was not her own little square room in Plumstead Cottage.

Her gaze came to rest drowsily upon an enormous basket of roses standing atop a dressing table. Her eyes flew open wide and she sat upright, staring at the bright bouquet. After a stunned moment, she threw back the satin coverlet and crossed to take a square white card from the heart of the red flowers.

Their color pales beside your lips, she read, and hardly drew a breath before looking at the signature. *Ruxart*. She let out a sigh and dropped the card carelessly upon the table.

A quick rap sounded upon her door. Before Helen could say anything, the door was flung open and the whirlwind known as Caroline Willoughby flew into the room.

"I'm so glad you are up!" she exclaimed. "I could not wait another instant to see your bouquet, for your maid told my maid they were delivered by Ruxart's man! Oh, are they not the most beautiful roses you've ever seen? And at this season! The viscount is a wonder, is he not?" Without pausing for an answer, she skipped to her cousin and snapped up the small card from where it had fallen. She read the message, her violet eyes widening.

"You have made a conquest, Helen!" she cried. "I confess, the way Ruxart smiled at you last night, I was quite eaten up with envy."

"Yes, but Caro, the smile never entered his eyes," Helen pointed out quietly.

"Oh, pooh! I should not care a button for that! Why, a wealthy viscountess doesn't need smiles from her *husband*!" Caroline twirled before the mirror, peeking through the roses to examine her sprigged muslin day gown with a critical eye. She leaned toward the glass to fluff her cropped blond curls and said with a laugh, "It is a great pity the viscount does not seem to care for fair beauties, for I should not hesitate to snatch him from you if I could. He is *the* catch of the decade, silly! And you want his eyes to smile!" With a pitying shake of her head, Caroline darted from the room, leaving her cousin standing with a line sketched upon her brow.

She did not understand, nor did she want to understand, such a fashionable view of marriage. For Helen, the union of two souls was only conceivable when blessed by love. It was, she feared, an emotion of which Lord Ruxart knew nothing. The memory of the cool calculation in his gaze returned and she shivered as she dressed in a becoming pleated percale gown of pale blue, with a high bodice and long, tight sleeves that accentuated the slimness of her figure. But she smoothed away the worry from her brow before removing to the breakfast room where she found her Aunt Elizabeth sipping from a Wedgwood teacup while Caroline busily spread a thin layer of marmalade over a biscuit.

"Good morning, dear. Caro was just telling me you were

up. I trust you slept well after the excitement of your first ball?"

"Yes, thank you, Aunt Liz," replied Helen, taking a seat opposite her cousin.

"Just think, Mama," said that lively miss, "Helen was not impressed with her roses! *I* should be positively overcome should I receive anything half so grand! And if Lord Ruxart had compared *my* lips to roses, I should be in transports of excitement!"

"Thank goodness Helen has more sense," said her mother dampingly. "It would not do, my dears, to take the viscount's attentions too seriously. It appears he's been much taken with Helen, but he's well known for his flirtations, and we must not expect this to be anything more."

"But if it *were*, Mama, just think how thrilling it would be!" said Caro before sinking her teeth into her biscuit.

"Well, there's no denying that it would be the greatest good fortune," admitted Elizabeth with a sigh.

"Oh? And why is that, Aunt Liz?" asked Helen in a voice carefully bland.

"Viscount Ruxart is the most eligible bachelor—" she began.

"I told her, the catch of the decade!" interrupted Caro before subsiding at her mother's quelling eye.

"Besides his title and vast wealth—some say greater even than the Golden Ball's forty thousand a year—he is the heir to his grandfather's title and all the Earl of Kerrington's considerable wealth as well. The connection is one of the oldest and most impeccable in the country; his estate stands on the ruins of an ancient fortification in Kent.

"Kerrington Keep," murmured Helen.

"Why, yes. When you consider what such a connection would do for your family, you cannot but be sensible of the good fortune such a match would bring. Imagine, dear, having all the burden of your family taken from William's shoulders! Why, I was quite bemazed to see how much he had aged in the years since your father died—one would hardly believe that he is not yet thirty!"

"He . . . he does have many cares, since Papa did not leave us provided for. And with Mama's health being so poorly . . ." Helen's voice trailed away.

"I suspect much of Dorothea's state of health is in her mind," returned Elizabeth sharply. "But I shan't speak ill of my own sister. If you married well, Helen, your mother could receive the best of medical care. And Clarence could continue his studies. It could also mean, I think, a bit of freedom for Jane. I'm sure no one could be more deserving of a chance for fun and ease! I was even more shocked by her spinsterish air than I was over William's staid attitude. Why, Jane is only six-and-twenty, and it's a shame to have her placed so firmly on the shelf!"

"I could not agree more, Aunt Liz! But when I begged her to come to London with me, she only laughed and asked me what an old thing like herself could do amid all the young belles and beaux! And she said William and Agnes and Clarence and Mama could not do without her."

"That, at least, I well believe," said Elizabeth through tight lips. She shook her head, as if to shake away the vision of her niece aged before her time, and spoke briskly. "But, of course, we are racing ahead. It would not do for us to get our hopes up on the basis of one basket of roses."

"But you would be the most envied woman in all England should Ruxart offer for you, Helen!" put in Caroline. "Last season, there was a jest that the recipe for a lively season consisted of one part balls and fetes, one part young beauties and one part Viscount Ruxart—then toss out everything except Ruxart, for the viscount alone would account for a lively time!"

"That is enough, Caro," reproved her mother.

Helen stared down at the rim of her plate for a few moments, then asked in a small voice, "I was wondering what you could tell me of the viscount's friend, Mr. St. Juste?"

"That cold fish!" cried Caro in disgust.

"Caroline, mind your manners! There is nothing so disagreeable as to receive unsolicited opinions from those who should know better than to express them," scolded Elizabeth. She turned to Helen and said kindly, "Mr. St. Juste may lack a title, but he is also most eligible, having a large fortune of his own. His father was one of the few French aristocrats with foresight. He left France before the worst excesses of the Revolution and though he forfeited his title—he was a Comte, I understand—and his property there, he brought most of his wealth with him when he emigrated. The father is gone now, but St. Juste's mother still lives on the estate, I believe. She's not been to town in years, but I remember her as a fiery Frenchwoman full of emotion."

Elizabeth pushed back her chair and stood, looking slim and quite youthful, despite the graying of her hair. "At any rate, should either of the two make you an offer, Helen, and should your inclination be to accept, it would be not only suitable, but a tremendous blessing for you and your family. But, of course, we must not count too much upon the circumstance of one ball."

"Don't forget the roses!" called out Caroline to her mother's retreating form.

Throughout the day, Helen received other posies and small gifts from admirers and dandies who were following Ruxart's lead in making Miss Helen the latest rage. And if she felt disappointed when none of the many offerings bore the card of Mr. St. Juste, Helen was most careful not to show it.

The day proved less than pleasing to the Viscount Ruxart

as well. It began with a morning call—at an entirely unsuitable hour for one who had not left the gaming tables at White's until past dawn—from John Fletcher.

When Goswick had informed Mr. Fletcher that his lordship was still abed and could not be disturbed, John simply brushed past him, ignoring the servant's lively protests, saying, "Surely, my cousin cannot be aware that the hour is so advanced! I shall wake him." He mounted the stairs so rapidly, Goswick only just kept up with him, coming nervously to a halt behind his shoulder when Fletcher thrust open Ruxart's door.

Lying on his side in an enormous poster bed, the viscount opened one eye, saw Fletcher standing in the door frame, and closed it again. "Remove him, Goswick," he said tonelessly.

"But my lord—"

"Don't be nonsensical, Nicholas," said John, whisking the servant's hand from his sleeve and advancing into the room. "It wants but a few minutes to noon, and you cannot wish to sleep the day away."

"Your concern overwhelms me," murmured Ruxart. He slowly opened both eyes, saw the determination stamped upon his cousin's face, and resigned himself to the unwanted interview. "Goswick, bring me coffee and a bottle of brandy."

"Brandy! At this hour!" exclaimed John.

"As you pointed out, it's nearly noon. I dare say by the time he returns it will be safely past noon and quite permissible for me to lace my coffee with brandy," said Nicholas, swinging his legs over the edge of the bed. "And, Goswick, send Oundle to me."

As Goswick disappeared, thankful to have escaped so easily, Ruxart moved to a small vanity where he poured water from a large pitcher ornamented with gold leaf into a matching ewer. After liberally splashing his face with cold

34

water, he turned to John. "Well, cousin, you've swept me from my bed. I ask myself, to what purpose?"

Before Fletcher could make an answer, the viscount's valet entered, carrying all the necessary items to shave his lordship. Ruxart dropped into a chair. Oundle wrapped a linen cloth around his neck and began to lather his cheeks. "Well?" inquired Nicholas again.

"You . . . you must know!" replied John, flustered. "It is on a private matter that I wish to speak with you!"

"I should be insulted if I were you, Oundle. My cousin does not think you are private. Do you wish to call him out? Shall I stand your second?"

Oundle permitted himself a smile at this jest before scraping his razor edge expertly down the viscount's cheek.

"Come, Nicholas! Your levity is misplaced," chided John. "As it was last night. I dare say you realize that all Lady Castleberry's guests could speak of was your dalliance with Miss Somers. It's shocking for you to play with someone's feelings to satisfy your own selfish purposes."

Ruxart's heavy lids hid the anger in his eyes, but his tone was harsh as he bit out, "One would think to listen to you, cousin, that I was out to ravish the chit, instead of marry her!"

"Oh, it is not your intentions I deplore—indeed, I'm quite surprised that you've at last realized your duty to your name—"

"Thank you!"

"But it is your manner of executing that duty, Nicholas, that is distressing. Your wager with St. Juste is an insult both to Miss Somers and to the seriousness of the wedded state. Marriage should not be entered into lightly, but only with a sense of respect and admiration on the part of those involved."

The earnestness of Fletcher's tone galled the viscount and as Oundle stepped back, his ministrations complete, Ruxart threw off the linen towel with an angry snap and stood.

"God, spare me your lectures! Why it is that you must always treat me like some younger brother, I cannot fathom—you seem to forget that I am eleven months the elder!"

"In age, yes, but you must permit me to say that you rarely act the elder."

"I do not permit you, cousin," said Ruxart through clenched teeth, "to say anything of the sort!" He spun round as Goswick silently entered and deposited a tray upon a Pembroke table. Ignoring the steaming coffee, he splashed brandy into his cup and tossed it off, knowing full well it would scandalize his visitor.

"Nick! Anything I say to you, you must know I say because I care about you and your welfare, and it is to keep you from making a great mistake that I am here today."

"Let me make my own mistakes, John! You've never kept me from one before—you should know by now you cannot. I've not forgotten our summers together at the Keep when we were boys, and indeed, it is because I hold you in some affection that I've not flung you bodily out of here for your impertinence to interfere in my affairs!" Ruxart leaned over the back of a chair and raised a hand to forestall Fletcher's protests. Though anger still glittered in his eyes, his tone softened as he said, "Yes, John, your damned impertinence! I've made up my mind to have Miss Somers for my wife and I will have her. And Armand's guineas, too. You may whistle down the wind for all I care, but I advise you—cousinly advice, you might say—to leave off, John, or you may press me too far. I don't wish to end by breaking your stuffy, righteous neck."

John looked thoroughly horrified, and his eyes darted from his cousin's stony face to the brandy bottle.

"Don't be a fool, Fletcher! I'm not drunk. One cup couldn't intoxicate a green youth. I'm merely tired of your prosy interference into my life!"

"My intention—"

"Oh, I grant you, kindness in itself. Very well, you have warned me! I am about to commit the greatest error. You may stand at the head of the line to tell me 'I told you so' afterwards, I assure you. And now, for God's sake, leave me alone while I still have some temper left to me!"

Fletcher stood motionless, the real hurt reflected in his hazel eyes annoying Ruxart far more than anything he had yet said. Then he turned on his heel and stalked from the room.

"Damnation! May all well-meaning, officious relatives be sent to hell!" exclaimed Ruxart under his breath as he signaled his valet to begin dressing him.

Once attired in a tightly cut morning coat of dark blue superfine and equally tight fawn pantaloons, the viscount set out in his curricle for what proved to be the second unsatisfactory interview of the day.

He called upon Miss Helen Somers in Brook Street where he found that lovely lady receiving visitors with the flighty Miss Willoughby. Though Helen smiled at him politely and thanked him for the roses, she did not seem overly touched by the gift. Moreover, she was so unreceptive to his attempts at conversation, leaving the burden of it to her cousin (who had no difficulty whatsoever in carrying the bulk of the discourse) that when he left, Ruxart was no longer so certain of the outcome of his wager with St. Juste.

Thus it was that Lord Ruxart pursued Miss Somers with a determination that set the *ton* buzzing. He sent her a fresh bouquet of flowers every day, each delivered with a flattering note tucked within the petals. The viscount called upon her every morning, took her driving through the park every afternoon and danced with her every night. For seven days, it was as if every other woman had ceased to exist. London's *haut monde* hummed with bemazement.

His pursuit extended even to the hallowed rooms of the sacrosanct Almack's, where his appearance occasioned a great deal of surprise, for it had been some years since he had last made use of his voucher to attend one of the weekly supper balls. Though his name had long topped the all-important List, his opinion of Almack's as being drier than a stack of Sunday sermons was well known and word of his arrival this night passed from ear to ear in a drone of conjecture.

One who watched his approach with pure amusement shining in her eyes was a handsome, vivacious brunette of scintillating wit. Many considered Lady Sally Jersey vulgar, but Ruxart was not among them. He stopped at her side and gracefully took her hand.

"Wonders never cease!" she laughed, lifting her hand to unfurl her printed silk fan. "And to what—or should I say, whom—do we owe this honor?"

"My dear Sally, I would like, I would very much like, to waltz with Miss Somers," replied his lordship directly, a lazy smile playing on his lips.

She snapped her fan shut and looked at him with eyes that sparkled with lively speculation. "So for once the gossip-mongers are in the right of it. I've a mind to deny you, Nicky, but I am even more of a mind to watch the excitement you shall dust up. Tell me, though, *are* you caught at last by the dazzling country beauty?"

Ruxart's hand closed over the fan. Her eyes flew upward to find his turned-down gaze filled with mockery. "Only you, dear Lady J., would dare to ask, though everyone else seems to want to. Let us say, then, that I may choose to be caught."

"Then by all means, you must have your waltz," she returned, extracting her fan from his grasp.

At the first strains of a waltz, they walked together to where Miss Somers had taken a seat, ready to sit out the dance that was still considered so daring, no respectable female could take a whirl without the approval of one of

Almack's patronesses.

"Miss Somers," said Lady Jersey with a wide, mischievous smile, "may I present the Viscount Ruxart as a suitable partner for this dance?"

With a nervous smile, Helen reluctantly rose to accept his lordship's hand. Lady Jersey did not linger, moving quickly on and thereby dashing Caro's hope that she, too, would be allowed to waltz.

Like a delicate flower exposed to too much heat, Helen's personality wilted in the presence of his lordship. She had become more accustomed to his smooth compliments, but unlike the majority of the *ton*, she did not believe Lord Ruxart to be in love with her. She had too often seen a look in his eyes so coldly calculating as to completely belie all the warm flattery he showered upon her. Once or twice, a passionate flame had blazed in the dark eyes raking over her, particularly unnerving to Helen because the fiery gleam remained somehow cold, like a block of ice set afire. At such times Helen fought down a rising fear by thinking solely of her family and their needs.

For his part, Ruxart found the ravishing beauty desirable, but she was so often inattentive, responding to his conversation with only the dullest commonplace observations, that he wondered if she were not loose-witted. It made not a whit of difference to his determination to have her as his wife. Having learned during the week from his man that, though the Somers' pockets were all to let, the Norfolk connection was unexceptional, the viscount resolved to win his wager. As his arms encircled her slim form, he thought of St. Juste's guineas and smiled rather kindly at Helen when they began to waltz.

Encouraged by the rare warmth of his smile, Helen ventured shyly, "I do not see your friend, Mr. St. Juste. Is he not with you this evening?"

"Lord, no! Nothing could persuade him to come here!"

"But whyever not?"

39

"Armand firmly holds there is only one reason to spend an evening at Almack's—to find a bride." As his partner flushed prettily, he asked, "Why else do you think they call this the Marriage Mart?"

She did not answer, feeling more intensely than before the burning where his hand rested lightly on her waist as they twirled dizzily around the room.

"You waltz delightfully, Miss Somers," he said at length.

"I—my sister taught me."

"Ah, yes, the estimable Jane," said the viscount cynically.

"Jane loves to dance and she is wonderfully light on her feet! She taught Maria and Clarence, too, though of course, it was all wasted on Clarence," explained Helen in a rush.

Ruxart stifled a yawn. It seemed that the only theme this chit warmed to was her infernal family and, in particular, her eldest sister, Jane. That so-worthy paragon sounded like a perfect match for his stick of a cousin Fletcher, he thought, before adroitly changing the subject.

Upon returning Helen to her aunt's side, the viscount inquired quietly, "Would you object if I called upon your aunt in the morning?"

"I . . . I would be . . . honored," she replied softly, her eyes cast upon her lap.

But naturally you would, he thought with a mental sneer. But he merely said a brief thank you before leaving immediately to search out some excitement elsewhere.

Elizabeth Willoughby nodded her head when, riding home in their carriage, she learned of his lordship's intention to call upon her. "Then you may depend upon it, Helen, he means to offer for you. What a blessing for your family!"

"It's too splendid!" cried Caroline, clapping her hands together. "When you are Viscountess Ruxart, will you get Sally Jersey to let *me* waltz? I swear I was fair eaten alive with jealousy to see you swirling about the room!"

When Helen remained mute, Elizabeth asked with a searching look, "Will you accept his offer, dear?"

"Mama!" shrieked Caro. "Of course she will! She must! You will, won't you, Helen?"

She looked dully from cousin to aunt and said hesitantly, "Yes, I suppose I shall."

A frown pleated her aunt's brow, but Caro bounced upon her seat. "How thrilling! My own cousin—the Viscountess Ruxart!"

Chapter Four

A blustery wind blew without as winter breathed its last in an attempt to delay the onslaught of spring. Because of the chill, a fire had been lit in the small sitting room in Plumstead Cottage—an unusual expense that had greatly displeased Agnes Somers and surprised her sister-in-law Jane. But Dorothea had insisted upon it before allowing her son William to assist her into the room.

The elder Mrs. Somers was stretched out upon the threadbare settee before the flickering flames, a light patched coverlet spread across her legs, her vinaigrette clutched in one thin hand and an opened letter in the other. Ranged about her on several ladder-back chairs were her children.

Her daughter-in-law Agnes was sourly watching the wood burning and mentally calculating the cost while her daughters, Maria and Jane, exchanged quizzical glances. Her sons each sat at an outer edge of the semicircle, William clearly impatient and Clarence soulfully inattentive.

"Here we are, Mama," said Jane. "What is this all about?"

"Yes, Mother," said William with his usual air of sobriety, "why have you gathered us together?"

"I have received," their mother declared dramatically, "a

letter! With some very important news!" The effort of her announcement apparently tired her, for Dorothea paused to take a whiff from the tiny bottle in her left hand before continuing. "Elizabeth has written that our little Helen is on the verge of contracting a brilliant alliance!"

"What!" ejaculated William.

"With whom?" demanded Agnes with a shriek.

Maria looked inquisitively at her elder sister, who gave a brief shake of her head. Of them all, only Clarence seemed unconcerned about his younger sister's possible nuptials as he scarcely raised his head from the small volume of poems in his lap.

"No one has applied to me for permission to address Helen," stated William with a hint of anger. Of average height and medium build, William might have been deemed handsome had he but smiled more often. He did not smile now, but stood and said solemnly, "I trust Aunt Elizabeth has not been encouraging some havey-cavey suitor!"

"It is nothing of the sort!" protested his mother, reviving enough to sit up. "Liz writes that he spoke with her—"

"She is not Helen's guardian!"

"No, of course not, William! He merely expressed his desire to court Helen and should Helen be willing, Elizabeth writes that the viscount intends to call upon you, as is proper."

"Viscount?" echoed Agnes eagerly, her pinched face aglow.

"Yes! Helen's admirer is none other than the Viscount Ruxart," proclaimed Dorothea with majestic triumph.

"Ruxart!" said four voices in unison, though each with varying emotion.

As William frowned heavily and Agnes clamored for details, Clarence continued to exhibit no interest. Maria alone noticed Jane's sudden stillness, the color draining from her high cheeks.

"Excuse me," Jane whispered, standing. "I feel . . . it is

very warm in here."

Frowning, Maria rose to follow her sister from the room, but her mother claimed her attention. Jane was thus left to retire in solitude. While below her, the family excitedly discussed the viscount's whirlwind courtship of Helen, Jane stood before the square wood-framed mirror in her tiny box of a room and gazed at the woman reflected there.

She saw a long, narrow face which to her gray eyes seemed utterly unremarkable. From the wisps of brown hair escaping the confines of her linen cap to the straight, patrician nose and overwide mouth, Jane saw nothing to recommend her face beyond the ordinary. Though her sisters insisted she was pretty, Jane laughingly affirmed she'd been the practice model God had made before presenting the lovely Maria and then His masterpiece, Helen.

In truth, the elder Miss Somers had much to recommend her. Her brown hair was not the deep, glossy chestnut that crowned her younger sisters, but rather a warm blend of soft browns much like the shine of well-polished walnut. The structure of her face was aristocratically delicate. Her eyes were finely cast, even and heavily lashed, though she thought them overly large for her thin face. She covered them for a moment with a pair of long, capable hands.

When Jane removed them, she no longer saw herself in the mirror. She saw a memory of a young girl in her London season, wearing an unbecoming pale gown and a nervous smile. She saw a young, darkly handsome man whose lank black hair scraped his collar as he turned to meet her. She saw a pair of haughty ebony eyes which looked through, rather than at, one. Could it be true, she wondered, could the same Lord Ruxart now be in love with Helen?

It came vividly, distressfully, back—the bright lights and brighter laughter of an overcrowded ballroom where she sat at the edge of gaiety. His back had been all she could at first see through the crowd, but from the moment she noticed the way in which his sapphire coat stretched across his broad shoulders, Jane had been irresistibly drawn to Viscount Ruxart. Her eyes had casually followed the progress of his superb athletic form and then, at last, he had turned.

A pair of cold ebony eyes pierced her with a brief, bored stare to devastating effect. She was stunned both by the arrogant assurance and the masculine allure of him. His presence became the sole object of her evening; she strained for even the merest glimpse of him and she ached with an unaccountable emptiness as she watched him whirl with one beautiful belle after another.

Her attention was momentarily claimed by a buxom matron bearing striking resemblance to an Egyptian pyramid when a shadow fell upon her lap. She stifled a small gasp as she raised her eyes to meet Lord Ruxart's haughty gaze. His lordship's evident ennui became pronounced as their tactless hostess forced the pair to stand up together in the set then forming.

Even now, as she stood before the mirror, Jane's hands trembled, as they had years ago, when placed into the viscount's gloved palms for that single, painful dance. She felt again the warmth of the color that stole up her neck as Ruxart fixed his chilling eyes upon her. She had stammered out a commonplace and he had slain her with a disdainful lift of his brow. The awkward girl she had been had withered with embarrassment into strained silence. The dreadful hurt of Ruxart's cut returned now to pierce her heart as Jane regarded her pale, stunned image in the glass.

There was a gentle tap at the door, followed instantly by the entrance of Maria. "Jane, are you all right? I was worried by your abrupt departure."

"It was nothing. I sat too near the fire, that is all."

"You're doing it much too brown," objected her sister. "You were never overcome by the paltry fire Agnes allowed to burn! You had best tell me the truth, you know, for I shan't leave off till you do."

"It wasn't very convincing, was it?" asked Jane with a

46

rueful smile.

"Not in the least!" replied Maria cheerfully. She sat on the edge of Jane's bed, tucking her feet up beneath her in a manner wholly unsuited to the wife of a dignified country curate. "Now what on earth made you look as though you would swoon?"

"Oh, surely not *swoon*, Maria!"

"Yes, swoon," she said firmly, though with a lively smile in her bright blue eyes.

Jane paused, then looking again at her reflection in the mirror said slowly, "I cannot imagine Helen becoming affianced to the Viscount Ruxart. He . . . he is cold and arrogant, not at all the type of man for Helen."

"Do you know him, then?"

"I met him during my season in London. He was very contemptuous of those whom he obviously considered beneath his touch. And he was the leader of the fastest set, forever setting the *ton* on its ears!"

"People change—and that was nearly eight years ago. He must have been quite young."

"But his reputation has not changed. We even hear tales of his doings up here! How could such a man be considered? . . ." Jane's impassioned words drifted into a pained silence.

"Dearest, you've said yourself that those who listen to the gossip-bearers are even worse," pointed out Maria finally. "How can you possibly judge the viscount without meeting him now? Jane, it's not like you to prejudge anyone."

The sisters sat quietly regarding one another, their closeness saying much that was not spoken.

"Tell me, what does the rest of the family think of Ruxart's offer?" asked Jane after a time.

"Well, William is not overly pleased. He agrees with you that a man of the viscount's reputation is not entirely suitable for our Helen. But Aunt Elizabeth wrote that he is wealthy almost beyond measure—"

"So Agnes welcomes him with open arms," finished Jane. "She'll soon bring William round, I'll wager you."

"She and Mama have nearly done so already! Poor William, I could almost feel sorry for him. And Clarence, of course, could not understand what all the fuss was about. He left the parlor muttering something about not wishing to be disturbed unless it was *important*!"

They enjoyed a laugh at this until at last Maria stood. "I must be getting back to my family! Thomas will be wondering what to do with the baby, you know, and I can only hope he did not let Anne make too much mischief whilst I've been away."

"Dear Mrs. Gaines!" said Jane, giving her a hug. "It is my consolation each time you leave that the rectory is only three miles away."

Maria returned the squeeze lovingly. "Promise me you will not continue to fret over Helen. I'm certain she'd not accept the viscount if he displeased her."

Having a clearer notion of her youngest sister's malleable temperament, Jane was not so certain of this, but she simply said, "Oh, I shall not do so. I was merely indulging in a fit of the dismals—something I am told we spinsters are allowed to do."

Her sister shot her a look of sharp concern, but said nothing more. Jane had always been the still water in a family more given to open simplicity; Maria would never intrude upon her true feelings. With a last quick hug, they repaired to the sitting room where they found their three relations still earnestly discussing the thrilling news.

"You must not let Ruxart have Helen until the settlements have been fully completed," Agnes was saying to William with rare animation on her drawn features. She then named a sum which staggered Jane.

She was shocked into protesting, "Helen isn't some article to be auctioned off to the highest bidder!"

An angry crimson blotched her sister-in-law's cheeks

while her brother hastily disclaimed, "No, no, of course not!"

Making use of the interruption, Maria bid her family goodday. After enduring a tearful embrace from her mother, she was at last permitted to set off in her shabby gig to return home to her own dear husband and children.

Upon her departure, Agnes returned to her raptures. "I knew economizing in order to send Helen for the season would be rewarded! With her beauty there was no doubt! Not one pound spent was wasted, unlike . . ." She stopped in sudden embarrassment.

"Unlike the money spent on *my* season," supplied Jane, amused at the other's obvious discomfiture. "To be sure, nothing was ever such a shocking failure as that—a pity it couldn't have been used for Maria instead!"

"Now, Jane, don't be nonsensical," put in her mother with agitation. "You know she could not be presented when we were in mourning for your dear, dear papa! And she was so set on throwing herself away on her curate that I dare say it wouldn't have done the least good if she *had* gone to town!"

"No, I dare say not," agreed Jane dryly.

"At any rate," continued Agnes briskly, "the question of settlements must be gone into thoroughly—however little Jane likes the idea."

Jane let this pass by, as she did most of the snide comments Agnes sent her way. Indeed, she often felt sorry for her waspish sister-in-law, for she knew Agnes's marriage had been a deep disappointment to her. Some three years after taking William's hand, the death of the elder Mr. Somers had saddled Agnes with an invalid mother-in-law, a spinster sister, a selfish, scholarly brother, and a young beauty whose sweet temper clearly showed the sourness of her own disposition. That she made them all feel the burden of the cross she bore generally mitigated any sympathy Agnes might have otherwise gained from Jane and today, looking upon the avaricious gleam in those pale eyes, Miss Somers felt quite

49

put out with her sister-in-law.

After trying unsuccessfully to find a suitable husband for her, the family had been greatly relieved when "The Problem of What To Do About Jane" had been settled by the young lady herself some ten months since. At that time, she had taken to wearing the mobcaps and austere gowns denoting the matron; thus having declared to the world her spinsterish state, Jane had entered into the role wholeheartedly, becoming her family's hub without ever seeming to step from the background of things. It was a role for which she had little liking, but one she accepted as her fate. At times like these, however, Jane wondered how she would be able to bear the dictates of fate.

She rose abruptly and excused herself to oversee the preparations for dinner, much to the relief of her relations, who wished to return to the one subject they found of consuming interest.

While in Norfolk the Somers family sat discussing the financial status of the Viscount Ruxart, in London, a determined lady was brushing imperiously past his lordship's manservant.

"Do not think you can put me off," she said with a wave of one gloved hand. "I shall stay here until his lordship sees me. And nothing, nothing shall budge me!"

"Er, yes, Madam. If you will just wait in the Blue Room," said Goswick tonelessly, throwing open a near door. Though he remained expressionless, Goswick mentally raised his brows at the absence of an attendant as his lordship's unexpected visitor sailed alone into the sitting room.

She stripped off her gloves, tossing them onto a chair covered in blue satin. They were followed by her fashionably frogged pelisse and Pamela bonnet, for she meant to make good on her declaration to stay as long as might be necessary. She moved restlessly about the elegantly decorated room, her deep green eyes darting from this object to that, her fingers running erratically through her copper curls cropped à la Titus. She did not take a seat, certain that Ruxart would soon appear.

She was right, for very shortly after, the door was flung open and his lordship greeted her with a haughty stare.

"Nicky!" she cried, starting to run toward him.

"Did you not understand my note, Pen?" he asked brusquely.

Mrs. Manderley paused, arrested by the harsh tone, but she decided to brazen it out. "The only misunderstanding, Nicky my love, is in your thinking you can dismiss me with a snap of your fingers!"

Ruxart came into the room, closing the door with a crack. "But indeed I can, Penelope. In point of fact, I have." His tone was so contemptuous that anyone else would have conceded at once, but his guest had never been one to yield easily. She took a rapid turn about the room, then faced him.

"But why? Is it that country beauty I've heard so much about? Darling, can she offer you what I can?" Her voice dropped to a sultry husk.

He made no answer, but merely stood eyeing her from beneath heavy lids. Little of her shapely form was left to the imagination as Penelope came slowly toward him, her hips swaying alluringly against the thin gown which clung tightly to her dampened petticoat. She raised her arms as if to embrace him, but suddenly Pen swung her right hand, palm open, toward his cheek. Ruxart's left hand lashed out, grasping her wrist roughly and effectively turning her hand away. His grip tightened painfully; he adroitly sidestepped and her kid half-boot kicked nothing but air.

"Tell me, were you so theatrical as a child?" he asked with a show of interest. "Or perhaps I should rephrase that: Will you be so theatrical when you grow up?"

"Let me go!" she hissed. "You're hurting me!"

The viscount quickly captured her flailing hand and, pulling her ungently into his arms, he brought his lips down to forcibly meet hers. It was a hard kiss, devoid of sentiment, and its effect was crushing to Penelope. It said all that he had not put into words. When he was done, he cast her savagely from him.

She stood, breasts heaving, trying to catch her breath and rubbing her reddened wrist. Pen stared at him with a pout, but her heart was pounding with excitement. The aura of violence about him had always enticed her. At last she said peevishly, "You're a beast, Nicky."

"Then you are well rid of me."

"How can you say that when you know how I feel about you?"

"Surely you don't expect me to believe your heart is broken or that you care a snap for me?" Ruxart asked in a bored drawl. "I was not the first to cuckold Manderley and I very much doubt I shall be the last, so have done, Penelope!"

"You know we are branches of the same tree," said Pen acidly, her pointed chin upthrust, "and whatever else we may feel, we'll always be drawn to one another."

"There is little point to this conversation," he said, his voice dangerously soft. "I'm not a man of many scruples, as you indeed know, but even I will not throw my mistress into the face of my fiancée."

"Fiancée!" Penelope audibly drew in her breath, then released it as two red spots tainted her cheeks. She was not one of the fortunate females to whom a flush was becoming and, looking at her stained, angry face, Ruxart wondered why he had ever been drawn to her at all.

"So it *is* the country mouse!" she sneered.

"It is," he confirmed flatly.

Again, she sucked in a sharp breath. Then she charged shrilly, "You don't love her. You're not capable of love."

"Understand this, Pen—what I feel is immaterial. I'll not have Miss Somers suffer any hurt. Should anything you do or say cause her the least embarrassment . . ." He let the unspoken threat hang in the air between them.

Collecting her clothes from the blue satin chair, Pen went slowly to the door. There, she turned to taunt him with a smile. "I'm willing to wager," she said confidently, "that however much you feel for your Norfolk nobody, my lord, you'll soon come back to me. You're as incapable of fidelity as you are of love and when you tire of her, you'll look to me for your pleasure."

She left him scowling at the slammed door. He was scowling still when St. Juste appeared later that evening. Armand stood staring speculatively at the viscount's obvious ill humor before venturing to ask, "And who is it you are calling out this time?"

"Oh, the devil! It's not that," said Ruxart, downing the contents of a wineglass at a toss.

Armand raised his quizzing glass and inspected his friend for quite some time, noting the unnatural glitter in the black eyes. Deciding his lordship was not yet castaway, however, he let the glass fall and inquired, "Dare I ask? Just what is it that has put you into such . . . shall we say, spirits?"

Nicholas flashed him a look that bespoke understanding, but answered moodily. "Pen paid me a call today, one of her usual melodramatic scenes. She said we're branches of the same tree, she and I, and I'm damned if she's not right!" When his friend made no response, he said more calmly, "At least Helen does not look as if she will enact me any Cheltenham tragedies."

With an inscrutable expression, St. Juste remarked, "Speaking of whom, you've only two days more to make good on your wager. You know, dear boy, when you let the first week pass by without even attempting to claim my thousand guineas, I quite feared you'd lost your touch."

As usual, St. Juste's dry observation made Ruxart forget his petulance. He threw back his head and laughed, then stood. "Your five hundred guineas are as good as in my pocket, Armand! Miss Helen will be saying yes with time to spare. In fact, I'm engaged to escort her to the Cowpers' this evening. Will you come?"

Though St. Juste was reluctant, Nicholas pressed him into accepting and a few hours later the two stood watching the ravishing Miss Helen step gracefully through the boulanger with a young coxcomb newly on the town. She looked, as always, breathtakingly beautiful. Her dark tresses were pulled to one side by a velvet ribbon that precisely matched the jonquil gown she wore. The curls cascaded down her shoulders, enhancing the creaminess of her skin as well as the fine structure of her cheekbones. Though some of the less gracious, or less lovely, females dismissed the simple style as too countrified, every male in the ballroom greatly admired its effect.

"It's as well her beauty sparkles so," commented Ruxart as his eyes followed Helen's progress about the floor, "for her wit does not shine at all."

"If she so displeases you," returned St. Juste on an unusually sharp note, "then choose another for your bride!"

"What, and lose my five hundred guineas?" laughed the viscount. "Not on your life! Besides, I've heard that for a wife to have more hair than wit is no bad thing. And Miss Helen's hair is superbly lovely."

St. Juste shrugged. "I do not find her to be so witless, but I dare say looking at it from a husbandly point of view makes one more critical."

He moved away before Ruxart could respond, leaving the viscount looking after his receding form with a thoughtful frown. He was unable to reflect deeply upon his friend's sudden acerbity, however, because he was immediately snared by his aunt, Lady Frances Fletcher.

"Ruxart!" she screeched. "I have been desiring to speak with you for days. Did you not receive the note I sent round to Half Moon Street asking for you to wait upon me?"

He turned a resigned, indifferent gaze upon her rounded features, focusing on her multiple chins. "I'm sorry, Aunt

Fanny, I was unable to get away."

She did not believe this for a moment and told him so bluntly. "But the fact is, Nicholas, I wonder what you are up to, trying so hard to fix your interest with that little beauty, for you've certainly never lost your heart! If you have a heart to lose—which I have doubted for years—you've kept it intact, for a man less in love I have yet to see!"

Ruxart gnashed his teeth at this, but knew the impossibility of trying to stem one of her lectures in midflow. He did not listen as she continued, but wondered where she found a dresser who would allow her out of the house with that repulsive puce turban wrapped around her head.

She regained his attention by rapping smartly on his wrist with her closed fan. "You will doubtless think me an interfering busybody—"

"Will I?" he inquired politely.

"But whatever game you are playing, Ruxart, I advise you to quit before the stakes become too deep!" With that Lady Frances trotted away, satisfied that she had set her nephew onto the right path.

Ruxart stared unseeing after her, then pivoted on his heel and went directly to where Miss Somers had just been seated, her face still delightfully aflush from the exertions of the dance.

"Miss Helen, I wish to speak privately with you," he stated, his tone directly abrupt.

"N-now?" she stammered, her eyes flying to meet his.

"If you please," he said, extending his hand.

She hesitated briefly, then placed her own slim hand in his and rose. As they moved together across the room, she knew this was the moment that had been expected all week and steeled herself to make an affirmative reply. She had looked in vain for some sign of affection from Mr. St. Juste, but had finally been forced to accept that his kindness to her stemmed solely from his friendship with the viscount. If she had to sacrifice herself for the good of the family, Helen would by far rather do so with the fair Mr. St. Juste or even, she thought sadly, with someone like the ridiculous Baron Alvanley whose wealth and eccentric pranks made him a regular feature in the *on dits* about town. But they were not about to offer for her as, she suspected with a sinking heart, Viscount Ruxart was.

His lordship stopped before a curtained alcove and stepped aside for her to pass through. He pulled the curtain closed when he entered, then turned his dark gaze upon her.

"Miss Somers—Helen—you must know what I wish to ask," he began in a brusque manner.

She tried to speak, but found she could not. She merely inclined her head shyly, which, had she but known it, tried his lordship's thin supply of patience to the utmost. He covered this by possessing himself of her trembling hand and, bending his head, lightly brushing his lips across it.

"I desire to make you my wife," he said as he straightened, "and if you will honor me with an acceptance, I will apply to your brother for formal permission to address you. Our future, my dear, is yours to command."

He had retained his hold upon her and she sat staring mutely at the two hands entwined before she finally raised her blue eyes to his square face. "I am certain you will find William happy to receive you," she said so softly he had to bend to catch it.

"You have made me very happy, Helen," Ruxart remarked calmly before returning her to her seat and setting off to collect his winnings from St. Juste.

Chapter Five

A small, slim boy burst through the door shadowed by an even smaller one. Their dark crops of chestnut curls and vivid blue eyes plainly proclaimed them as Somerses. The elder, a child of possibly seven or eight, skidded to a stop and the younger crashed into his back.

"I say!" cried the first. "There's a ripping carriage coming up the road!"

"Frederick," said Agnes sternly, "that is no way to enter a room. You and George go out and see if you can enter like little gentlemen."

"But, Mother!"

"No buts, Frederick, if you please. Now do as I say."

The boy stalked out, followed quickly by his little brother, whose stubby legs could not keep up with his sibling's. The pair marched back in, quietly this time, to their mother's austere approval.

"What were you saying about a carriage, Freddy?" asked his Aunt Jane, looking up from her needlework.

"It's a bang-up rig," said the boy knowingly, "and it's got a capital crest on the side!"

"Where do you pick up such terms?" Agnes wondered, but

at the same moment Jane said, "I think I hear something."

"That's the carriage!" exclaimed Freddy. He ran to the window and stood pressing his nose to the pane while George stretched on his tiptoes beside him.

Jane laid aside the linen she had been mending and rose to stand behind her nephews. "Indeed it is," she confirmed. She turned a puzzled look upon Agnes. "And it's stopping here!"

Agnes joined the others to peer out the window in time to see a private coach drawn by four bay horses pull to a halt before their cottage. The outriders sprang to the ground, opened the door and let down the steps to help the occupants emerge. A young lady's maid clutching a square dressing case stepped out first, then stood waiting for her mistress.

Freddy was the first to see her. "It's Aunt Helen," he declared while George clapped his chubby hands together. Jane ran lightly to the door and outside to meet her sister.

"Helen! Why didn't you let us know you were coming?"

"I did not know myself before yesterday," she answered with a happy laugh as she threw her arms around Jane's neck. "There was no chance to send word before Aunt Liz packed us off!"

Followed discreetly by the Willoughby's maid, the two came arm-in-arm into the house where they were met by Agnes. "Whose coach is this?" she inquired keenly.

An indecipherable expression crossed over Helen's face before she answered tonelessly, "It is my Lord Ruxart's. He kindly offered it for my journey."

Jane cast her a sharp look, but was constrained from saying anything while Agnes continued to greet Helen. She did so with such a degree of warmth that her young in-law was prompted to ask if she was feeling quite the thing.

"Oh, you precious child!" Agnes replied with a false titter. "How could we not all feel happy for your joy! It is the best of good news, and we are most impatient to hear all the details of your romance." She ended this speech by tapping on the door of Dorothea's bedroom and saying as she entered, "Mother Somers, look who has come home!"

Mrs. Somers lay upon her bed surrounded by her bottles of hartshorn and Hungary Water; her vinaigrette reposed next to her hand and was grasped instantly upon their entrance. She sat upright with astonishing energy and cried, "Oh, my sweetest! My love! Such a triumph! It was precisely what I expected of you, though of course we were most surprised when Elizabeth wrote of your brilliant catch. If only your dear, dear papa could share in your happiness, for I am sure the salvation of the family would have saved his life!"

Such reasoning brought an amused twinkle to Jane's eyes, for dear Papa had met his untimely end by falling from his horse during a drunken celebration for the winning of a bet, the winning being a far more unusual circumstance than the drinking. The twinkle soon disappeared, however, for within the hour Jane was certain that her sister was not in love, nor even very happy over her forthcoming betrothal. Helen confirmed that his lordship had indeed spoken and would be traveling to Sloley in the next day or two to speak with William and make his formal declaration. She stated this so matter-of-factly, with such a resigned set to her pretty lips, that Jane was nearly overset with anxiety to be alone with her.

There was no opportunity throughout the remainder of the afternoon, for Dorothea engulfed her daughter in her arms and continued to monopolize her, pausing in her raptures occasionally to sniff at her vinaigrette or to question Helen sharply about the season's *on dits*, the latest fashions, and all the myriad details of fashionable life on the town.

By the time her mother at last relinquished her, Helen was thoroughly convinced that she had been right to make this noble sacrifice, for matters were far worse than she had ever realized. Though Mama had not been vulgar enough to mention such subjects, Agnes had referred repeatedly to such mysterious things as settlements and mortgages until Helen was assured that only her marriage stood between the

59

Somerses and the poor house.

This notion was reinforced over their family supper when even William admitted that his lordship's offer was a fortunate one, indeed. He mitigated this slightly by adding, "If I find his character is not all as is reputed, I shall be most happy to give my consent to this match."

"If!" shrieked Agnes. "What can you mean? Of course you will consent!"

Observing that Helen, who could not bear arguments or dissension of any kind, was turning pale, Jane intervened, saying quietly, "It shall all be settled soon enough. Helen, dearest, do tell me where you came by that fetching bonnet you wore today! It became you extremely."

The subject having been successfully turned, little more was said regarding Helen's betrothal and gradually the color returned to her cheeks. But her sister remained dissatisfied and impatiently awaited the time when they would retire to the tiny bedroom they had shared for years.

At last, however, the moment came when Jane sat on the edge of Helen's bed, regarding her seriously with concerned gray eyes.

Helen did not meet her gaze directly and chattered nervously about her stay in London, her trip home in the viscount's luxurious coach and her happiness to be back in her own little room until finally the flow of words faded awkwardly away.

"Why are you entering into this engagement, love?" Jane asked gently then.

"Why—why it is a wonderful match! His lordship is—is handsome and most flattering! You cannot imagine how attentive he has been! It will be a most agreeable marriage, I assure you."

"Stuff!" said Jane in sisterly affection. "It's as plain as a pikestaff you are not in love."

"Oh, Jane!" Helen responded airily. "Surely you do not still believe that people marry for *love*! Is that why you've

60

never got off the shelf?"

There was a shocked silence while Jane struggled not to show her hurt.

"Jane, dearest, I'm so sorry!" exclaimed Helen in great distress. "I never meant—"

"It does not signify."

"But it does, it does! I am so *sorry*!" Tears spilled from her lovely eyes as Helen flew into her sister's arms.

"You silly peagoose! It was nothing," said Jane, giving her a hearty squeeze. "Now dry your eyes. As regards the other, you must do as you feel is best, dear. I only spoke out of concern for your happiness."

"I know! I know! I'm a wretch to have spoken to you so," she sobbed on a muffled hiccough.

"Nonsense!" Jane countered bracingly. "Now let us say nothing more about it." She blew out the candle and, wishing Helen pleasant dreams, climbed into her own bed to lay awake for quite some time.

During the days which followed, they spoke no more of the betrothal for Helen's manner did not invite confidences and Jane was far too wise to press upon her. She was tempted once to speak when, three days later, Agnes came into the parlor wreathed in smiles to announce that William had received a note from the Viscount Ruxart. The note had been sent from the inn in nearby Worstead where his lordship had put up with his cousin, Mr. Fletcher. Helen accepted the news that Ruxart would be calling upon them in the morning with such a strained smile that Jane had to bite her lip to keep back the exclamation that sprang to mind. Her sister's only comment, however, had been that they should like the viscount's cousin very well, for Mr. Fletcher was a nice, quiet gentleman.

That Ruxart had journeyed to Norfolk with his cousin John had come about as a result of an argument with

Armand St. Juste. Though not generally of matutinal habits, the viscount had risen early the morning of Helen's departure to pay a call upon his friend. He was ushered into St. Juste's sunny breakfast room where the beau sat leisurely perusing his morning correspondence. As Ruxart was announced, Armand set aside the stack of papers and took up his eyeglass.

"I fear I shall have to make my apologies to Dobbs," he observed. "I made quite certain he was mistaken. But there! You see that I can be in error, after all."

"And what," inquired his lordship as he sat, "can you be in error about?"

"Being well aware of the hour, I informed Dobbs, when he told me you were calling, that he was of course mistaken," he explained. As Ruxart laughed, he continued on a drawl, "I don't believe I've previously had the privilege of seeing you before noon, Nick. To what do I owe this unprecedented honor?"

"You know Miss Somers leaves today," said Ruxart, stretching out his legs. "I'm set to follow in a day or two. I should like you to come up to Norfolk with me."

St. Juste paused in the act of putting his coffee cup to his lips. "Why?" he asked without expression.

"Oh—because the prospect of being stuck in the country for days on end with my beautiful but boring fiancée and a parcel of her relatives leaves me cold."

Fixing his green eyes upon his massive ruby ring, St. Juste remarked in a weary tone, "I cannot be chasing into Norfolk at the height of the season—even to oblige you, my friend."

The viscount bestowed a puzzled frown upon St. Juste, but said easily enough, "I doubt there will be much of a season with its finest beauty and biggest rogue out of town. Come, Armand, we could find a week's entertainment together—even in Norfolk!"

"Selecting your bride is as far as I am able to exert myself," drawled St. Juste without moving his gaze. "I believe the effort of wooing her for you is beyond me."

"Don't come that damned manner of yours with me," returned Ruxart, too softly.

"I am afraid I must decline your invitation, Ruxart. Other matters press."

Anger flashed in his eyes as Ruxart scraped back his chair. He stood motionless a moment, then said tautly, "As you wish."

He strode to the door but as he reached for the handle, St. Juste looked up from his steady contemplation of his ring and said gently, "Nick, you shall do much better without me."

Ruxart left without responding. He had stood upon the street slapping his gloves together with a heavy frown. His groom, holding the heads of his lordship's spirited grays, kept his face immobile, though he wondered what had occurred to erase m'lord's sunny mood. Jem's curiosity, when the viscount presently pulled to a stop before Mr. Fletcher's lodgings in Curzon Street, was even greater.

His lordship whisked past Fletcher's manservant before that astonished man could do more than drop open his mouth. Ruxart's irruption upon Fletcher in his bedchamber caused John to cease knotting the muslin about his neck to turn and stare at him in imitation of his servant.

"Good morning, John," said the viscount casually as he came forward.

His cousin, taken by surprise, greeted him with a lessening of the stiff manner he had maintained toward the viscount since their last falling out. Feeling sure that nothing less than calamity could induce Ruxart to be about at this early hour, he inquired anxiously, "What's wrong, Nick? Is it Grandfather? Is he—?"

"Lord, no! I don't doubt that he'll dance on my grave," he replied with a thin smile. "Nothing is wrong, John. At least, nothing I despair of mending." He threw down his gloves and hat while watching the rigidity return to Fletcher's bearing.

"Then how may I be of service?" he asked with reserve.

"I'm to go into Norfolk in a day or so and would like you to accompany me."

"I fail to see what purpose could be served by my coming along for your courtship," said John, motioning for his guest to be seated.

"Oh, I well know you don't approve of this match," Nicholas said, continuing to move about in his restless way, "but I had thought we might use this journey to put an end to the rift between us."

Fletcher wavered. He wanted nothing more than to be on terms with the cousin he had always, secretly, looked up to. But at the memory of their recent argument, he remained stiff. "I think I'd best not come. My presence could only be an interference into your affairs."

"For God's sake, man," bit out his lordship heatedly, "don't hold my words against me! You know what I am like when angry!"

A smile suddenly crossed Fletcher's face. "After knowing you all my life, Nicholas, I must confess that I do."

Ruxart paused in his pacing, then gave an answering laugh. "Then you'll forgive me and come?"

"I suppose I must," said John in friendly resignation, "for I know your determination when you wish for something."

"Good. It shall be deadly dull, I dare say, but there's an elder sister, I'm told—"

"You're never playing matchmaker!"

"Devil a bit!" denied Nick, not without humor. He proceeded to collect his hat and gloves, then flashed his cousin his most winning smile. "I'll see you in, say, two day's time?"

John nodded his agreement and Ruxart left the room as suddenly as he had entered it. His lordship's groom was gratified to see that m'lord had regained a better frame of

mind, a mood which was miraculously maintained throughout the next few days and even through the day's journey
into Norfolk.

The cousins had arrived in Worstead on the Friday, each
feeling in good humor with the other. Fletcher had tactfully
refrained from criticizing his lordship's reckless handling of
the ribbons, while for his part, Ruxart had thoughtfully
driven his curricle at an unusually moderate speed.

If Freddy had been enthusiastic about the viscount's
coach, he was ecstatic when he saw his lordship's curricle,
which he called all the crack and from which he could not
take his eyes. He was quite cast down at being sent up to the
schoolroom with his brother, but brightened somewhat
when his Aunt Jane whispered a hurried promise to bring
him down later.

Jane had spent the majority of hours since the receipt of
the viscount's note in a flurry of preparations for the
momentous visit, working with Agnes and Mrs. Beedle, their
cook, to get ready. Insisting that the future viscountess must
not sully her hands, Agnes refused to let Helen do anything
beyond the lightest dusting with the result that she nearly
fainted with panic. Jane, however, shooed Helen into the
capable hands of Aunt Liz's maid. Once everything had been
scrubbed, dusted, washed and polished, it only remained for
Jane to make a last-minute tour of inspection.

As she stood in the small drawing room, she vividly pictured a pair of turned-down ebony eyes staring with haughty
disdain at the worn drapes, the shiny thin chair coverings,
and even at her own olive merino gown which was at least
four years out of fashion. An embarrassed warmth crept up
her neck. The thought of Ruxart's arrogant appraisal of her
home, and the low opinion she was certain he would hold
upon seeing the mended linen and threadbare carpets, sent
the heated flush up over her cheeks. It was the only sign, as
their guests arrived, that Miss Somers was not her usual
calm self.

Years of being the mainstay of the Somers family, however, had given her considerable control over her emotions and it was with the semblance, at least, of composure that Jane rose to meet Viscount Ruxart. She met his scrutiny squarely and did not reveal any of the inner turmoil that overcame her when she saw him again mentally dismiss her as he had done years before.

His eyes passed over her swiftly as Helen continued making introductions very prettily in her low musical voice. Elizabeth's maid had dressed her dark curls in a fashionable topknot which was left unadorned. Betty had then suggested that Miss Helen wear a simple cream gown of twilled cambric with azure ribbons circling its high waist; she wisely left all else to her charge's own natural good looks. The viscount had much admired the results, setting both Mrs. Somerses firm in the belief that his lordship was contracting a love match.

Helen drew Ruxart's attention to the final member of her family present, her brother Clarence. His every objection—and these had been numerous—having been overridden by the females of his family, Clarence was indeed there to meet his future brother-in-law. He noted the set of the viscount's superfine blue jacket upon his broad shoulders, the mirrored gleam of his tasseled Hessians, the intricate knot of his jauntily tied cravat and dismissed him instantly as one of the sporting set. Clarence sat down wearily, prepared to be bored out of mind.

His feelings were echoed precisely by Ruxart, who notwithstanding, proceeded to charm the majority of the family with his easy good manners. William was most favorably impressed and began to believe Agnes had been, as usual, right to set his lordship's reputation down to vile tale-bearers who jealously embellished his every youthful peccadillo. He was equally pleased with Mr. Fletcher and was gratified to see Jane speaking quietly with the gentleman, though it was a pity she had worn her cap today.

The elder Mrs. Somers, having drawn on every reserve of her spare strength, sat in the center of the room, much like a queen holding her court, and it was she who dominated the conversation.

"My dear Lord Ruxart, I am sure I need not tell you how pleased and honored we are by your visit to our little home!" she said regally as soon as he was seated. "Though, of course, this is not the manner in which the Somerses have always lived. No, indeed. I quite remember the gay times we had in London when Mr. Somers and I were first married! General Sir Grenville Somers is my brother-in-law, you know, but poor Aubrey! Well, you know how it is with younger sons."

"I am pleased to be here, ma'am," put in Ruxart when she paused to take a breath.

"My dear late husband always used to say, before he met with his fatal accident, that his luck would come about, and I feel quite certain that were Mr. Somers here today, he would be telling us that it had, at last!" Dorothea rattled on brightly. "But I always knew something wonderful would come about with our little Helen. She is the dearest child, so sweet, so good-natured. She'll make you a lovely viscountess, mark my words."

"Indeed, ma'am, I shall mark them immediately," the viscount murmured rather dryly.

"Please, Mama," interjected Helen softly, a delightful rose caressing her cheeks.

"It is only the simple truth, love! You are all that his lordship could wish for in a wife."

"Mother," said her eldest son as a purple flush climbed up his neck, "may I remind you that the matter is not yet settled. Lord Ruxart has not yet applied to me."

"Oh, pooh, William! It's as good as settled! Is it not, my lord?" she inquired with an arch wag of her hand.

"I've no doubt that you've indeed settled it, ma'am," said Ruxart, a sardonic smile playing on his full lips.

The hands laying folded upon Miss Somers' woolen lap

67

suddenly clenched and the fire of her anger blazed into her eyes. She could scarcely repress her rage over his lordship's arrogant mockery, her fury over her family's willing acceptance of his barely concealed insults.

A few moments later, Ruxart was endeavoring not to yawn when he chanced to glance her way. Black eyes met gray and held. His attention was firmly caught by the fierce glare being focused upon him. He lazily looked her up and down. Miss Somers sat quietly, her long hands resting in her lap and her face expressionless, but those overlarge gray eyes were clearly filled with hostility. The viscount found himself wondering what was going on behind the impassive face with the smoldering eyes and how he should discover it.

He was recalled by Dorothea, who inquired sharply if he meant to make a formal announcement immediately. He answered that it was his intention to do so and the conversation proceeded as before. When he rose some few minutes later to take his leave, he discovered that the sister with the angry eyes had slipped from the room. Shrugging off his unaccountable disappointment, he agreed to return later for a private interview with William and followed his cousin outside.

Fletcher mounted the curricle and Ruxart was about to climb in beside him when his name rang out. He turned to see Miss Jane Somers standing on the front step with a small boy attached to each of her hands. He looked at the two children, then at the tall young woman between them. A challenge shone clear in her expressive eyes.

"Lord Ruxart, I should like to make you known to my nephews, Master Frederick and Master George Somers," she said directly.

The two little boys bowed solemnly, each with eyes rounded in awe of the man who had driven the magnificent curricle.

"How do you do?" asked the viscount, just as seriously. He extended his hand.

Freddy shook it gravely, but the younger boy took his aunt's skirt in his grubby hand and hid shyly behind it. With a lift of one black brow, his lordship noted that she seemed neither to mind nor even to notice the damage being done to her gown. The elder boy tugged at her gown, too, and Jane bent while he stood on tiptoe to place his lip against her cap. Of a sudden, Jane's laughter filled the air. Ruxart's raised brow was joined by its mate, for it was not a tinkling society titter, but a warm, throaty laugh that was as enchanting as it was infectious.

"I think, my dears," she said with a tilt of her linen mobcap, "that you must ask him yourselves."

The boys' brilliant blue eyes widened even further. Freddy's mouth opened soundlessly.

"May I perhaps be of some help?" prompted his lordship.

"I—if you please, sir!—me and George would like to ride in your curricle! It's a bang-up rig, sir!" rushed Freddy. He looked for approval to his aunt, who nodded her head with such a twinkle in her gray eyes as they came up to meet the viscount's that Ruxart found himself saying, "It could be arranged. Perhaps tomorrow after church, if your mother is agreeable."

He did not stay to share in the boys' ecstasy, and when he and John were finally away in his curricle, he wondered again what it had been about those gray eyes that had caused him to assent to taking two young brats into his most prized vehicle. "I must be," he remarked aloud, "getting old."

To which mystifying comment his cousin had no reply.

Chapter Six

The few persons who chanced to travel along the high road in the countryside beyond Sloley the following morning were met with the edifying prospect of Lord Ruxart bowling along in his curricle seated between two small boys. Jem nearly fell from his perch when his lordship placed the Masters Somers on the seat of his vehicle; he was moved enough to later forcibly remark to the stableboy at Worstead that he'd never seen nothing like it, no, nor thought to see again!

John Fletcher had been let down at the front step of Plumstead Cottage where he stood with Miss Jane Somers watching the curricle pass out of sight. He much admired the modest neatness of her plain attire; he had no liking for the extremes of fashion and was, indeed, much shocked by the practice of the more on-the-go women to damp the petticoats of their sheer gowns. His eyes had more than once wandered to her tall, trim figure during church services that morning and they now focused warmly upon her.

"I wish I might know the secret of your success, Miss Somers," he said with a kind smile as they moved inside.

"My success?" she repeated quizzically.

"My family and I have been trying for years to do what took you only a bare moment—to get Ruxart to follow one of our suggestions," he explained in a teasing tone.

"But I assure you, Mr. Fletcher, I did not 'get' his lordship to do anything. This was an arrangement between my nephews and him. Indeed, his behavior toward the boys has been such that I fear I've been doing him an injustice," she said frankly. Jane was in the act of seating herself upon the settee in the deserted parlor and thus did not see the puzzlement cross Fletcher's face.

"What sort of injustice could you be doing to Ruxart?"

"Oh, well . . . I cannot say I am pleased about this match, Mr. Fletcher. In fact, I must confess to having conceived a misliking for it from the moment I first learned of it. But I knew his lordship by repute—"

"Lord, who does not?" he laughed.

She answered him with her own warm laughter. "Yes, but I must now own to having prejudged his lordship. I'm determined not to do so again."

"I still long for your secret, Miss Somers, for at the risk of destroying my cousin's good name with you once again, I must tell you that Ruxart would never be spending his morning driving children in his curricle solely for their pleasure. He generally obliges only himself and to the devil with all else. Although," he added thoughtfully, "he does occasionally allow himself to be ruled by one other."

"May I ask by whom?"

"Our grandfather, the Earl of Kerrington. He more or less raised my cousin and he can still bring Nick in line. But, Miss Somers," he said, smiling once more, "tell me why you were not at supper with us last night? I did wonder, when we sat down and you had not appeared, if you were perhaps feeling unwell?"

"No, it was nothing of that nature. I quite often take my supper in the schoolroom with my nephews; I did so last night," she replied a trifle self-consciously. In truth, she had

72

not been able to compose herself for another encounter with Ruxart last night. She recalled vividly how her pulse had raced yesterday when he stared at her with his brows raised in that odd fashion and she was grateful when Fletcher turned the conversation to more neutral topics.

The viscount's curricle returned some twenty minutes later and they went out to greet it. As Ruxart lifted Freddy down, the young boy exclaimed, "Auntie, you will never guess! He let me hold the reins a bit, he really did! *And* he said I had good hands!"

Fletcher received this pronouncement with all the astonishment it deserved and could only believe his cousin's action to stem from the fact that the horses were local cattle and not his lordship's prized grays.

Miss Somers, however, was unaware of the magnitude of Ruxart's gesture and the look she bestowed upon him was not one of surprise, but one of friendly gratitude. Looking at her in turn, all thought of informing Miss Somers of the impossibility of his repeating the excursion died stillborn on the viscount's lips.

George joined Freddy on the ground and the pair rushed into the house, eager to tell everyone of their splendid adventure. Jane watched them dash out of sight, then turned to the viscount.

"Thank you, Lord Ruxart. You've been very kind."

"You mistake, Miss Somers," he drawled with just a hint of a smile, "I am almost never kind. Just ask my worthy cousin!"

"There is no need. He has already informed me that you generally oblige no one but yourself," she said, shooting a twinkling look at the unfortunate John. "I understand that your feeling is 'to the devil with all else.' Have I that correct, Mr. Fletcher?"

Ruxart's smile gave way as he tilted his head back to laugh. John was unable to reply, but sent her a humorously reproachful glance before leaving them to enter the cottage.

"You are an unusual woman, Miss Somers," said the viscount, putting out his arm. As she laid her hand lightly upon it, he asked, "Tell me, why were you so angry with me yesterday?"

The hand upon his sleeve nervously jerked; it stilled on the instant, but Ruxart had noted it and stopped to look directly at her. "Come, can you not bring yourself to tell me what grave solecism I committed to put you so out of sorts with me?"

His black eyes were quite free of the cold haughtiness Jane could not bear. Disconcerted by his unwonted warmth, she removed her gaze to her fingers. "You must forgive me, my lord. I rather thought, you see, that you were enjoying some private fun at my family's expense."

He did not respond and she looked up to find the distant chill once more in his eyes. "I am sorry," she began.

"Do not apologize," he cut in curtly. "You were quite right and I ask your pardon."

She was bereft of speech; he thought she was again angry and with a swift step he left her side. Jane stood bemazed, considering this surprising depth in the man she had once dismissed as arrogantly shallow. When she at last entered the house after him, he had already joined his cousin and her brother in the parlor. She hesitated at the door, then with a firm shake of her head, continued to the back of the house.

In the parlor, William was discoursing cheerfully, the usual stern set of his lips for once relaxed, upon the new pups his best hunter had sired, even offering his lordship one. Conversation continued on like topics until Agnes interrupted the gentlemen. She positively beamed upon the viscount as she said with an arch look that he might prefer the company in the back morning room. She continued to beam as he left, for all that was needed for the betrothal of Miss Helen and Lord Ruxart to be completed was the formality of his addressing the young lady.

The greater portion of the afternoon and evening of the

previous day had seen William closeted with the viscount. Though she had been in an agony of fear that William would be taken advantage of, even Agnes had to admit that the settlements were more than fair. They would finally be pulled out of the River Tick into which the late Mr. Somers had plunged them, William had explained to the family that morning, and with a substantial amount to spare. Helen had accepted the news with a sinking heart, for she now realized she must do nothing to annoy the man who was to save the family. She was again telling herself this as she sat where Agnes had left her, artfully promising to deliver her suitor as soon as may be.

Like every other apartment in Plumstead Cottage, the back morning room was small, shabby and sparsely furnished. Thus, when Ruxart entered to find Helen seated upon a faded sofa in a picturesque pose, the lovely lady far outshone her setting. She wore an aqua muslin gown cut low across the bodice, affording his lordship a teasing view of soft, creamy breasts. The sleeves were short and squared and she wore no gloves, exposing her slender arms to his inspection. He lingered only an instant on the threshold, then strolled forward to place himself beside her.

"I've come bearing gifts, my love, so you had best beware," he said with a sensual smile. He held out his closed fist, gradually unfurling it to reveal a brilliant ring composed of small diamonds clustered round an enormous sapphire so deeply blue as to seem black. The gems winked at Helen as the sunlight danced over the ring's surface. She stared at it, dumb-struck.

The viscount swept up her unresisting right hand and gently slid the ring onto her finger. "There. That seals our bargain," he said lightly.

"Thank you," she murmured, finding her voice at last. "It is . . . my lord . . . it's the loveliest ring I've ever seen. Thank you!" She raised her vivid blue eyes, shimmering with pleasure, and a flame leapt into Ruxart's eyes in answer.

"No jewel could surpass your own loveliness, my beauty," he said huskily. He leaned close and drew her into his arms. She briefly saw the fiery passion in his face as he brought his lips warmly to hers. His kiss was ardently moist and Helen could not repress the shudder of fear that shook her slender frame.

Ruxart instantly pulled back, frowning at her with such a dark scowl that Helen cried out, "I am—I am sorry, sir! I-it—I was not expecting it!"

Some of the menace left his dark eyes, but the gelid gaze returned to them and Helen did not know which it was she dreaded the more.

"There is no need to apologize," he said curtly.

Noting the creases marking either side of the viscount's set mouth, Helen feared she had made him terribly angry. "But there is!" she protested in agitation. "I mean to be a . . . a dutiful wife, my lord."

"Don't you think, my dear, it's time you called me by name?" he asked with a mocking curl of his lip.

"Please, my—Ruxart—I did not mean to make you angry! I will not do so again, I promise," she said, sounding like a contrite child.

Annoyance, impatience and resignation flitted in rapid succession across his lordship's face. He finally responded flatly, "Do not be overmuch concerned, Helen. I'm all too often angry, usually without just reason. It is I who should beg pardon for having frightened you. Such was not my intention. And now, I believe it is time for me to take my leave of you."

She put out a trembling hand to restrain him from rising and turned her face up. She closed her eyes and waited, her body rigid with tension. Her air of the martyr brought a fresh scowl as Ruxart studied the long fringes of lashes dusting her delicate cheeks, the rosy lips that formed a heart of desire. He leaned forward. His lips grazed hers and he was standing.

"I'll see you tonight, my love," he said coolly, then left.

Having done what she could to help Mrs. Beedle in the kitchen, Jane now crossed the hallway on her way to her room. Wisps of brown locks peeped around the ruffled edge of her linen cap, and a light sprinkling of flour graced the front of her gown. Her cheek bore the imprint of her baking while upon the tip of her nose, a spot of white powder sat proudly.

She was about to turn up the stairs when she heard a door open and looked over her shoulder to see Mr. Fletcher coming out of the parlor. She smiled at him pleasantly and placed a foot upon the stair.

"One moment, Miss Somers," he said, coming forward with a smile. He drew a large square of linen from his pocket. "You've been at work in the kitchen, I perceive."

"What?" Her hand whisked to her cheek and returned lightly dusted with flour on the tips. "Oh," she said, observing them. "I must look a frightful sight!"

"You look charming," he countered, tilting her face up with his fingertips and dabbing gently at her cheek with his kerchief.

This agreeable scene was viewed with something less than enjoyment by Lord Ruxart who stood in the shadows of the hall watching them narrowly. Their apparent companionship further exacerbated his lordship's already ruffled temper and when his cousin began so tenderly to attend to Miss Somers' cheek, the viscount had reached his limit.

"Have you quite done, Fletcher?" he demanded crossly as he came forward.

Startled, Jane tried to pull from John's fingers, but he checked her by resolutely applying the linen to the tip of her nose. "In a moment, Ruxart," he said, calmly removing the last of the flour from her face. Finally he stepped back. "There you are, Miss Somers. All right and tidy."

"Thank you," she said quietly. She was intensely aware of Ruxart's set jaw, his eyes blazing beneath his drooping lids.

77

His lordship now strode to the door and, with a rueful smile at Miss Somers, Fletcher joined him. All the way to Worstead Inn, he was subjected to a series of the viscount's animadversions on the impropriety of flirting with country spinsters who did not understand the rules of the game. John wisely kept from responding, though he mentally raised his brows at his cousin's vehement outpourings.

Jane had stood motionless until the door had fully closed; she then went directly down the narrow hall to the morning room from which Ruxart had exited. Stepping through the doorway, she saw her sister standing staring out the window.

"Helen, what has occurred? The viscount—"

"Oh, la," broke in Helen, sounding precisely like her cousin Caro, "is he not the most extravagant dear? Just look at the ring he has given me!" She spun from the window to exhibit her hand, continuing spritely, "Such generous manners and such address! He is forever saying the most flattering things! I vow and declare I am the most fortunate girl there ever was!"

Jane examined her sister's face with a look of searching inquiry. "Lord Ruxart did not look as if he'd been paying you flowery compliments, Helen. He wore a thunderous frown when I saw him."

Remembering her cousin's precept, Helen said blithely, "Oh, as a rich viscountess, I shan't need to look for smiles from my *husband*!"

Her sister revealed none of her shocked dismay, but said quietly, "You need not go through with this. It's not too late to cry off."

"Do not be going into *that* again, I beg of you!" returned Helen, turning away from Jane's steady gaze. "Indeed, you are becoming a regular Sour Peg, Jane, and you'd best take care not to become a positive nag!"

This airy speech had its effect. "Very well, Helen. I shan't say another word on this subject, I promise you." Jane stared silently at her sister a moment more, then turned from the room.

Immediately, Helen threw herself onto the bare sofa to shed tears of self-pity. She felt alone, misunderstood, the magnanimity of her noble sacrifice unappreciated.

Since the prospect of a bride frightened by his advances did not amuse him, Ruxart returned to Plumstead Cottage that evening determined to be patient, gentle and charming with Helen. His resolution was apparently rewarded for the young miss treated him to a display of artful coquetry to rival any seasoned lady about town. She greeted him with more animation than he had yet seen, twirling lightly in her soft rose gown to gaily introduce her sister Maria and the curate to whom she had been happily wed these past six years.

Bowing to the young woman presented to him, Ruxart instantly liked what he saw. Maria Gaines was dashingly pretty, though not, he thought, the equal of her younger sister, but she had a cheerful openness with a foundation of sense about her that he recognized and admired. He left her with one of his best smiles to greet her husband.

Thomas Gaines looked more like an overgrown school-boy than a sober man of the cloth. His was a sunny counte-nance in a round face with juvenescent lines, but his gaze sized the viscount knowingly as they clasped hands. Though he had scandalized his valet by leaving him in London—Oundle being convinced his lordship was incapable of dress-ing himself—Ruxart had nonetheless managed to present a creditable appearance in his neat unostentatious evening dress. Gaines approved the lack of ornamentation, later tell-ing Maria he had to own his lordship was no fop.

Ruxart's ready charm again captivated both of the Mrs. Somerses as easily as it had the night before; Maria, too, seemed taken with his lazy smile and gracious manners. If the viscount wondered at the absence of Miss Somers, he did not remark upon it. Fletcher, however, was quietly asking Helen where her eldest sister might be when the lady in question made her entrance.

She wore her best gown for the occasion, a plain indigo kerseymere, the severity of which was softened by a touch of creamy lace at the collar and cuffs. Despite her careful tucking, soft brown tendrils escaped the confines of her laced cap to spill charmingly over her ears. Within the glow of the candlelight, she no longer looked like the plain spinster she professed to be.

In front of her stood a brightly pretty child with a mass of tumbling dark brown curls and a much smaller toddler wobbling on two short, stubby legs.

"I hope you will not mind," said Jane with an apologetic smile, "but it did not seem quite fair to deny them a chance to meet our guests when Freddy and George have already done so." She moved quickly forward, ignoring the disapproving glare from her sister-in-law, to present her niece and nephew to their visitors.

No other woman of the viscount's acquaintance would have cared a button what the children thought fair and Ruxart looked warmly from Miss Anne Gaines' gray eyes to those of her aunt. He found Miss Somers regarding him with cool disapproval and redoubled his efforts to charm, swinging young Daniel Gaines onto his knee. Though this action endeared him completely to Maria, Jane remained distantly cool. She soon removed the children with barely a smile of appreciation for his lordship.

Throughout dinner there was no opportunity for the two to converse, Ruxart having been placed to Dorothea's right where he soon fell victim to one of her ongoing monologues cataloguing her sufferings since the loss of her husband. He observed his cousin talking easily with Miss Somers at the far end of the table and was surprised at the annoyance he felt, but he put this down to the insufferable boredom of his own dinner partners.

Helen, in her attempts to please his lordship, called upon every flirtatious method she had ever seen her cousin Caroline employ, thereby quickly wearying him and distressing her sister Jane. Having long been the object of feminine wiles, Ruxart began to wish the meal over midway through the second course. His air of impatience was noted by Jane and she fumed at his lordship's obvious ennui. She had known how it would be when he met her family. But she had not suspected how much it would hurt her.

At last the interminable meal was finished; the ladies withdrew to the parlor and the gentlemen were left to enjoy their port and snuff in peace. The port was quite passable and its effect was apparently soothing for even the viscount seemed restored to good humor when they rejoined the ladies. Miss Somers was sitting in the far corner, her head bent over a small book. She did not look up as the men entered and was quite startled when she was addressed.

"And what fault do you find with my behavior this evening, Miss Somers?" Ruxart inquired as he took a chair beside her.

Despite a sudden dryness in her mouth over this unexpected query, she managed a steady reply. "What possible fault could I find, my lord? You have been all that is charming and gracious."

"Your eyes tell a different story. They are filled with disapproval each time they set upon me."

"I do not disapprove of your actions tonight, my lord, whatever you think my eyes are saying."

He studied her for a time, his lids half-closed. "Still, you dislike me," he said flatly.

"Of course I do not dislike you," said Jane, glancing away in sudden confusion. His frankness disarmed her for it was not at all what she expected of the arrogant peer. When she was emboldened to turn her eyes to the viscount once more, she found the cynical glaze returned to his gaze. She followed the direction of his cold stare and discovered he was looking directly at Helen. A spasm of anger shook her and she said in an undertone of disdain, "It is your intention toward my sister I dislike, my lord."

The viscount focused that forbidding look upon her, the lift of one heavy brow indicating his question.

"I dare say it is a lovely ring you've given my sister, Lord Ruxart," she said in a furious whisper, "but I do not believe it is sincere."

"What do you mean?" he demanded with a quick frown.

"Only that neither you nor Helen will convince me that there is any love involved in this match. Doubtless, you have your reasons for wanting to marry my sister—"

"Oh, doubtless!"

"As she must have for accepting your offer, but there is nothing of the deeper feelings necessary for happiness together about either of you! To marry you would be the worst thing imaginable for Helen—"

"Thank you!"

"And for you! To continue with this marriage is a grave mistake for you both."

"Thank you for the warning, Miss Somers!" said Ruxart on a scathing note. "May I take leave to tell you that I stand in no need of your interference?"

"Of course you may, my lord, since it is obvious at any rate," responded Jane tranquilly. Having vented her anger, she no longer wished to antagonize his lordship. Indeed, she felt quite sheepish for having spoken to him so bluntly. She held out her hand with a friendly smile. "I'm afraid my habits of speaking are as plain as my looks, but I truly meant no offense. Don't let my disapproval of the match be taken as a sign of enmity! Let us remain friends, especially if we are soon to be relatives."

The viscount had no choice but to take her outstretched hand and after a quick, firm shake, Miss Somers rose to join

Mr. Fletcher and Clarence on the other side of the room. She had most certainly surprised his lordship, whose experience of disapproving relations had led him to expect a lengthy sermon to be rung over his head. As he moved toward his fiancée, he contemplated Miss Somers' smile. It occurred to him that she was, perhaps, not so very plain after all.

Chapter Seven

Plumstead Cottage oppressed Jane. The notion of having to endure another day of Ruxart's company suffocated her. Helen had begged and Mama had virtually insisted that she be included in the picnic proposed for that afternoon; the stunning effect of the two shedding tears together over her wilfulness had finally wrung from Jane a reluctant agreement to chaperone the excursion.

Following this trying scene, Jane helped Mrs. Beedle pack up a basket, then slipped quietly from the house. She felt the need of time to compose herself for the projected outing. She went purposefully for the stables and was soon perched happily in the loft playing with six little balls of fur nestled in the hay, naming each kitten and complimenting the mother on her excellent taste in babies.

While doing so, she reflected upon the oddity of her sister's betrothal. It was obvious that Helen did not love the viscount—and Jane could only wonder at such singular taste!—for she could not seem to bear being alone with him. Jane did not know what had occurred between them yesterday, but last night's performance had not deceived *her*, she thought as she absently stroked the softly mewling kittens.

Altogether, Helen appeared frightened and unhappy, his lordship alternately exasperated and bored. Jane had tried to convey some of this to Maria last night, but when she had mentioned Helen's unhappiness, Maria had given her a puzzled look.

"Helen seems quite happy," she said. "She was certainly filled with gaiety tonight."

"Overly so, I fear. Her manner wasn't the least natural. You must see that they don't suit!"

"I see, dearest, that you are refining too much upon her nervousness. I well remember how I was when Thomas proposed! I'm sure I was cheerful beyond bearing! As for the viscount, I've seen nothing whatever to fault and much in him to admire. I think you must forget whatever prejudices you have against him."

Jane abandoned the attempt then and did not speak of the matter again before the Gaineses departed for their own home in the morning.

So her thoughts whirled round and round with always the same ending: Helen was to marry Lord Ruxart, happy or no. And there was nothing to be done about it. With a heavy sigh, she at last kissed the smallest of the kittens and returned them all to their watchful mother's side. She then reluctantly began the descent of the steep wooden ladder. She hitched the hem of her brown gown up and was halfway down, her hands still on the topmost rung, when an imperious voice said cuttingly, "I believe, Miss Somers, you were engaged as a member of our outing?"

She cast a surprised eye over her shoulder to discover the viscount standing below her, his brows pushed together over his snapping eyes. Having been informed by his fiancée that they could not leave without her sister, Ruxart had gone searching for Miss Somers and his ill humor had heightened with each step. He knew the chit did not like him and to be confronted with the prospect of a full afternoon of the Somers sisters and his cousin Fletcher for company was the outside of enough. Even the sight of two shapely ankles in white knit stockings did nothing to lessen his resentment and he stood glowering as she hung motionless on the ladder.

"A *gentleman* would remove whilst I came down," she said finally.

"A *gentlewoman* would not be standing on a ladder with bits of straw sticking to her gown!" he retorted, anger beginning to give way to amusement.

Jane looked down the front of her dress and her hand slipped slightly. Ruxart stepped quickly forward, extending his hand.

"Let me help you down, Miss Somers," he commanded.

She hesitated a heartbeat, then let him take her hand to steady her descent. His touch ignited her with the devastating desire to let herself fall into his arms. She firmly ignored this improper urge, though she found she could not ignore the searing warmth of his hand on hers.

Ruxart's ill temper ebbed further still as she negotiated the last few rungs, though he fully expected to be the recipient of her womanly wrath. Certainly, Penelope would have delivered the first volley of an explosive charge, but upon touching the ground, Miss Somers released his hand and merely said, "One moment, if you please, my lord."

His amusement grew as he watched her prosaically pluck the straw from her gown and he actually smiled when she continued with her usual air of composure, "I'm sorry I put you to the inconvenience of having to find me." As she was at this moment twisting her lanky frame in an attempt to remove the straw clinging tenaciously to her backside, Jane did not see the last vestige of temper fade completely from his lordship's eye.

"Are you never disconcerted, Miss Somers?" he asked softly.

She looked up from her endeavors, her brow raised quizzically. "Should I be?"

"Ah, well, I trust you were alone in the loft," the viscount answered mischievously, taking her arm as they moved from the stables.

"To tell the truth, sir, I was not alone."

He halted to turn a sudden frown upon her. "What are you saying?"

"Merely that I have been seeing an old friend," explained Jane as she continued to walk on. When she tossed a merry smile over her shoulder she found his lordship was scowling in earnest, so she too stopped, adding with a laugh, "My cat has had kittens! And though Whiskers is a very protective mother, she kindly allowed me to pay them a call."

Ruxart's brow cleared; he came to her side with a roguish laugh.

"Whatever can you have been thinking, my lord?" Jane asked, widening her large eyes in pretended innocence. As they had come upon the rest of the party on these words, the viscount had no opportunity to answer, but displayed a broad smile. Seeing it, both John and Helen sighed with relief. His lordship had left them in such ill humor that the two had despaired of the picnic ever coming to pass.

When she saw Ruxart's cheerful mien, Helen was able to say quite happily, "Thank you, my lord, for finding Jane! Our picnic would never have been the same without her!"

"I'm much inclined, my love, to agree with you," he responded as he handed her up into the phaeton.

Though this ancient vehicle appeared to be not too well sprung, it was of a generous size and could easily have accommodated the four on their airing, but the gentlemen elected to ride beside the carriage. As they spent the journey exchanging bantering compliments, each trying to outdo the other, the party arrived in a mood of convivial companionship. They chose a gentle slope which fanned beneath a small grove of trees. They were soon settled upon the grass, enjoying the fine, warm spring day and the sumptuous luncheon extracted from the wicker basket.

The auspicious beginning seemed destined to blossom

into an agreeable time for all. Congenial conversation flowed easily throughout the meal. Jane described the stable loft's new residents; the cousins reminisced about childhood picnics on the manicured grounds of the Keep; Helen contributed the secret of the dandelion wine she had prepared for the party. By meal's end, the viscount's engaging good humor had nearly relaxed his bride-to-be. In turn, her simple manner, free of the overshy missishness that so annoyed him, had Ruxart thinking they would suit well enough after all. It was unfortunate John chose to remark that he hoped they should have a day as fine as this for their wedding day. Color swept instantly over Helen and as instantly fled. In a scarce whisper, she stuttered that she hoped so, too.

A look of wearied irritation passed over Ruxart's face, though he made no comment. Jane then had the happy notion of sending her sister off to pick a bouquet for their mama. John attempted to mitigate his previous error by offering to accompany her. Once left alone with the viscount, Jane rummaged through the basket, pulling a slim volume from its depths.

"This is Lord Byron's latest work and though Clarence will hold that it's not worth reading—he favors the classics of antiquity, you know, and anything not at least two hundred years old is too modern for him!—I count myself fortunate to have procured this copy," she explained as she braced her back against a tree. "Shall I read aloud, sir?"

"By all means, Miss Somers, do so if you wish," he answered, stretching out over the grassy knoll. He lay on his side, propped upon one elbow, watching her expressive face as she read the verse. He decided her voice lacked the musical quality which made Helen's so unique, but its mellow tone had a soothing effect that he quite liked. Studying her face, he found much to admire, though she was clearly not a beauty. He was particularly taken, he decided, with her ever-changing, oversized gray eyes.

"Do you know," interrupted Ruxart on a drawl, "your

eyes are like a misty morn? As mysterious and as enticing."

Her voice paused for the merest instant, then Jane continued to read with all the placid air of one who had not just received her first flowery compliment.

"Miss Somers, you are not listening!" he complained.

"No, of course not," she concurred calmly, looking up from her book. "If you wish, sir, to practice the pretty things you intend to say to Helen, I would rather you do so upon Anne, for she would like them prodigiously. She is at that age, you know."

"Practice the . . ." said he, dumb-struck.

"Perhaps you are not practicing," she admitted, "for I dare say you have said such things so often, they now come naturally to you, whether or not there is the least cause. At any rate, you must see the effort is completely wasted upon me."

"Yes, I do see," he agreed, warmth gracing his dark eyes.

The leather volume again claimed Jane's attention, but she had not read much beyond the next stanza when the viscount again cut in.

"Why do you object to my betrothal to your sister?" he inquired, staring fixedly at her.

His serious tone quite unnerved her, but she replied evenly enough, "I have already—"

"You must be aware that many marriages not founded on love turn out well enough," he broke in impatiently. "I fear your objections go beyond that! Tell me, why is my suit so repugnant to you?"

"Well, there is your money," she said slowly.

"You object to my *money*?" queried Ruxart, disbelieving.

"It is not your money, my lord, but what you do *with* your money that is so distressing. Why just last year, the Laytons returned from London full of the tale of your having lost five thousand pounds at one sitting. Five thousand pounds! Gambling such a sum away seems sinful to me."

"I see," he said, his full lips pressed firmly together. "Is there anything else, ma'am?"

"I do not think this discussion should be continued. There is no point in making you angry—"

"Come, Miss Somers! I've been the object of censure for years. Your plain speaking, as you put it, does not in the least disturb me!"

As his face was at that instant filled with wrathful resentment, Jane wanted very much to laugh. The attractive young man was rapidly giving way to the disdainful peer. Perhaps a set-down to his esteem was called for, after all.

"Very well, my lord," she said calmly. "Your style of living is not altogether pleasing—devoted as you are to the pursuit of pleasure. Besides your passion for all forms of gaming, your various escapades have set the *ton* on its ears for years! And, of course, one constantly hears tales of your many mistresses."

"And what," he prodded crossly, "do you think I do wrong with my mistresses? Beat them?"

"Why, no," replied Jane thoughtfully. "I suppose you make very pretty love to them."

"What would *you* know of love, Miss Somers?" he snapped.

If he had slapped her, the sting could not have been sharper. The book tumbled from her hands and her fringed shawl slid off her shoulders. Jane did not notice either one. A fierce flush spread over her cheeks as she struggled to find a response to his insult.

Discovering that there was, after all, one blushing virgin very much to his taste, Ruxart immediately lost all desire to further wound her. He jumped to his feet and came to her side. "Forgive me! I should not have said that!"

"There is no need to apologize, my lord," said Miss Somers, also rising. "It's not your fault I'm a spinster and therefore unversed in the ways of love."

"Don't! I deserve that frosty tone, but I'll not have you place yourself in the ranks of the matrons—"

91

"*You*, my lord, have nothing to say to the matter. I've been placed among the matrons for years. And now, if you will excuse me—"

But Ruxart entrapped her wrist before she could move away and they stood, unspoken emotion exploding between them. He searched Jane's face as if it held the secret to his own unexpected consuming need for her approval. The fading stain of embarrassment contrasted oddly with her defiant eyes. He had seen that same discordant mixture of chagrin and contempt before; gazing at Jane, he suddenly saw a much younger girl in a gaudy gown whose scornful eyes had belied her obvious discomfiture.

"I've met you before."

It was not a question, yet Jane felt compelled to answer. "Yes. During my come-out season," she said without expression. "We danced at Mrs. Northrup's supper ball."

"You wore some godawful pink thing," he said slowly, running his eyes over her figure.

Her heart stopped. "You remember that?"

Ruxart did not reply as he continued to look at her in an inscrutable manner. In his mind, he pictured the lanky, awkward girl whose hair pinnings had threatened to come undone, who had stammered at their introduction, who had, he vaguely recalled, bored the boy he had been. In those days, he thought ruefully, nothing but a diamond of the first water had been worthy of his attention. Again meeting Miss Somers' deep gray eyes, Ruxart knew a flash of regret for the damnable folly of youth.

As he held her captive, staring so intensely, Jane saw the memories pass through his restless eyes and she trembled with an abrupt desire. Aware that he had suddenly, in some inexplicable way, found her attractive, she longed to throw herself into his arms and show him precisely what she knew of love. But Jane resisted temptation, knowing that for all his wild ways, the viscount would despise such impetuosity. Where his hand encircled her wrist, Jane's pulse throbbed violently. She tried to snatch free of his burning clasp, but Ruxart tightened his grip.

"Miss Somers, please! Let me ask your pardon—"

"For not remembering me, my lord? You needn't cry pardon for that, for I assure you I did not expect it of you."

Though her tone was matter-of-fact, it cut him to the quick and he reacted with a flare of temper. "No, of course you did not! How could you?"

"How could I, indeed?" she retorted, pulling her wrist free at last. "When one is as selfish and arrogant as you, my lord, one need not remember those so unworthy of notice."

"Thank you! Your assessment of my character is most enlightening. But let me tell you . . ."

Ruxart got no further, for Fletcher returned just then with Helen, their arms overflowing with wildflowers of all descriptions. Both immediately knew something of moment had occurred. Jane stood with her shawl slipping unnoticed from her shoulders and her face unusually flushed, while beside her, the viscount's stony aspect was abnormally pallid.

John saw the smile fading from Helen's lips and stepped forward, saying with false heartiness, "Our expedition has been most successful!"

His words smoothed over the uncomfortable moment, but the return to Sloley was beset by a heavy air of constraint. When the old phaeton rolled to a stop before the cottage, Jane alit before either man could dismount to assist her. She went directly to her room without taking leave of them and they soon departed for their lodgings in Worstead without again seeing her.

The viscount offered his cousin no explanation and John knew far better than to press for one. He did not see his lordship again until Ruxart appeared from his room that evening, ready to escort the Somerses to a supper ball given by the local squire, Sir Richard Layton. The sight which met Fletcher's startled gaze was a vision to behold.

For once, Ruxart had spared no pains with his appearance. His satin knee breeches and black velvet evening jacket enhanced his lordship's dark coloring and muscular build. John enviously wished that he might show to such advantage, but knew it was not the fine clothes that made Nick so devilishly handsome. It was perhaps a pity that Oundle was not attendant upon the viscount, for he would have been highly gratified to discover a diamond pin stuck neatly into the folds of Ruxart's impeccably tied cravat, while a gold signet ring graced the little finger of his lordship's right hand. Altogether, Ruxart looked very much the lord of the realm that he was and Fletcher acknowledged this fact with a firm whistle.

"I must say, cous', I'm dazzled," he said, smiling "You'll lay all the country girls out flat, you know!"

"I'll wager there's *one* I don't impress, for she'll very likely say this proves I am nothing more than a dandified fop!"

"What can you mean? Miss Helen—"

"No, it's the sister I mean," explained Ruxart shortly. "It's easy to see why the two of you deal so well together—you have in common the utmost disapproval of my life style!" he added between gritted teeth as they left the inn.

Fletcher digested this in silence, wondering what game his volatile cousin was hatching now, for he knew that Nick in a temper would stop at nothing to get his way. And it was clear that the temper of the afternoon had not abated a jot. It did not promise for a pleasant evening, and John began to wish heartily he had never come to Norfolk.

In truth, Ruxart was intent upon showing Miss Somers just how wrong she was, that he could, in fact, be the very soul of social decorum. She would soon see that the Viscount Ruxart was a man her sister should feel honored to marry, and he hoped she would then be regretting her condemnation of his character.

Disappointment awaited him, however, for Miss Somers was not a member of the evening's party. Nothing said to her during the afternoon could prevail upon Jane to attend the Laytons' ball. Both Mama and Agnes were going and that, she said firmly, meant she must stay to watch over the boys for they all knew Clarence was next to useless and Mrs. Beedle, though a very fine soul, could not soothe away George's nightmares as she could. Agnes was not inclined to disagree, but William, thinking he had detected a certain warmth in Mr. Fletcher's attitude, had uttered a protest. It had been in vain. Jane was staying home.

Ruxart's polished manners covered over his frustration at the news of her absence, but John noted the lines pulling at the edges of his mouth and thought for an instant of pleading a sudden bellyache. He gave it up and was soon rolling along with the Somerses in the viscount's elegant coach, listening with resignation to Dorothea explain just which combination of restoratives had enabled her to make this excessively exerting and, to her view, decidedly dangerous outing.

The progress of the carriage was watched from Jane's bedroom window until it could no longer be seen. She then took herself to her nephews' room, where she passed an agreeable hour playing the damsel in distress for her two heroic knights. After tucking the boys into bed with a story and a kiss, Jane tried to while away the hours with a book. When she found herself reading the same page for the third time, she set it down and took up her needlework. When she pricked her finger while pulling out a set of badly placed stitches, however, she gave up all attempts to occupy herself and went up to her room. There she spent a considerable amount of time sitting before her mirror, but at last she decided with regret that there was nothing of a mysterious misty morning about her eyes and, with a melancholy sigh, climbed into bed.

Moonshadows slid across her face as she lay remembering each word, each look his lordship had given her that day. She vividly brought forth the timbre of his voice, the light in his ebony eyes, the tilt of his dark head, and she burned with a longing to show him how well she could read him. *She* would not tremble at the passionate promise of those full lips! Slipping a hand beneath her cheek, she turned on her side and tried resolutely to put such thoughts away. But they would not refrain from popping out of the darkness with haunting clarity. She felt her only hope lay in his rapid removal to London and yet desired nothing less. She pictured Ruxart whirling through the squire's ballroom with her beautiful sister in his arms and did not even bother to wipe away the tears as they rolled silently onto her hand.

Those who attended the Laytons' party found it, for the most part, sadly insipid. The country dances were nearly as boring, remarked the viscount to his cousin, as the belles dancing them. Nothing met with his approval and when he had raised a disdainful brow for the fifth time to some encroaching guest, Helen could barely control her increasing anxiety. It was an unhappy fate that led Ruxart to decide it was time to settle upon a wedding date. When he mentioned the matter as they were sweeping the room together in a waltz, his fiancée fell to stammering nervously, forgetting all the modish airs she had been trying desperately to wear all evening.

"I—I have not thought of it," she replied miserably in answer to his demand for her to name the day.

"Well, my dear, it must be thought of!" he said in a cutting tone. "See if you can bring yourself to do so by morning. We shall discuss the matter then."

She thought him very annoyed with her and all attempts to hide her wretchedness withered. She barely got through the last of the waltz and later wondered how she managed the rest of the evening. Though nothing had yet been announced, she had been forced to endure the sly congratulations and knowing looks from their neighbors and to receive them with some semblance of happiness. Helen longed only for her bed throughout it all and she fairly flew up to her room, with only a hurried goodnight whispered to his lordship, as soon as they returned home.

She crept as quietly as she could about the room, trying not to disturb Jane in the next bed. But Jane was still fully awake; she lay silent, however, not wishing to hear about the evening, not wishing to reveal her own depressing thoughts. It was not until she heard a muffled sob emerge from the other bed that she sat up; on the second such sob, she slipped from her bed to the edge of her sister's.

"Helen, dearest, whatever is wrong?" she asked softly.

"N-nothing!" claimed Helen, giving way to tears in earnest.

"Shh, you silly babe," murmured Jane. She gathered the quivering girl into her arms and held her firmly until the weeping died away. "Now, tell me what happened to make you cry."

"It is the viscount," said Helen on a hiccough. "He—I—I made him most monstrously angry with me!"

"Well, *that*, let me assure you, is nothing to cry over! It is his lordship's habit to lose his temper with everyone. Why, you must know he was very angry with *me* just this afternoon."

Her light tone calmed Helen considerably and she was able to continue with some composure, "He asked me to set a wedding date and when I told him I hadn't thought of it yet, he—he looked at me with his lids dropping over his eyes as if—as if I were—oh! some contemptible toady and said—oh, *so* coldly! that I must give it thought and that we should discuss it in the morning!"

Recalling her promise not to again tease her sister about the folly of this match, Jane squeezed Helen tightly and said,

"You must not let him frighten you so. You must simply give him the stare direct and tell him to quit being so nonsensical."

"B-but he was quite odious! He looked like a very d-devil!"

"He is no more of an ogre than Freddy! He is just a spoiled, impatient boy, much used to getting his own way."

"Now it is you who are being nonsensical!" returned Helen, achieving a tremulous smile. And Jane privately agreed.

Chapter Eight

The occupants of the crowded breakfast room at Plumstead were silent. Clarence's attention was, as usual, riveted upon the tome propped up before his plate, his unattended food growing cold, while Jane sat beside him watching Helen's food progress slowly from one side of the plate to the other as her fork nudged it listlessly along. Jane's own sparse breakfast—a cup of tea and a slice of buttered bread—joined the forces of the ignored as she pondered the latest developments in what promised to be Helen's calamitous courtship.

The melancholy of the night before had lifted as Jane's calm good sense reasserted itself. She might suffer from unrequited love, but she would not, like some heroine in a Minerva novel, fall into a decline because of it. She had her family to occupy her and though her future might not be termed bright, it was by no means bleak. It was Helen's future that so deeply furrowed her brow; Helen's future that darkened her normally bright eyes.

At the head of the table, William did nothing to spur conversation amongst his family; he alone was busily discussing his breakfast with a vigor that more than made up for the apathy of the others. His wife was eating with his mother (whose habit it was to break her fast in bed), leaving him free to devote himself to his meal; ham, eggs, fish and bread were swept rapidly from his plate to his mouth.

Thus, coming upon the scene some minutes later, Maria Gaines found her family very much self-absorbed and not at all social.

"You might all be rehearsing for one of Shakespeare's tragedies! Whatever is the matter with you all?" she asked cheerily as she came in. She was surprised when her sisters both started at her quip; she was even more so when she saw the color fade from Helen's face.

"Hullo," said William between gulps. "What brings you here?"

Slipping into the chair opposite Clarence, Maria cast a surreptitious glance at Helen as she explained, "I've brought Daniel over for the day. I trust you shan't mind, but Anne had the fever all last night, and though she seemed more fussy than ill this morning, I thought it better to remove the baby. You know how the least little sickness overcomes him!"

"Oh, poor Anne! Is there anything we can do for her?" inquired Helen in quick concern.

"No, she's already on the mend. I've no doubt Anne will be her usual pert self by evening."

"Have you time for a cup of tea?" asked Jane, rising.

"Yes, thank you, though I cannot stay too long. Thomas will be anxious, you know, for he has not the least notion of how to go about settling Anne when she fusses."

"Well, I'm very sorry Anne is poorly," Jane said as she moved from the scarred mahogany sideboard to place a steaming cup before Maria. "But I shall be glad to have the baby. I was amazed at how well he is walking! The next thing you know he will be dancing," she said teasingly.

"Speaking of dancing," said Maria over her teacup, "it's a great pity you weren't at the Laytons' last night to see the stir the viscount caused."

"I can well imagine it," she murmured tonelessly.

"His dress, his elegance, his air all set the neighborhood talking! Helen was the most envied person there, I can tell you."

Helen bent her head in embarrassment, but before she or Jane could make a response, Clarence astounded them all with one of his abrupt observations.

"I'd not have thought," he pronounced precisely as if he were discoursing upon some abstract subject and not his sister's fiancé, "that one of Homer's Cimmerians would have suited Helen." Without waiting to see the effect of his comment, Clarence retreated once more into his book.

Though his comparison had completely mystified the majority of his audience, Jane, who was of a more bookish bent and had actually read many of the classics, was much struck with the aptness of the description. Seeing Helen's stricken look, however, she decided the less said about the Viscount Ruxart this morning, the better, so she turned to Maria and asked whether she had yet seen Mama.

"Yes, I took Daniel to see her before handing him over to Mrs. Beedle. She and Agnes were recounting last night's social triumph. Mama positively gloated over paying off an old score with Mrs. Hatchett by refusing to make her an introduction to Lord Ruxart."

Jane laughed at this, though somewhat perfunctorily. Maria's tone changed when she continued, "Dearest, *why* weren't you at the squire's?"

"I am well past the age of parties—"

"Nonsense!" cut in her sister soundly. "You are no such thing! Why, Mr. Bickford asked specifically after you, Jane, and you know he would only need the merest encouragement to declare himself, for he has been dangling after you this age and more."

"Please! I dare say I was not meant for marriage—"

"Pooh! You should be caring for your own babies, not mine!"

"What's all this talk of marriage?" demanded William, looking up from his plate to swivel his gaze from one sister to the other. "Has Bickford made you an offer, Jane? Why have I not heard of it?"

"No, no, it's no such thing. It's one of Maria's fancies, nothing more." Jane pushed back her chair and stood, saying with a fixed smile, "Do not tax me further, Maria, I beg of you. Though I dearly love you, not even for you would I consider a connection with a man whose nose continually drips. Send us word when all is well with Anne."

She removed from the room before any could stop her and paused in the hall to compose her trembling. To speak of marriage and babies pierced her heart with a pain that was unendurable! Firmly pushing away the image of dark, troubled eyes in a strong, square face, she breathed deeply and went directly up to her mother.

"Ah, Jane, the very person we need!" exclaimed Dorothea from amid her pillows as her daughter entered the room. "My dear, we *cannot* decide if the wedding should be at Sloley Church or St. George's in Hanover Square. Which do you think it should be?"

"I think, Mama," she replied, planting a kiss upon the proffered cheek, "that it is far too soon to be making such a decision. Helen and Lord Ruxart need more time together before they settle their plans."

"You surely cannot expect us to wait until the last moment to make all the necessary arrangements," Agnes objected sharply. "There should be nothing havey-cavey about this marriage!"

"Oh, I quite agree," responded Jane, undisturbed. "That is precisely why I do not think the marriage should follow the betrothal with undue haste."

The pair before her seemed much struck with the force of her argument and Jane seized the moment to put forth a suggestion. "I've been thinking, Mama, that if you feel up to it, it would be no bad thing for you to take Helen on a round of morning visits. We shouldn't want the neighbors to say she is already putting on airs and coming the grand lady."

Her mother sat up, her ruffled peignoir spilling forward. "No, indeed we do not! Why, last night I had to protect Helen from the most prying questions, though I nearly suffered megrim doing so. And though I shall no doubt find it excessively exhausting and not at all what my constitution needs, I would not have it said that I would not make the supremest sacrifice for my child's future happiness!"

Since all of this had been said with a great deal of vigor, her daughter did not evidence the least concern for her health, but merely agreed, "No, of course you would not."

Thus, within a mere two hours and amid all the flurry attendant upon one of her outings, Mrs. Somers set out with her youngest daughter and her daughter-in-law to pay morning calls. It was, she informed them all after a reviving whiff from her vinaigrette, a notion she had been happy to conceive for Helen's sake, despite the no doubt dire consequences for herself. Sitting beside Dorothea in the old phaeton, Helen looked quite pretty, if slightly pale, in a twilled morning gown of light blue cambric and a chip bonnet with blue ribbons to match. She was reluctant to accompany her mother, fearing that Lord Ruxart would be out of temper if he arrived to find her gone, but was persuaded to go by her eldest sister's brisk arguments.

"Don't be a goose!" said Jane with a quick kiss. "He'll be pleased to find you know your social duty—such a quality is essential in a viscountess, you know."

As it happened, his lordship did not appear for his promised morning call. After returning to his room at Worstead Inn the previous night, Ruxart, ignoring his cousin's heavy protests, had broached more than one wine bottle with an intensity which precluded any early morning socializing. It was, therefore, well past noon when he rode over to Plumstead with Fletcher to be met with the news that Mrs. Somers and her daughters were not at home. Grimly thanking Mrs. Beedle, he turned to leave when he was arrested by a young voice.

"Hullo, sir!" called out Master Frederick from the top of the landing where he stood looking over the banister, while beside him George stood peeping through the railings. "Have you come in your curricle?" he asked hopefully.

"I'm sorry, Freddy, but we rode over today," answered the viscount. Suppressing his desire to laugh at the crestfallen look of disappointment which covered the boys' faces, he added, "But it's fortunate that you appeared, for Mr. Fletcher was just saying how much he'd like to take you and George for a ride on Thunderbolt."

Fletcher had no time to protest; Freddy was flying down the stairs crying, "Oh, would you really?" before he could do more than send his cousin a glare. But he took it in good stead, answering in the affirmative with a ready smile. The boys were then ushered out, Master George riding on the viscount's broad shoulders, and soon mounted on the back of Fletcher's roan.

Ruxart sent them off with a mischievous smile that was not lost on John; he then wandered aimlessly about the lawns of the cottage, feeling oddly out of sorts. He would not have thought the disappointment of not seeing Helen would be so great. Yet he had to admit he *was* disappointed, sorely so.

Rounding the corner of the house, Ruxart saw Miss Somers playing on the grass with her youngest nephew. Her laughter rang out warmly as the toddler took a clumsy step then collapsed, surprise stamped upon his round face. She tilted her head back as she laughed; her white cap stood out against the brilliant blue of the sky like a suspended cloud. She caught Daniel in her arms and stood, revealing bright green grass stains smearing the front of her plain muslin gown. To his giggling delight, she swung the small boy around, causing her ridiculous mobcap to slide askew and escaping ringlets to tumble into her face. Sunlight rippled warmly over the flyaway curls as she spun and, watching, the viscount reflected that he had never seen so charming a woman as Miss Somers was just then—grass stains, crooked cap, tumbled curls and all.

Twirling Daniel around once more, Jane caught sight of Ruxart as he stood watching her. She jerked to a halt, her laughter dying. Caught unaware, she felt ridiculously vulnerable. She slowly set the child down and busied herself with adjusting her cap as she strove for composure. When he approached, she glanced over his muscular form, so well displayed in a buff riding coat and buckskin breeches, and then away.

"I trust you will excuse my lamentable appearance, Lord Ruxart," she said with the semblance of calm.

He noted the guarded expression in her eyes. "Your appearance, Miss Somers, is delightful."

"Now you are pitching it much too strong, my lord!" she laughed. "Having made your notions of a gentlewoman's appearance well known to me, I am sure you are quite excessively shocked—but too much the gentleman to show it."

"Ah, but you have made it very plain that you do not consider me a gentleman at all," he returned with a wicked smile. "I therefore take leave to tell you again, Miss Somers, that you look charming."

Puzzlement flashed through her gray eyes as she wondered just why he should want to turn her up sweet with pretty flattery, but she let it pass, turning the subject by saying, "I trust, too, that you will excuse Helen for having gone out, but you must know that it was essential she pay morning calls."

"I must if you say so, but I confess I fail to know why."

"Why, otherwise our neighbors would be saying Helen was too high in the instep and thinking herself too good for the likes of them, and *that*, you know, we could not let happen."

"Of course not," he agreed solemnly.

She thought perhaps he was mocking; there was a definite twinkle in his dark eyes. "You may laugh, but it wouldn't be at all comfortable to be on bad terms with our neighbors."

Baby Daniel, having lost interest in this conversation, had taken a few tottering exploratory steps. Just as his short legs were about to buckle, his aunt recaptured him and swept him into her arms. With Ruxart keeping pace beside her, Jane now moved toward the house. A pudgy hand gripped the ends of ribbon under her chin and pulled with surprising strength.

"No, dearest," she scolded, catching the dirty hand and playfully kissing the offending digits.

"I, for one, applaud Master Gaines' worthy attempt to rid you of that preposterous cap. Why do you wear such things?"

"Oh, for protection," she replied self-consciously.

"Protection, Miss Somers?"

"From all the matchmakers, you see. Even though I'd been on the shelf for *years*, I was forever being told to make myself agreeable to men with spindly legs or dripping noses. None of whom could be considered a *catch*, of course, but then, I should know not to look too high for a husband! No one knew quite what to do with me, you see, but once I put on the caps, such attempts to settle my future ceased. The relief felt by all was immense, I can tell you."

He heard the anger behind the light words and was conscious of a desire to kiss her bitterness away. Before Ruxart could even understand the depth of his unexpected emotion, Miss Somers was saying in her usual tranquil tone, "I've a favor to ask of you, my lord, one which will be absurdly easy for you to fulfill."

Jane paused and shifted the weight of Daniel in her arms while letting her eyes rest on the viscount's face. He recognized the challenge in them.

"You fill me with foreboding, Miss Somers. What is this absurd favor?"

"I should like you to delay discussing your wedding date with Helen."

He said nothing, but turned one sardonically raised brow upon her. She thought how arrogantly scornful that brow made him look. "I'm not trying to interfere, but I think perhaps you might consider how precipitate your demand may be. My sister is . . . Helen is easily influenced and at this point, whatever day you wished for, she would agree to, regardless of her own feelings. What is more, she'd fear to displease you with the wrong choice. Surely, it's not too much to ask that you wait a little longer to press her on this matter."

"For someone not trying to interfere, you're doing exceptionally well at it," he commented dryly. "Try to believe that I do not intend to bully Helen into anything distasteful to her."

"I did not mean—indeed—"

"There is no need for you to explain yourself," he interrupted. His eyes were shuttered as he held open the door for her. "I've no wish for a bride who fears me."

Jane passed into the cottage with a crimson stain upon each cheek and gratefully left his lordship to Mr. Fletcher's company in the parlor while she shepherded her three nephews upstairs.

By the time she came to rejoin the men, her hair neatly tucked back under her cap and her stained gown exchanged for her brown wool, the morning callers had returned and were removing bonnets, pelisses and gloves. Jane quickly noted that the fingers untying the pretty blue ribbons of Helen's bonnet were shaking, but before she could reassure her sister, Lord Ruxart strolled to the young girl's side.

"Did you enjoy your round of visits, my dear?" he inquired as he firmly put her quivering hands aside and undid the knotted bow. He lifted the hat from her glossy curls and tossed it carelessly onto a nearby pie-crust table, adding, "Well?"

Thinking this was a criticism of her absence, Helen bent her head, fixing her gaze on the exquisite shine of his boot, and replied timidly, "I—I am sorry, sir. I meant to be here—"

"You needn't apologize!" he cut in rather impatiently. Her eyes flew up to his face; he clearly read the fright in them and though he mentally expostulated, he forced himself to say kindly, "Come, Helen, tell me about your visits."

She allowed herself to be drawn next to him on the settee and dutifully related the morning's social round. If his lordship was not interested, Helen could not detect it, though she suspected he did not actually care what Mrs. Dawlish had said with regard to Mama's spasms or how Miss Lettice Layton had stared at her new ring. When she had brought forth all she could think to tell, the pair sat silent, Helen nervously toying with the frills of her gown while the viscount intently studied her.

"I have been thinking," he finally said, "that perhaps it would be best to wait upon your return to London before inserting the notices of our betrothal." He looked at her searchingly and wondered if that was indeed relief he had seen in her eyes.

"If that is what you wish," she responded hesitantly. She licked her heart-shaped lips, then suggested timorously, "We could perhaps make the announcement at my ball."

"What ball is this?"

"My Aunt Willoughby has planned a come-out ball for me at the end of the month."

He presented one of his winning smiles. "An excellent notion, love. And shall we wait until we are together again in town to select our wedding date?"

"Oh, yes," agreed Helen, happily returning his smile.

"What are you two speaking so seriously of?" demanded Mrs. Somers archly from across the room. "Though I'm certain no one could blame you, my lord, for wanting to keep Helen all to yourself, you must wait a while longer for that privilege!"

"We were just discussing the announcement of our betrothal, ma'am," Ruxart answered pleasantly. "We rather thought we'd wait until Miss Helen's come-out ball to break the news."

"But why?" asked Agnes rather sharply.

"But for the impact it would have, of course," he replied easily. The viscount's eyes moved from Agnes to Jane, where he met with a look of warm gratitude. Beside her, John sat regarding his cousin in wonderment, for not three hours ago his lordship had made vividly clear his intent to have the matter settled today. If Nicholas were waiting on Miss Helen's whim, it would be, thought Fletcher, the most astonishing element yet of this whole incredible business.

"But quite right," Dorothea surprisingly approved. "It would be just the proper occasion for such an announcement. Why, it puts me in mind of when dear Mr. Somers disclosed *our* betrothal at the Yardleys' Christmas ball."

The arrival of William cut short his mother's reminiscing, much to the relief of the rest of the party. "Did you ride over, Lord Ruxart?" he inquired after making his greetings. "You may be spending the afternoon with us—the clouds are gathering outside. We shall soon be in for a severe storm, mark my words!"

A distant crash of thunder gave emphasis to his prediction and filled Jane with dismay for she wondered how she could manage to keep the relaxed mood between Helen and his lordship from dissolving. The solution was delivered from an unlooked-for source when Clarence wandered absently in behind his brother, remarking, "This is the kind of day I remember we used to spend hours playing at slip-groat. Remember that, Jane?"

"Indeed, I do," she answered, smiling.

"And what," queried Ruxart, "is slip-groat?"

"Have you never played?" asked Jane in return. "Oh, that's infamous! It was once a game of kings, you know—"

"I believe," interrupted Clarence, "we still have the old

board about here, haven't we? Perhaps we could find it and show his lordship how to play."

A search of the attic was rewarded with an antique wooden playing board, which was thoroughly dusted in a matter of moments; the viscount volunteered the shillings for the game and the challenge was on. Clarence soon displayed an astonishing skill and he confessed with a sheepish grin on his handsome face, "I've not spent *all* my time at my books, you know!"

The room filled with merry laughter as Ruxart and Fletcher made their first clumsy shots. A wager was suggested by William, but his lordship rejected this. "I rather think not," he drawled. "Among family I play only for . . . love, shall we say?"

When it was Jane's turn to play, she demurred, saying blandly, "Since I know nothing of love, I fear I've nothing to stake." Try as she might, Miss Somers could not refrain from looking at Ruxart as she said this.

He was clearly amused. "Come, Miss Somers," he coaxed, "We shall gladly let you play for nothing more than your own whim!"

The others joined his attempts to persuade her and Jane was at last prevailed upon to take her turn. She judged her shot to a nicety and with a quick press of her palm sent her shilling sliding neatly into a bed for a point.

"I am relieved I did not bet against you," commented Ruxart with a crooked smile.

"You know it is said only a fool wagers against an unknown," she rejoined on a knowing laugh, "and you are certainly no fool, my lord."

"I must disappoint you," he said as his smile faded. "I have wagered on an unknown."

"Oh? And did you win or lose?"

Fletcher inhaled sharply as he watched his cousin answer wearily. "Oh, I won the wager, Miss Somers. But I fear," he added beneath his breath, "I may have lost the game."

Chapter Nine

It was not to be expected that the spirit of cheerful festivity be sustained for long, but Jane was at a loss to understand just what had so utterly ruined the viscount's pleasure in the game. Though he continued to play and converse easily, his dark eyes no longer smiled and his face bore his more usual aspect of restless discontent. The game had ended without giving her an answer and as they kept country hours at Plumstead, Jane was forced to quit the room immediately after in order to help Mrs. Beedle prepare for dinner.

A fierce staccato beat against the windows as the clouds delivered the promised rain in full force. Somers pressed his guests to remain, saying, "You certainly can't wish to ride out in this storm and you needn't worry about changing for dinner *here*. We don't stand upon ceremony, especially with family."

Fletcher, too, had noticed his lordship's saturnine humor, but he was given no opportunity to speak privately with Ruxart until well after the simple but savory supper. The two were finally left alone at the table, each reposing with a glass of hock, while William descended into the cellar in search of a very special bottle of port he had been saving, he insisted, for just such a time as this.

"I think, Nick, I should offer you my congratulations," remarked John diffidently. "Things have turned out rather well for you." He raised his glass to his cousin, then watched Ruxart over the rim as he drank.

With great deliberation, the viscount reached for the decanter and slowly refilled his glass. He sat gazing into the liquid for some time before responding flatly, "Before you become too effusive with your felicitations, John, you might remember that you were opposed to this match from the outset. I cannot recall your precise words, but you made your views of the wager perfectly clear. I may have pocketed St. Juste's five hundred guineas, but each time I suffer through a conversation with my beautiful, bird-witted fiancée, I wonder just what I lost!"

Ruxart looked up from his contemplation of his drink to find his cousin staring beyond him, shocked dismay stamped ludicrously on his face. Nicholas glanced quickly over his shoulder. Miss Somers stood in the door frame, her large gray eyes fixed scornfully upon him. Before he could collect his wits, she pivoted sharply and disappeared.

"Damnation!" Turning his fury on the unfortunate Fletcher, he demanded wrathfully, "Why the devil didn't you warn me?"

"I didn't see her 'til it was too late! And if you insist upon making such comments about your fiancée, something like this was bound to occur!"

"What I choose to say about Helen Somers is my business alone!" Ruxart enunciated through clenched teeth. He pitched the full glass of wine down his throat and set the empty glass onto the oak table with a thump.

Ignoring this danger signal, John said in a tone of deep disapprobation, "I foresaw how it would be with a match founded upon a wager!"

"Don't you see it's all of a piece!" snapped the viscount savagely. "All of life is a toss of the dice. Do you think I'd have fared any better submitting meekly to the earl's choice of a bride?"

"No, but I do think having chosen this imprudent course, you could be more gracious to your bride-to-be! Your displays of ill temper—"

"For God's sake, John! Had she not desired to marry me, Helen only had to say no. But whether for my charm of manner or for my fine fortune, she chose to play out this hand. You must see that I cannot now forfeit the game."

This was said with such a bitter edge that John forbore making further argumentation, and they sat in strained silence until Somers reappeared.

Proudly displaying a dark bottle covered with a film of dust, William stood where his sister had been an instant before. "Just wait 'til you taste this, gentlemen! I'll swear you've never had a finer port in any grand house."

Fletcher returned a courteous response and attempted to keep a smooth appearance up while William busied himself with the decanting and serving of the wine. It was not easy, for his lordship was barely civil.

Ruxart's only thought now was to see Miss Somers, to explain the situation in a way that would somehow erase the contempt from her eyes. Upon being handed a glass of the red port, the viscount downed the contents with an impatient toss. This cavalier treatment of so fine a wine scandalized William, but he said nothing, merely assenting in a strangled tone when his lordship brusquely suggested they now rejoin the ladies.

As they entered the sitting room, Ruxart rapidly searched the small room. Jane was not there. When he inquired of Helen where she was, he was told she had retired for the night. Such a heavy scowl crossed over his features, Helen wondered fearfully what she had done to have so violently offended his lordship.

At that moment, Jane was striding furiously up and down the length of their tiny bedchamber. Her rage surpassed that of the storm outside as she reviewed every despicable facet of Ruxart's vile, detestable nature. She thought fondly of the bygone days of the French Revolution when aristocrats were very properly guillotined and visualized with relish a certain lord's head being severed from his body. She decided it was much too good for him.

Over the past few days she had begun to think him likable and even, in many ways, actually kind, but she now saw clearly that he was far worse than the cold, arrogant beau she had originally thought of him. That he should claim Helen for a *wager* was an infamous act of wickedness which left Jane feeling sick with anger.

Such a consuming wrath soon spent its force and Jane sank quietly to the edge of her bed, trying to determine what she should do. In the end, she realized there was little she could do. To tell Helen was unthinkable, while William, with Agnes and Mama behind him, would undoubtedly turn a blind eye to the matter. The insult would have to be borne in silence, but she, at least, vowed never to forgive the viscount.

While Miss Somers conjured up a series of intricate and exceedingly gruesome deaths for Lord Ruxart, he sat below suffering polite, meaningless conversation, pondering how he would convince her he'd meant no harm. Used all his life to women whose deepest concerns were the latest fashions and most current *on dits*, Ruxart felt himself to be at point nonplus with the tall, intelligent creature whose good opinion had suddenly become all-important to him.

As soon as it was possible to do so, Ruxart made his excuses and departed. Though it was no longer storming, a fine drizzle accompanied the cousins on their way back to Worstead Inn, perfectly matching their dampened spirits. The short journey was made wordlessly, but as they neared the inn, Fletcher broke the silence. His apology was stiffly given and as stiffly received. The companionable mood which had been building up between them during the week now appeared destroyed.

The constraint between them had not lessened by morning. They prepared for their return to London in leaden silence and so drove back to Plumstead Cottage to make their farewells.

It was his lordship's intention to have it out with Miss Somers before he left and it was with a grim frown that he learned she was not at home. She had gone out, he was told, on an errand of mercy, delivering a basket of foodstuffs to a sick tenant. He suspected she had gone to avoid seeing him and a martial gleam sprang into his eye.

The viscount had been quite right. Jane left the cottage as early as she could manage, for, she told herself firmly, if she never saw Lord Ruxart again, it would be too soon for her. Her anger had abated somewhat, but the disgust and disappointment were felt as vividly as in the moment she had heard that hateful voice disclosing his lordship's true nature. She walked slowly along, reluctant to return home, afraid he would not yet have gone and still, somehow, equally afraid that he would.

The rapid pounding of horses' hoofs drummed in the distance. Even as she moved to the side of the road, Jane knew who it was. She did not look behind her, but continued to walk steadily along, her head held high, her heart keeping beat to the rhythm of the horses' gait. The curricle dashed past her; Ruxart skillfully steered it to an abrupt halt across the road some feet before her, effectively blocking her way. As she neared, he commanded curtly, "Get in."

She stood, weighing the possibility of denying him and trying to walk on. She knew this would be a hopeless attempt on her part, resulting in the kind of scene she most wished to avoid, so she shifted her empty basket to her left arm and extended her right hand to meet his lordship's outstretched palm. With a nimble movement, she mounted to sit rigidly beside him.

"You are, Miss Somers, a woman of rare good sense," remarked Ruxart as he expertly backed his horses onto the road and proceeded on the way. Jane did not respond. He cast a sideways glance at her. She sat erect, only the rapid rise and fall of her bosom disclosing her furious state of mind. "I wish," he said earnestly, "to explain my remarks last night."

"There is nothing, my lord," she said in frozen accents, "to explain. Your arrant contempt for my sister is all too evident."

"But I did not mean—" he began.

"What you meant, sir, was obvious! To marry my sister on the basis of a wager is—is odiously wicked."

With a curl of his lip, Ruxart responded coldly, "I believe the majority of your family would feel that my fortune—if not my title—more than compensated for any lack of finer sentiment."

"Must you insult us all?" she exclaimed in heat. "Have you not the least shred of decency?"

Her biting words and disdainful tone kindled his ever-ready temper as the viscount invariably met anger with anger. "I am aware—as indeed, you have not made the least attempt to disguise it—of your disapprobation of me, of this match. I'm willing to admit I should not have wagered on my choice of a bride, but you needn't fear I'll treat Helen with any disrespect."

"But you have already done so! What you do not realize, however, is that Helen is not so brainless as you would believe. In fact, the only *bird-witted* thing that I know she has ever done is to have agreed to marry you!"

"I take leave to tell you, Miss Somers, that Helen stands in no need of your defense! I shall treat her with the utmost respect and kindness. I shall treat her as befits the Viscountess Ruxart."

Jane sat perfectly still, her eyes blazing and her back held rigidly straight. He cast his eyes at her once, then away as he made a fresh attempt. "I do not often make apologies—"

"That I can well believe!"

"But I'm offering you my sincere apology for having

116

offended you," he finished stiffly.

"Do you not understand, Lord Ruxart, that it is not I to whom you should make your apology, but to Helen, whom you have offended most gravely! Helen's nature is so sweet, so kind that *she* would undoubtedly forgive you. *I* cannot," she declared in a colorless voice.

Ruxart said no more and devoted his attention, seemingly, to the road. His jaw muscles flexed erratically and lines etched deeply beside his set mouth, but Jane did not see this for she kept her eyes resolutely fixed upon her lap. She vowed not to give him the satisfaction of seeing her eyes blur with tears.

When he pulled the curricle to a sharp stop before Plumstead Cottage, his groom ran quickly up to help Miss Somers alight. She entered the house without so much as a backward glance, wondering at the perversity of her own heart which was at this instant knocking painfully against her ribs at the departure of one whom she thoroughly detested.

"Tell Mr. Fletcher I am waiting!" rapped the viscount to Jem, who emitted a soundless whistle as he ran to obey this stern command. He could only conjecture wildly as to the cause for m'lord's ugly mood.

When John climbed into the vehicle, he could not keep from inquiring, "So Miss Somers did indeed overhear us last night?"

"Yes," replied Ruxart shortly.

Curiosity unwisely prodded John. "And?"

"And Miss Somers could give you lessons in the art of dressing me down," he answered with a ghost of a laugh.

Fletcher subsided and Jem saw that it was to be a very uncomfortable sort of journey home. He took mental bets with himself as to when his lordship and the gentleman would have a regular set-to, for it was clear m'lord greatly itched for one. However, it appeared Jem would lose his bets for by the time the viscount's curricle rolled beneath the stone arch of the Rutland Arms in Newmarket, the two were conversing, if somewhat uneasily, on neutral subjects.

It was an unlucky stroke that, as they renewed their progress the following morning, John chanced to remark, "You know, that Miss Crandall we met at the Arms last night put me in mind of Miss Somers."

"Don't be a fool," said Ruxart instantly. "Miss Crandall was by far too well-mannered."

"Miss Somers is a very good sort of woman. I've rarely met better. She is worth a dozen Penelope Manderleys!"

"I suggest," his lordship said crushingly, "we leave Mrs. Manderley's name out of the conversation."

"How can I? When your name has been coupled with hers more often than a cock to a hen . . ." Fletcher's peeved voice trailed off as Ruxart turned a quelling glare upon him, thereby thwarting Jem's hopes of seeing m'lord plant his priggish cousin a proper leveler.

London was reached none too soon for either of the travelers, neither of whom had spoken a word beyond the barest necessity for the remainder of the trip. One look at his lordship's face as he admitted him into the house was enough to inform Goswick that the sojourn out of town had not been a success. If he did not actually tiptoe around the viscount that night, it was the only precaution not taken in an effort to avoid stirring up his well-known and much-feared temper. All such efforts failed signally as Ruxart found fault with everything and everyone who had the misfortune to come his way. No, decided those belowstairs to a man, his lordship had not enjoyed his stay in the country.

Lord Ruxart was in the act of putting foot to boot the following morning when Armand St. Juste was ushered into his room. His lordship paused, his stockinged foot poised as his eyes met the cool green gaze of his friend. Then he wordlessly slid his foot into the Hessian and yanked it on. He reached for the mate and put it on while St. Juste critically surveyed him.

"Those are very fine boots, Nick," he said lazily at last. "Hobe made them, of course?"

"Of course."

Leisurely strolling into the room, Armand turned his rare smile upon his friend. "I came to welcome you back and to discover the particulars of your excursion into the bosom of your in-laws."

"You might," pointed out Ruxart acidly, "have known from the outset."

"Still displeased with me, Nick? I fear I would have been very much . . . shall we say, *de trop*? Confess, you'd have done as well without your cousin along!"

His lordship was not impervious to St. Juste's charm. "Oh, God, yes!" he agreed as he stood. "In fact, we ended with a fantastic row, as usual. I rather doubt the good John will have much to say to me for several weeks."

"I believe it is said that some good comes out of everything," his friend commented dryly.

The last vestige of their previous falling out was wiped away as Nicholas laughed outright.

"But I am waiting to hear about your adventures in Norfolk! How and why did you come to—er, no, how stupid of me! *Of course* you quarreled with Fletcher. But tell me the rest."

Shrugging into a snug morning jacket of bottle green that stretched handsomely across his broad shoulders, Ruxart waved away Oundle and faced St. Juste to lament comically, "I've been saddled with a damnable pack of relatives I wouldn't care to foist on anyone this side of Hades! Armand, how *could* you?"

"My dear boy, surely you cannot hold me responsible!" protested St. Juste, smiling.

"Oh, can't I, though?" As they descended to the spacious

119

breakfast parlor, he set to describing his future in-laws. "The mother is one of those semi-invalids who gloat over each new symptom, the half of which are devised—"

"You begin, my friend, to fill me with remorse," cut in Armand apologetically.

"Lord, I've scarcely begun! There's a bookish brother who, at first glance, set me down as a mere brawny fellow not worth the noticing—though I rather fancy I made a recovery in his esteem with my skill at slip-groat—"

"Slip-groat?"

"Ah, you see what you have missed!" Ruxart took a long sip from the coffee that had been mutely set before him and considered before continuing. "And there's another brother whose main concerns are hock and hounds. *He* at least would be tolerable if it weren't for his wife. *She* is a rapacious, pinch-faced shrew whose greatest pleasure seems to be directing thinly veiled barbs at the eldest sister."

"That would be, I collect, the estimable Jane?"

"Yes," confirmed Nick curtly. One of St. Juste's fair brows languidly rose and upon seeing it, Ruxart added crossly, "She took me in dislike."

"What? And you did not use the infamous Armytage charm to overcome her?"

"Miss Somers found my charm totally resistible. I strongly suspect she would gladly welcome the news of my early demise."

"Now, Nick, you interest me greatly. Tell me about this Miss Jane Somers. Is she a beauty?"

Nicholas sat still, staring blankly as her image rose clearly before him. "No, she's not a beauty," he answered with a rueful smile. "She is rather plain, though her eyes are . . . expressive . . . and her smile is . . . pleasing. She's a regular Long Meg—quite a head taller than Helen, in fact—and has a trick of looking down her nose that sets one in place right enough! She, at least, doesn't attempt to veil her barbs, preferring to make the hit direct."

"And were you . . . hit?" Despite the casualness of the query, St. Juste watched the viscount closely from under half-closed lids.

"She learned of our wager," he said by way of answer. "And I rather fear she'll not easily forgive me."

"And Miss Helen, did she learn of it as well?"

"No—no, and I don't think Miss Somers will tell her."

They sat mutely for some minutes, each seeing a vision of a woman. But Ruxart was somewhat disconcerted when he realized he was picturing an oversized pair of clear gray eyes beneath a muslin mobcap, and he pushed his chair abruptly from the table.

"I've a week before my fiancée arrives to claim my attention, Armand, and I've a strong desire to kick the country dust from my heels! Shall we begin at White's or Watier's?"

"I believe a view of the cattle at Tattersall's to begin," drawled St. Juste. "Then, of course, we must take a turn through the park as a prelude to an evening at the tables of White's."

This pleasant program proved to set the pattern for Ruxart's week. The viscount was seen everywhere from Cribb's Parlour to Carlton House in such a heavy round of socializing that St. Juste was moved to cynically comment that it was apparent Nick was more intent on kicking up dust than on kicking it off. But Ruxart merely shrugged and continued to clutter each day with a hectic schedule, beginning and ending every engagement with a level of restless energy previously unmatched.

Chapter Ten

Lady Frances Fletcher was not the person in whom one confided a secret, for in general news given her was no sooner taken in than it was revealed. It was as if she were but a resting house where news paused briefly before galloping on to visit the rest of the *ton*. But such was her utter disbelief over the tidings delivered by her son that her nephew had indeed offered for the country nobody that Lady Frances had for once kept her own counsel. After making several fruitless attempts to corner Ruxart during the week, she finally sallied forth to Half Moon Street, where she brushed majestically past Goswick as he opened the door.

"Do not be trying to deny Ruxart to me! I'm going to see him if I have to sit here the entire day!" Upon her declaration, she removed her pink kid gloves and thrust them at the impassive butler as one throwing down a gauntlet.

"I think, m'lady," he intoned with a wooden face, "that his lordship will receive you in the yellow morning room." He led her across the black-and-white marbled foyer to hold wide a door.

With her befeathered head erect, Lady Frances marched in. The room, though not large, was well-proportioned with a bright and cheery setting; like every other room in the viscount's house, it was finely decorated with an understated elegance. Her admirable surroundings had no effect upon Lady Frances, however, for her thoughts were fully occupied with the incredible intelligence that her nephew meant to marry at last.

She placed her short, stout body plumply on a chair covered in shiny yellow-striped satin, with every expectation of being kept there at length. But Ruxart was not one to avoid any unpleasantness. He had accepted with resignation Goswick's message that he was entertaining a morning call from his aunt and he stepped immediately toward the yellow room.

His aunt had her hands raised to gently lift her hat from her head when Ruxart entered. As this monstrous structure was a straw tower of what appeared to him to be the entire plumage of some once-proud bird, he watched with amusement her intricate maneuverings as she contrived to bring it safely from atop her gray curls to the seat beside her.

"Quite right, Aunt Fanny," he approved, strolling forward when she had at last accomplished the removal of her bonnet. "You are wise to divest yourself of that thing— shall I summon Goswick to banish it from our sight?" She managed only to drop open her mouth in wordless outrage before he went lightly on. "You really ought to get rid of your dresser, my dear. She lets you go abroad in the most appalling headgear."

She eyed him with hostility as he sat easily across from her. "That hat is quite the *height* of fashion, Ruxart!"

"Fashion is at a low ebb these days."

"Really, if you choose to be disagreeable, there's no sense in talking with you!" Her nephew's brief hopes were dashed, however, as her double chin folded in an earmark of obstinancy that he well knew. "But I've come to discover if what John has told me can indeed be true! Have you truly offered for the Somers chit?"

Ruxart studied the toe of his boot. "Yes, my dear aunt, I have."

"There is no understanding you, and so I've always said! You surely do not claim to love her."

His lordship made no attempt to deny this charge. "I should have thought," he drawled instead, "that you would be overjoyed to learn I've at last awakened to my sense of familial duty."

"Of course, of course, but *why* that little nobody?" As his head came up with a quick frown, she added crossly, "Oh, she's quite the loveliest girl to be seen in years, I'll give you that! But she has neither fortune nor position to recommend her."

"She has, nonetheless, one thing of import to recommend her, dear aunt."'

"And what is that, pray?" she demanded waspishly.

"My ring as pledge upon her finger." The viscount stood and looked down upon his aunt. "I'll have Miss Helen treated with all the respect due the Viscountess Ruxart."

"Naturally—I did not mean—and if it is *indeed* true . . ." Lady Frances halted in her flustered attempts to explain herself and gathered her dignity to inquire with more composure, "But why have you not published the notice of your betrothal?"

"But imagine, if you will, the stunning effect when we announce the news at Miss Helen's come-out ball."

She appeared satisfied and in quite a mollified tone inquired, "When is the wedding to be? John was so close I swear I was ready to box his ears!"

"We've not yet decided upon a date," he replied as he moved to stand with one foot upon the polished steel grate.

Lady Frances stared at him with narrowed eyes, wondering what could be behind that colorless tone. "Well, I do not say that you couldn't have done better—though indeed you could have if you'd but come to me—but that is neither here nor there." She broke off hastily as she saw his eyes darken.

"But I for one shall welcome the dear girl with a grateful heart, for she has at least put an end to your liaison with that dreadful Penelope Manderley. *That* woman is as bad as Caroline Lamb, you know, and you are well rid of her! The scandalous gossip alone—"

Her steam was clearly up and Ruxart let her disperse it for quite some time. At length, however, he could take no more. He turned a suppressive gaze upon her and said dampingly, "Forgive me, Aunt Frances, but I've yet to discover how my personal affairs are any of your business and I'll thank you to cease your interference in them. Ah, yes, you are affronted! I suggest you take yourself off to find a sympathetic friend to commiserate over what shocking bad manners your nephew has."

When she and her bonnet had departed in a huff, Ruxart could only wonder that, with such a mother, his cousin John had retained his sanity into manhood.

Whether he was spurred by his well-meaning aunt or by his own sense of devilment, only the viscount knew, but it was certainly with an eye to making mischief that he rode to the side of an elegant town-barouche in Hyde Park that afternoon. With the slightest hesitation, St. Juste reined in beside him to view from narrowed eyes the touching reunion between Lord Ruxart and Mrs. Penelope Manderley. It was to be observed that Mrs. Manderley's alabaster hand trembled as it encountered his lordship's, but she managed a tolerably casual air.

"What a delightful surprise! My Lord Ruxart, Mr. St. Juste, you are acquainted with lady Granville, are you not?"

"But of course," responded Ruxart promptly, his eyes never leaving the seductive emerald gaze of Mrs. Manderley.

"You must know," put in St. Juste in a dry tone, "that Ruxart is known to every female in town—and a great many beyond."

A round of laughter met this sally, to be followed by more commonplace conversation. After some five minutes, his lordship straightened in his saddle. "A pleasure to see you again."

"Were I not engaged to be at Vauxhall tonight," said Pen coyly, "I'd gladly give you the pleasure of my company again."

Ruxart regarded her from beneath drooping lids. "But, my dear Pen, I don't recall asking for that, er, pleasure." He bowed curtly at the waist, ignoring Penelope's sharply audible gasp, and rode off.

As they cantered on through the park, St. Juste casually examined his friend. "Forgive me—perhaps I was not attending—but did you not tell me this affair was quite finished?" he inquired with an air of languid interest.

"It is. Are you worrying over me?" asked Ruxart, smiling.

"Not at all, dear boy, not at all. I was merely," he explained lazily, "ascertaining the facts of the situation."

"Well, Armand, the fact is I was of a mind to see how the passionate Pen has been faring without me, nothing more."

It might have remained nothing more, but that night chanced to be the first since his lordship's return to London that was not overflowing with engagements. Ruxart dined alone and long after the last plate had been cleared from the delicate lace covering the lengthy table, he sat gazing unseeing at the flames pirouetting upon the candletops of the branched silver candelabrum. His long legs were stretched out before him as he sprawled within his chair, one hand draped over the wooden arm while the other idly twirled an empty crystal glass.

He meant to write the news of his betrothal to his grandfather and was thinking of how his message would be received when out of the candle flames came two very vivid, very unpleasant images. The first was that of his dashing fiancée shuddering with repulsion as his lips fell upon hers, the second, the look of pure scorn directed at him from Miss

Somers' gray eyes. The crystal ceased to spin. The viscount's hand clenched, snapping the long stem of the glass in two.

"My lord!" exclaimed the footman as he started from the shadows behind the viscount's chair.

"It's nothing!" said Ruxart crisply. He wrapped the linen napkin about his hand, though the ruffled wrist of his shirt had already been stained with his blood. "A scratch—nothing more! Tell Goswick to have my carriage brought round, if you please." He stood, staring a moment more at the broken shards of glass, then turned roughly from the room.

Lord Ruxart was shortly to be seen amongst those ambling through the walks of Vauxhall Gardens. From the rotunda the strains of an orchestral concert could be heard as all manner of people passed along the delightfully graveled walks and through the triumphal arches. Class distinctions did not apply to the pleasure gardens. Anyone with the shilling for admission came to enjoy the beauty of the groves festooned with thousands of lamps, to watch the fireworks or to listen to the many concerts given each night. Everyone from ruffians to royalty, from the lightest light-skirt to the grandest grande dame was to be seen there. Viscount Ruxart paid little attention, however, to the many attractions; as a holder of a silver season ticket, he had seen it all before. But as he drew near the boxes which opened onto the colonnades, he evidenced rather more interest, pausing to scan the occupants through a ribboned quizzing glass.

In one box, supping in splendor, sat a copper-haired beauty wearing a daring green silk gown with a plunging *décolletage* that clung enchantingly to her fine figure. A spangled shawl slid artfully off her bare shoulders; sapphires hung from her ears and circled her throat. Her cropped curls were ornamented with a gold band from which two soft feathers extended, accentuating an altogether ravishing sight. When the beauty at last caught sight of him, her surprise was apparent for the color faded from behind her rouged cheeks and she turned rapidly to make conversation with her blond companion. Ruxart sauntered slowly forward, a mocking satisfaction playing upon his lips.

"Lady Granville, Mrs. Manderley," he said with a slight bow to each as he neared. "I must confess my amazement at seeing two such charming beauties dining alone. I must ask, have the men of the *ton* gone blind?"

Giggling, Lady Granville hid behind her painted silk fan. Her laughter heightened her ruddy complexion, already nearing the shade of her beribboned cochineal gown. His fulsome compliment was not, however, so thoroughly enjoyed by Mrs. Manderley. She eyed him coolly and commented cuttingly, "You were not moved to say such pretty things this afternoon. Have you had perhaps a change of . . . heart?"

He smiled, an attractive, appealing smile that yet escaped his eyes. "I've been told I haven't got one. Would you mind if I joined you? Or are you indeed waiting upon someone?"

"Why, no, my lord," giggled Lady Granville as she dropped her fan to protest. "Should we be likely to wait upon anyone else when we might have your company instead?"

He responded to this flirtatious quip with a kiss upon each lady's hand before turning to come round the box. The instant he stepped away, Pen leaned toward her friend and said beseechingly, "Can you make some excuse to be absent for a time?"

Promising nothing, Lady Granville looked knowingly at her, but stopped short of winking. When Ruxart joined them, she endured a fulminating glance from Penelope as she playfully tapped his fingers with her closed fan. "You did not linger long, my lord! I declare, 'tis said, where there's haste, there's a randy man, to be sure!" On this vulgar shot, she rose. "I must stop to chat with friends I've chanced to see. Do not be doing what I should not, Pen!" she added with an arch wag as she exited through the back of the booth.

His lordship took her vacant seat. "That woman shows clearly to be the cit's widow she was before Granville married her money. I wonder that you've taken her up, Pen."

Penelope knew all there was to know about throwing out the lures with which to catch a man's interest, but for once she did not make use of such tricks, saying instead with simple sincerity, "I've not given up hope of your returning to me, Nick. Am I wrong to dare to hope?"

This worked as feminine wiles would not have done. The viscount captured her slim wrist, encircling it with his square hand. "That depends, my dear."

She caught her breath. "On what?"

Ruxart pressed his mouth warmly on the point where her pulse wildly coursed. His deep dark eyes then rose to meet hers. "On how much you tempt me to want you."

"Oh, Nicky, how I've missed you!" she whispered as his head bent over her wrist once more. Her eyes drank in the vision of him, moving from the lank black hair past the firm jawline to the full lips nuzzling her skin. As he released her wrist, she noticed the cut along his palm. "What happened to your hand?"

A cloud passed over his features. "It's nothing. I was careless and cut myself." He rose abruptly to stand behind her, running his hands restively along the creamy flesh of her shoulders. He bent to drop a kiss upon the back of her bare neck when from the corner of his eyes he caught sight of a tall, slim woman in a drab olive gown. Stiffening, Ruxart raised his eyes.

Across the spacious, well-lit lawn he saw Miss Jane Somers, her smile fading as she recognized him. Cold distaste crossed clearly over her face. Nettled, the viscount pressed his lips on Pen's neck with slow deliberation. For good measure, he followed this with a kiss planted firmly on her shoulder, but when he looked up to see the effect, Miss Somers had gone.

"Darling," murmured Pen, twisting her head to face him,

"Shall we leave?"

"I think," he answered, sitting back down beside her, "that I'd much rather stay and enjoy the pleasures of Vauxhall."

She hid her disappointment and smiled gaily as he filled their wine glasses, but she ached to be alone and in his expert arms once again. She ran her hand along his cheek and though he caught her hand and kissed it, she had the oddest notion that he did so absently. It now seemed to her that his attention was devoted to the passing crowds and Pen set herself to be as tantalizing as she well knew how to be.

Despite her efforts, his lordship was considering leaving the booth to wander through the gardens, wondering if he could again sight that olive gown amongst the various groves and lanes, when a man unexpectedly entered the box behind them.

Soberly, but fashionably, dressed, he was of medium height and a build that had once been athletic, but now tended to the paunchiness of middle age. The hands gripping his gold-topped walking stick had whitened and he bore an air of suppressed rage.

"One might term such a touching scene intimate," he rasped through tightened lips, "but I believe intolerable might be more apt."

"Robert! What a fright you've given me!" exclaimed Penelope rather shrilly. "Coming in like that!"

"I do not doubt, madam wife, that you did not expect me," he responded acidly. "But I found no occasion to remain in the country once I learned of a certain lord's return to London."

Robert Manderley was quite some years older than his wife; his lined face seemed older still in the glaring light of the box as his anger engraved each line more deeply. His eyes continued to bore through the viscount as he stood rigidly facing him.

Ruxart gradually unfolded himself to stand before the older man. "I do not like your tone, sir, or your implication," he said in a voice devoid of emotion.

The walking stick jerked up, but whatever Manderley meant to say or do was never known. On the instant, the door to the box again swung open and Jane Somers stepped in saying brightly, "Dear Lord Ruxart! You were quite right! The Grand Cascade was indeed a wonder to behold! Was it not?" She applied to her sister for affirmation.

Entering behind her, Helen nervously agreed that it was indeed a wonder, just like a real waterfall, and Jane smiled brilliantly upon them all before focusing her radiant attention on the stunned Penelope. "Mrs. Manderley, it was most kind of you to include us in this expedition. The gardens are all I've ever read or heard they were." As no one seemed inclined to speak, Jane directed an inquiring look at the graying gentleman scowling fiercely at her. "I don't believe I know . . ."

With a blatant look of admiration, Ruxart performed the necessary introductions, causing Jane to exclaim, "Oh, Mr. Manderley! You are so fortunate to have the dearest wife! No one could have been more kind to my sister or me during our stay here in town. Though it's not yet been made public, Helen is betrothed to the viscount, you know, and we've met with graciousness from all his friends, but most especially from dear Mrs. Manderley."

While dear Mrs. Manderley sat in wordless dismay, Helen put in a tremulous, "Yes, indeed, so kind," which earned her a derisive glare from Pen's husband.

There was nothing Manderley could do but accept the situation Miss Somers had thrust upon him, though he did so with ill grace, whispering harshly to the viscount, "Do not think, Ruxart, that this makes an end to it!"

His lordship replied with surprising calm that he thought no such thing, but his apparent amusement only served to further infuriate the outraged husband and Ruxart decided it was perhaps time to absent himself.

"Did I not see," he said, interrupting Jane's spritely flowing chatter, "your Aunt Willoughby here? Should we not join her?"

"If you wish," answered Jane. Taking Pen's hand, she said in a voice dripping of honey, "I know that when Helen and Ruxart are wed, they shall have you often to visit, so I look forward to seeing you again. Goodnight, Mrs., Mr. Manderley."

Ruxart accompanied the sisters out of the box, leaving Pen to face her husband's frustrated fury alone. His own enjoyment of the situation was clipped short some twenty feet from the box when Jane rounded on him, her eyes flashing. "If you've no thought for your own reputation, you might do well to remember Helen's!"

"Please, Jane, don't," begged Helen, turning ghostly pale. "There is no need—I am not—"

"There is every need!" objected her sister wrathfully. "Someone must tell this fatuous—"

"I'm quite certain you shall do so, Miss Somers," broke in the viscount, "but I don't think you wish to do so here. Unless, of course, you wish to create precisely the kind of scene you've been working so strenuously to avoid."

Miss Somers appeared to have lost the power of speech as her mouth fell soundlessly open. She allowed his lordship to lead them to her aunt's booth, not listening to the steady stream of inconsequential comments he addressed to Helen. By the time they joined the Willoughby party, she had regained enough of her usual composure to greet them steadily.

Three pairs of eyes scrutinized Ruxart, each with a different measure of curiosity. Caro's violet eyes were openly agog with interest; Elizabeth's examined him in consternation; it was left to John Fletcher's eyes to provide the disapproval which his lordship had expected. Throughout the brief time he remained with them, Ruxart was treated to a display of frigid disdain from Miss Somers, while he saw readily that he would soon be subjected to another inflamed interview with his cousin. His fiancée was unexpectedly courteous and before he parted from them, he pressed her hand and said softly, "I must ask your forgiveness."

"It's nothing, I assure you," she responded quickly. "But, please, Ruxart, do not be arguing with Jane! I—I do not think I can bear it!"

With a greater degree of warmth and understanding than she had yet had from him, Ruxart assured her that he desired nothing more than to be on good terms with her sister. He left them on a promise to call in Brook Street the following day.

Jane fumed in silence until they at last returned to the Willoughby's town house. After tapping once sharply on the door of her sister's room, Jane stormed in to demand, "How *could* you be so pleasant to him? Was it not the outside of enough that we must debase ourselves with his mistress?"

"But, dearest, *you* suggested it," Helen pointed out timidly.

"To avoid a scandal! It was apparent Manderley meant to challenge Ruxart and a fine thing it would be to have him involved in a duel over Penelope Manderley a week before he's betrothed to you! Though if he'd been killed it would have served him right!" she added with bloodthirsty relish.

"But, Jane, if *I* do not mind his connection with Mrs. Manderley, I do not see that *you* have any cause to complain! You must remember that ours is to be a modern marriage, like the French marriage of convenience."

Jane stared unbelieving at Helen then stated firmly, "Even so, I know that if he were *my* fiancé, *I* would not suffer the likes of Pen Manderley!" So saying, she retired with a slam to her own room to scheme with satisfaction all the cutting things she meant to say to his lordship on the morrow.

Chapter Eleven

Adroitly maneuvering his restive pair of grays through the heavy morning traffic on Bond Street the following day, Viscount Ruxart was startled to espy a well-known ruffled mobcap progressing down the street, apparently quite alone. He pulled roughly on the reins, causing Jem to protest loudly, "M'lord! To be yankin' at the horses' mouths like that!"

"Get down and hold their heads," ordered Ruxart tersely as he leapt lightly from the curricle. Three swift strides brought him to the side of the tall, slender figure wearing the mobcap, where he said without preamble, "Come with me. I'll see you home."

Jane Somers turned slowly to face the owner of that hated voice. "Thank you, but I am not yet going home," she said.

"Where is your maid?" he demanded.

"I have none with me."

"Then you are most assuredly going home with me now." The viscount put out a pre-emptory hand; Miss Somers saw no option but to take it.

She was soon seated beside Ruxart in his curricle as it proceeded toward Brook Street. As they drove through the crowded streets, his lordship rang a pithy peal over her head

135

on the improprieties of young ladies strolling down Bond Street unescorted during the height of the season until at last Jane could no longer restrain the laughter burbling up within her.

"And what," he turned and thunderously demanded, "are you laughing at?"

"Why, at you, my lord!" she answered through her merriment. "Anyone less suited to be lecturing on propriety, I cannot imagine!"

"Your reputation, Miss Somers, is no laughing matter," he said bitingly.

"But, surely, Lord Ruxart, I am well past the age of such considerations."

"Well past . . . my god, you are worse than the greenest schoolgirl! If you've no more sense than to wander about town attracting the attention of the vulgar, then your reputation should be left to its own deserts!"

One glance was sufficient for Ruxart to realize that Miss Somers was wholly insensible to the gravity of her morning's solecism. The mirth clearly sparkled in her eyes and it appeared that only by pressing her lips firmly together was she able to refrain from again exhibiting a display of hoydenish laughter.

Jane was indeed amused. It was not in her nature to remain out of temper for long and the white fury of the night before had dimmed with the first bright rays of sunlight. With calm reflection, she had decided that her best course lay in seeing as little of her sister's fiancé during her stay in London as possible. That she had run almost directly into him on her first expedition about town was humorously ironic; that he should issue such a lecture was, to her view, nearly a cause for hysterics.

Though he managed to remain remarkably expressionless as he stood behind the fascinating exchange between m'lord and the lady, Jem had difficulty restraining himself when, as they pulled up before the Willoughby's tall town house, the viscount again jerked at the ribbons in a manner quite unlike his usual gentle handling of his grays. He was further surprised when the lady climbed nimbly down and attempted to forestall m'lord by thanking him for the ride.

"Although I do think perhaps I should make you explain to my cousin why I've arrived home without the lavender water I promised to procure for her!" Her humor turned to alarm as Ruxart began to follow her down. "No! Sir! There is no need!"

"You mistake, Miss Somers," he countered as he took one elbow and guided her along. "There is plainly a need for your aunt to be informed of your excursions. I'm quite sure she is completely ignorant of your doings."

She had the grace to flush and allowed him to lead her up the steps. Pausing at the top, Ruxart added, "And I had promised to call upon Helen today."

"My sister," began Jane before breaking off abruptly.

"Yes?" he prompted.

"Is much too good for you!"

"If you mean to argue with me, my dear girl, you must do better than that. It is a point which even I cannot argue," he said with a provoking smile.

He held open the door and Miss Somers passed into the house without responding. But as she began to mount the stairs, she halted to cast a speculative look at him. "I did say, did I not, that you were no fool."

With that, she continued on her way. Ruxart watched until she had gone out of sight, a smile of appreciation tugging at his lips. He was recalled to his surroundings by the discreet cough of the servant behind him and was soon announced to Miss Helen.

Seated upon a long, low, armless settee of Egyptian design, as was the current rage, Helen favored her fiancé with a bashful smile as he entered and set aside the issue of *La Belle Assemblée* with which she had been occupying her time.

"Do you hope to find the fashion to perfect your beauty?" he asked lightly as he saw the magazine. "You should not bother, for it cannot be done. Yours, my dear, is already the very perfection of beauty."

She tried to laugh this off, for as always, his flowery tribute set her in an embarrassed quake. "No—no! I am merely passing the time."

Ruxart sat down easily beside her, watching her fingers nervously entwine themselves together. "Helen, about last night," he began.

"You need not explain!" she broke in quickly. "I was not the least upset, I assure you!"

"I must nevertheless beg your forgiveness," he persisted soberly.

"There—there is n-nothing to forgive," she whispered.

"I give you my word, Helen, that you need never fear being put in such a position again."

The young girl stared down at her hands, caught the glimmer of the diamonds about the glossy sapphire and seemed to gather up the courage to speak. Taking a deep breath, she raised her eyes to meet his and said, "My lord, let us understand one another. I do not intend to be a bothersome sort of wife. This is—this is to be a marriage of—of convenience, is it not?"

His downturned eyes seemed to slant even more than usual. Her direct speaking surprised and perversely annoyed him, for he was in the habit of making women love him through no effort at all, and the thought that he was to marry one who, to all appearances, did not love him in the least affronted his vanity to no little degree. For no accountable reason, his lordship instantly blamed her sister Jane for this, and wondered briefly how he would bring the interfering Miss Somers to regret her negative influence upon his fiancée.

None of this showed on the viscount's dispassionate face. He answered quite smoothly, "Of course it is, my dear. Have you, as yet, given any thought as to a suitable wedding date?"

"I have always thought the—the autumn a—a beautiful time for weddings," she stuttered hesitantly.

"Autumn!" He saw her face pale at his exclamation and swallowed his opposition. "Very well, if that is what you wish," he said instead. "It's longer away than best pleases me, but I'd not object to September."

Helen rapidly assented to September, fearing the temper she saw lurking behind the hard glint of his eye should she put forth a suggestion of October or, more preferably, November. Ruxart did not remain long after this, leaving Helen alone on the Egyptian settee, where she reflected with melancholy on how quickly five months could pass.

From having seen, in Lord Ruxart's well-expressed opinion, rather too much of Miss Jane Somers, fashionable London fell to seeing practically nothing of her at all. She busied herself with the preparations for her sister's ball, which she had been reluctantly persuaded to attend, and with keeping at a distance from the viscount. Other than trips to Elizabeth's dressmaker for gown fittings, Jane's few excursions were sightseeing outings with John Fletcher.

It was on the afternoon of their tour of the Tower of London that the subject of his lordship's recent grievous behavior was broached, Fletcher stumbling over an apology for his cousin.

"I expect someone said something to set him on," remarked Jane thoughtfully. She read the question in her companion's eyes and continued, "The wager about my sister—did you, perhaps, lecture Ruxart about it?"

"I *spoke* to him, naturally," replied Fletcher stiffly. "I could not stand by—"

"And was this before or after he actually followed through with this scheme?"

"Before, but—"

139

"There you see! It's little wonder he's as rash as he is, with you to spur him on!" She put up a hand to silence his protest. "It's true, you know. It quite puts me in mind of Agnes and Freddy. If they were to pass a tree walking to church of a Sunday, she would promptly adjure him not to dirty his good clothes by climbing that tree—a thing Freddy would have no thought of until that very moment. Naturally, Freddy would be climbing that tree directly. He'd need, you see, to prove himself to be his own person. It is the same, I dare say, with your cousin."

"That may well be true, but Ruxart had entered upon the wager before I spoke out against it. At least, I was there when St. Juste offered him the wager. I did protest, but . . ." Fletcher floundered into silence, remembering how his words had, indeed, seemed to encourage Ruxart's devilment.

"I did not mean to sermonize and must ask you to forgive my interference," said Jane with an apologetic smile.

"What you have said, you've no need to apologize for. I'm only too afraid that you've hit upon a truth I should have seen long ago."

They walked on, a meditative frown marring the set of John's straight mouth. After passing through the mint and the armoury, where they viewed with interest, among other things, the sword used to decapitate Anne Boleyn, Jane suggested they quit the Tower, having seen, she felt, quite all worth seeing therein.

Rolling home in the sensible equipage Fletcher had deemed suitable for the excursion, they conversed on various topics, lighting at length upon the upcoming ball.

"The great wonderment of it, for me," said John with a good-humored smile, "is that my mother has not spread word of the betrothal abroad, for she is the greatest rattle."

"Speaking of rattles, *I* have been overcome with amazement at Caroline's discretion, for I fully expected her to trumpet the news throughout the *ton*!" she laughed.

A guarded expression settled over Fletcher's countenance.

Jane studied him, an understanding gleam gracing her eyes, but it was with only the barest hint of amusement that she said, "I have noticed—I hope you won't think me impertinent to mention it—but I have thought I detected a certain warmth in your regard toward Caroline."

With no little effort, she gradually drew the tale from her reluctant escort. It seemed that he had, indeed, once cherished a fondness for Miss Willoughby, but he had been, he informed Jane, brought to his senses before matters had progressed too deeply.

"She has a levity of mind that I cannot admire," he stated in a severe tone. "And she suffers a sad want of conduct."

"Surely, you judge her too harshly. She is but seventeen, and the delights of the season to one just out of the school-room can indeed be heady."

"When I tell you that I once—just once, ma'am—asked her to forego the pleasures of a party to spend a quiet evening with my family, and that her answer was to dance the night away, you will readily see how little Miss Caroline Willoughby cares for my regard!"

Jane turned her gaze upon her lap, hiding the ready laughter in her eyes from Fletcher's outraged view. Judging it wisest to let the matter rest for the time being, she began to speak of inconsequential things and so easily passed the rest of the journey home.

In the meantime, having at last prevailed upon St. Juste to accompany him on one of his daily visits to Brook Street, Ruxart dispensed easy advice to Elizabeth Willoughby on the methods best suited to make her ball that epitome of success, a dreadful squeeze, while leaving Helen's company to his friend.

When a lull fell in their discourse, Helen took a deep breath and confessed on a rush, "I am exceedingly glad you have called today, Mr. St. Juste. I'd begun to fear that you were displeased with the thought of Lord Ruxart's marrying me."

"How could you think, my dear Miss Helen, that I would

ever be so foolishly lacking in taste as to be displeased with you?" he inquired with the drowsy smile which so fascinated her.

"That was prettily said!" Helen's lovely lips parted in a smile far different from the strained one with which she received the viscount's compliments and its effect on St. Juste was intense. He exhibited no trace of his usual weary manner as he leaned toward her, his green eyes shining darkly.

"I am not, in general, one to give advice, my child, but if you wish to make a success of your marriage—"

"I do wish it," she interrupted gravely. She stared at the magnificent ring flashing on her finger and added resolutely, "I would welcome any advice you honored me with, sir."

St. Juste hesitated. Then, with a glance at the viscount sitting casually across the room, he said slowly, "Ruxart does not respond well to criticism. Should you attempt to lecture or nag at him, he will invariably run counter to your wishes. At the same time, you must not be afraid to speak your mind. Do so, directly, then leave the matter, and Nick will respect you the more for it."

"Do you know, sir, that my sister gave me much the same advice?" The faint lifting of a thin blond brow evidenced his interest and she went on with a smile, "Jane told me that whenever the viscount does what I should not like, I should look him in the eye and tell him to quit being so nonsensical."

"I begin to perceive, child, that your sister is a woman of extraordinary sense," he drawled. "I must confess to a longing to meet Miss Somers."

Crossing toward them, Ruxart had caught this last and said with rare affection, "I, too, long to see such a meeting! But Miss Somers has virtually disappeared—I've not had the fortune to see her all week. Where has she been hiding?"

"Why, she has been touring the sights with Mr. Fletcher," answered Helen without regarding her effect. When she went on to innocently inform Ruxart of the constant attention his cousin was devoting to her sister, she was unaware of the depth of his displeasure, for he covered it well. He asked in an even tone where the two of them ventured.

"I do not know precisely where they have been each day, but I do know that today they were to see the London Tower. Jane has a guidebook, you see, which tells about all the sights to be seen in the metropolis."

"Do you think, Helen, that there is anything . . . of a serious nature . . . between them?" Ruxart asked with a casual air.

"In truth, I have been wondering. . . ." she replied slowly. Then looking at him with a tremulous smile, she added, "But would it not be the most tremendous thing! We could perhaps have a double wedding!"

This pleasant prospect did not appear to afford his lordship much satisfaction. Perceiving this, St. Juste led the conversation onto a less volatile path, helping to surmount any obstacles during the remainder of the visit.

Though he lingered as long as was socially acceptable, Lord Ruxart was again denied the opportunity of seeing Miss Somers, for she had not returned before he and St. Juste rose to leave. The viscount strenuously suppressed an impulse to travel home by way of the London Tower, proceeding instead to Gentleman Jackson's Salon in Bond Street, where he expelled his excess of repressed choler by sparring with the great man himself. Jackson was heard to remark that m'lord would do better if he could but keep his passions out of the business. Had he so desired, Mr. St. Juste could have enlightened Jackson, for he well knew that Nicholas Armytage never kept his passions out of any matter.

The Viscount Ruxart was not alone in his disparagement of the possible pairing of his cousin Fletcher and Jane

143

Somers. Caroline Willoughby had grown increasingly downhearted during the week and upon Jane's return from the Tower, she loudly announced she had the headache and flounced from the sitting room. Jane accepted her young cousin's departure with equanimity and sat talking with her aunt for a full half hour before excusing herself to make her way upstairs.

Entering Caro's room before the sound of her knock had died away, Jane found her cousin sitting before her gilt dressing table, staring morosely into her mirrored reflection.

"I trust the headache is better?" asked Jane as she came to stand behind Caro.

"Yes! Thank you!" sniped the girl.

"You know, Caro, I had the oddest notion that you were suffering from something quite different."

"Did you?"

"Well, yes, I must own I've been thinking you to be in love," admitted Jane apologetically.

"Love—ha! And with whom, I pray you, should I be in love?"

"Oh, someone like . . . Mr. Fletcher, perhaps?"

"Mr. Fletcher," enunciated Caro firmly, "is stuffy! He—he thinks I am nothing but a sad flirt!"

"Well, and so you are," agreed Jane. Before the indignant young lady could remark to the contrary, Jane went serenely on, "But you are not *wild*, Caro. Mr. Fletcher knows this, surely."

"He is stupid and stuffy and I'm sure I do not care in the least what he thinks!" she declared dejectedly. After a moment she added in a depressed tone, "At any rate, I have been thinking Mr. Fletcher has shown a decided partiality for *you*, Jane. Have you—have you not formed a *tendre* for him?" she asked in the voice of one not desiring to receive an answer.

"Oh, Caro, don't be absurd!" was Jane's laughing reply. "I am no longer of an age for such fancies."

Though many would have argued this point, Caro seemed much struck with the force of this sensible argument and a smile spread over her lips. In a moment, however, an unhappy thought effectively removed the smile.

"Still, it is apparent that Mr. Fletcher has formed one for you," she insisted glumly.

"Well, you know, I've not wanted to mention it, Caro, not knowing how you would feel about such a thing, but it's my belief that Mr. Fletcher has been escorting me about town just to have an excuse to call here and perhaps see you. His eyes always follow you when you're in the room, you know."

"No—do they?" breathed Caro.

"Indeed they do," assured Jane, smiling. "Mr. Fletcher needs only to realize what a very well-behaved girl you can be to get over his priggish attitude."

Caro cupped her chin in her hand and stared thoughtfully at her cousin. "You think that if I act prettily and don't flirt overmuch at Helen's ball, Mr. Fletcher will no longer hold me in dislike?"

"Yes, I do."

"Oh." She sat digesting this. As Jane rose to leave, however, she broke from her reverie to ask, "Would you like to wear my silver ribbon at the ball? You may—I shan't be wearing it!"

Jane accepted her cousin's burst of generosity, then left her to ruminate further on the arts of catching a man, even a man as stuffy, as obstinate and as, in Caro's view, adorable as John Fletcher.

Chapter Twelve

One pale hand brushed a blond lock off his brow as St. Juste listened to the viscount's description of his afternoon session at Manton's Shooting Gallery. They stood within the Willoughbys' elegantly formal withdrawing room, both wearing the finest full evening dress. The stark black favored by St. Juste heightened the ethereal effect of his pallid coloring, while Ruxart's deep blue velvet intensified his own darkling good looks. His lordship appeared even more than usually restive, but this, it must be supposed, would be natural in a man on the night of his public betrothal.

The opening door disrupted Ruxart's tale as the men turned to watch Elizabeth Willoughby glide forward. "Forgive us! Shocking in us to greet you so late, I know, but we've been at sixes and sevens the whole of the day!" Her broad smile charmed them both as with a swish of her aqua empire gown she sat upon a rosewood sofa with scroll end.

Entering quietly behind her aunt, Helen was utterly dazzling in a white India muslin gown embroidered with gold thread and with a long train coming off the shoulders. She curtseyed in a very pretty manner, then said as she gave her gloved hand to her fiancé, "Caroline and Jane send their apologies—a last minute tear in Caro's gown has delayed them, but they shall join us directly."

"Dear child," put in her aunt with a comic smile, "if I live through this ball of yours, I swear I'll not give another! Caro shall have to make for Gretna Green. You cannot imagine, my good men, what last minute crises I've been put to to averting all day!"

Her light-hearted air set the conversation traveling along droll lines as they awaited the rest of the dinner party. Soon the drawing room doors opened upon a liveried servant who made the stentorian announcement that Lady Frances Fletcher and Mr. John Fletcher had arrived.

Remembering their last meeting only too clearly, Lady Frances greeted her nephew with the merest inclination of her elaborately turbaned head as she swept past him to place her plump form next to her friend Elizabeth. By contrast, she extended a regal hand to Armand and begged him to favor her with the name of his tailor, for whatever may be said of him, no one could ever fault the cut of his clothes and John would do well to call upon St. Juste's tailor as soon as may be.

Having long ago acquired the art of charming ladies, old and young alike, Ruxart promptly presented himself before her and, bowing with an exaggerated flourish, said teasingly, "You see before you, dearest aunt, a miserable nephew, anxious to make amends. He is even willing to go so far as to praise vociferously that golden headdress which now reposes so brilliantly upon your glorious curls."

His tone was engaging; his smile even more so and Frances could not resist. Slapping at his wrist with her carved fan, she exclaimed, "Oh, Ruxart! You are a sad rogue, indeed! It's a wonder that Miss Helen is willing to have you, and so I declare!"

"I quite agree—it is a great wonder," he murmured as he straightened to salute his cousin.

The latest breach between John and his titled cousin had

never been properly healed, but outward relations between them had remained cordial enough. Tonight, however, it was to be noted that his lordship was decidedly cool toward Fletcher. Ruxart's humor did not improve when, on the opening of the double doors, John became rather more keenly attentive. It was not to be known that the cause for his sudden interest was the pert blonde in the dashing primrose evening dress flounced with lace, for Miss Somers entered directly behind her, to stunning effect.

With his quizzing glass raised to view her, St. Juste lamented to his friend in a sleepy undertone, "But, my dear Ruxart, you told me she was quite plain."

The viscount did not reply. He simply stood and stared.

Feeling her age no longer required the unbecoming pastels demanded of a debutante, Jane had chosen a gauze gown decorated with silver rosettes worn over a dove gray satin sheath, the color of which perfectly matched her enormous eyes. A silvery gauze shawl was cunningly draped over her arms and allowed to trail behind her, providing adornment as no amount of jewelry could have done.

But it was her hair that commanded his lordship's attention. Having previously been hidden by a succession of spinsterish caps, the soft brown radiance had been unexpected. Like Helen's, Jane's hair was not fashionably cropped, but kept long in a profusion of gentle curls. For the occasion, she had piled her hair into an artful topknot, threaded with the silver ribbon so generously offered by Caro, with tendrils tumbling over her ears. Gazing at the warm blend of color, Ruxart was reminded of the patina of some richly mellowed wood.

Helen darted forward to take Jane's hand, guiding her to the gentlemen, where she shyly introduced her to Mr. St. Juste. He took Miss Somers' hand and held it for a still moment as he searched her eyes.

"I am honored," he remarked at last, lightly caressing her fingertips with his lips.

149

Jane, for her part, examined him just as directly. Despite the studied languor, she recognized the intelligence behind the sleepy eyes and the strength of character beneath the elegant clothes. She decided that, wager or no, she liked what she saw.

"The honor, Mr. St. Juste, is mine," she replied. "I've heard a great deal of you, you must know, and have long anticipated this pleasure."

A smile gradually graced his lips. "Ah, but you must put aside whatever you have heard, my dear, for the half of it, I am persuaded, can do me no justice at all, while the other half does me rather too much justice."

Her honeyed laughter enchanted him as much as it had the viscount. His lordship took the moment to make his own greeting of her, saying, "It is becoming a novel experience to see you, Miss Somers. Have you quite finished with all the sights to be seen in the metropolis?"

"Oh, I am quite certain, my lord, that you could show me a few not even mentioned in my guidebook," she returned, laughing.

Their attention was captured just then by the announcement of dinner and the small party proceeded to the formal dining room to pass a pleasant interlude preceding the ball. Sitting at opposite ends of the lengthy table, Ruxart was granted no further opportunity for speech with Jane, but throughout the meal, his eyes wandered often toward the spot where she sat next to John. Conversation was light and witty, the food savory and fulfilling; the small company at length rose from the table satisfied with it and each other.

Within the hour, Brook Street was the scene of a bustling fervor as carriages, coaches and vehicles of all kinds rolled forward to dispense their occupants at the front of the well-lit town house. Footmen ushered the arrivals within, removing cloaks and capes, walking sticks and hats, before each guest mounted the stairs to formally greet their hostess in the threshold of the elaborately decorated ballroom.

Not wishing to copy Mrs. Knight's recent success with silk hangings, or to resort to following Lady Holland's lead in festooning her rooms with fresh flowers, Elizabeth had shrewdly struck upon the notion of placing mirrors throughout her rooms. The prismatic reflection of shimmering candles, sparkling gems and splendid gowns was stunning. In addition, small bits of mirror hung from the ceiling with ribbons, creating a celestial glitter much admired by her guests.

Music penetrated the air as Lord Ruxart led Miss Helen to the head of the first set. Other couples fell in behind them, and Jane was gratified to see her cousin wreathed in smiles as she took to the floor on the arm of Mr. Fletcher. Mindful of Jane's advice, Caro behaved with an unsurpassed decorum and was so gracious toward her partner that the two were soon in perfect charity with one another.

Sitting on one of the armless Sheraton chairs lining the walls, Jane placidly watched the colorful activity about her.

"May I request the honor of this dance, Miss Somers?" a lazy voice inquired.

She turned her head to behold the lithe figure of Armand St. Juste. "I do not intend to dance, sir," she replied.

"Ah, then I intend to sit with you," he drawled. He put his words easily to action, settling beside her. "I have heard, Miss Somers, that you hold Lord Ruxart in dislike."

She followed the direction of his gaze to study Ruxart as he moved with graceful ease through the dance with Helen. She then turned to scrutinize the long, thin face of her companion before saying tranquilly, "You have been misinformed."

"Indeed?"

She ignored this weary inquiry to observe, "I'd not have thought that the two of you would make close friends."

"Ruxart is somewhat . . . shall we say, energetic."

"But he is your friend nonetheless," she persisted.

"He is my friend."

It was simply said, but she was conscious of a sudden desire to change topics. Several impartial subjects were covered, with Jane being kept much amused by St. Juste's air of fatigue, when toward the end of the first set, he commented, "I trust you will change your mind about dancing, Miss Somers."

"Oh? Why is that?"

"I fear you shall be hard put to find enough excuses for not doing so," replied St. Juste while surveying the room through his beribboned glass. "I find I must apologize for putting you in such a position."

"*You* apologize! Whatever can you mean?"

"It will have been observed that I've been conversing with you for the whole of this dance," he explained apologetically. Dropping his glass, he looked at her with the air of one slightly beset with worry. "You shall—I'm sorry, my dear— be plagued with requests the rest of the evening."

"I shall?" questioned Jane, smiling her disbelief.

"Undoubtedly."

St. Juste came to his feet as Ruxart and Helen emerged from the crowds. It appeared his lordship was in one of his kind moods, for Helen was smiling happily. With a silent sigh of relief, Jane rose to join her sister and the two ladies were soon surrounded by an admiring circle of eager young beaux.

A thin white hand on his sleeve detained Ruxart from joining that circle. His face was a mask of ineffable boredom as St. Juste mused, "I perceive, Nicholas, that I've made a mistake. You are far too dark for Miss Helen! Perceive what a striking couple we should have made with my fairness emphasizing her dark beauty and vice versa."

"Most definitely vice versa!" laughed Ruxart. "Don't expect me to apologize, St. Juste—you chose her for me after all!"

"So I did, dear boy, so I did," returned Armand in tones of utter ennui. "It behooves me to permit the *ton* a glimpse of

152

what might have been." So saying, he wandered over to solicit Helen's hand for the next quadrille.

Pressing past two youthful and well turned-out exquisites who stood arguing for the honor of leading the protesting Miss Somers into the set forming, Ruxart presented the lady with his own petition. She declined politely. He persisted, but she was not to be persuaded, insisting she meant only to watch the dancing of the evening. Lady Frances swooped down to claim her nephew's attention before he could make an issue of the matter, and much to Jane's relief, he was drawn inexorably away.

When, some few minutes later, Ruxart chanced to see Miss Somers stepping lightly into the quadrille with Fletcher, his anger, he felt, was justified. To give her her due, Jane had tried to deny Mr. Fletcher, but in his way, John was as obstinate as his cousin, and as no one had swept mercifully forth to rescue her, her objections had at last been overcome.

Once she had succumbed to Mr. Fletcher's entreaties, Jane gave herself up fully to the pleasures of the quadrille. She loved to dance and executed even the most intricate steps with the lightest of grace. When, as St. Juste's prediction proved all too accurate and she was presented with the novel experience of having men encircle her, vying with one another to partner her for each dance, Jane forgot altogether her intention to remain on the sidelines as became the matron she considered herself to be. She favored one zealous gentleman after another, stepping happily to the music and thoroughly enjoying her astounding success.

Her enjoyment was observed by Ruxart with a mixture of amusement and annoyance. His annoyance, however, grew as Miss Somers continued to elude him. The more she seemed to prefer the attention of others, the more securing a dance with her became an object with him. He found himself needing to know the feel of her in his arms. When he saw her dancing with his cousin Fletcher for a second time, annoyance gave way to anger.

He waited impatiently, watching them moodily from beneath half-lowered lids as he struggled to keep from striding forth and tearing her from Fletcher's side. When, after what seemed to him an interminable length of time, the dance came to an end, Ruxart met the guilty pair with a heavy frown.

"I had thought, Miss Somers," he said tight-lipped, "that you had chosen not to dance this evening."

She strove to keep her voice light as she replied. "Indeed, my lord, such was my intention. But as Mr. Fletcher overcame my every objection—"

"I had not realized my cousin could be so determined," he cut in with faint derision. "Come, Miss Somers, I believe the next dance shall be mine."

Dimly aware of the first strains of a waltz being sounded and thinking she could not bear to be in Ruxart's arms, Jane shook her head in wordless protest.

"I am certain this is our dance," he repeated in a tone that brooked no denial.

"But I am persuaded you would much rather stand up again with Helen," she countered, turning to her sister beside her.

"Oh, no," said Helen unhelpfully. "You must dance with him, Jane! You have not done so once tonight."

Miss Somers looked from her sister to his lordship, then firmly set aside her mounting panic and quietly agreed. It was only, she told herself resolutely, a dance. Though the hand she set upon Ruxart's velvet sleeve shook slightly, Jane appeared calm as they moved into the swirl of couples waltzing.

Beneath the gleaming mirrors, they paused and faced one another. His gloved hand clasped hers and the room dissolved into a kaleidoscope of colors. A startling tremor of desire passed between them as Viscount Ruxart took Jane

154

Somers into his arms and twirled her into a blur of time and essence. She saw nothing but the dark passion burning within his eyes; she heard nothing but the erratic leaping of her heartbeat; she felt nothing but the heated touch of his hand resting on her waist.

Though they did not speak, it seemed to Jane as if the sudden acknowledgment of their love had been shouted through the room. Nothing would ever be the same again.

The music faded to stillness. Ruxart stood motionless, staring at her. Then abruptly, he turned and strode away.

Her fingers still trembled where he had touched them. Her every breath was taken with effort. She stood where he had left her and knew again, nothing would ever be as it had been before.

Some twenty minutes later Nicholas Armytage, Viscount Ruxart, formally announced the plighting of his troth to Miss Helen Somers. Amid the outpouring of felicitations, his lordship looked not at his new fiancée, but stared at Jane with such searing intensity that she was forced to make her excuses and retire straightway from the festivity.

She lay down fully clothed upon her bed and stared dully up into the darkness, trying to understand what had just happened. That Ruxart now loved her she had no doubt. As the gay melody of the Duke of York's Quick Step floated faintly up to her, she tried to decide if the knowledge of this love was a painful joy or a joyous pain.

Out of the shadows came one clear thought: Their love could never be fulfilled. She knew that for all his wildness, Ruxart was an honorable man. He would not jilt Helen. And Jane thought it highly unlikely that her timid sister would ever cry off from a betrothal so publicly announced. She wondered bleakly, as she had so often before, what had prompted Helen to accept the offer of a man she so clearly

155

did not love.

It was at this point that a tap on the door disturbed her woeful meditations.

"Jane? I do not mean to hector you," said Helen quietly as she closed the door and moved to her sister's bedside. "Ruxart sent me to discover if you are all right, which was very kind in him, was it not?"

For some seconds, Jane made no response. Then she said woodenly, "You may tell his lordship there is nothing to be concerned about. I am unused to such excitement, that is all."

She seemed unwilling to elaborate so Helen lightly kissed her brow and backed toward the door. "Do get some rest, dearest," she whispered as she left her sister to the dull comfort of the darkness.

Jane did not know how many hours had trudged by when another rap sounded upon her door, to be followed by a cropful of blond curls.

"Jane, dear, are you awake?" inquired a voice full of suppressed excitement.

She forced her lips to part, her tongue to move. "Yes, Caro."

"Oh, thank goodness!" she exclaimed, rushing in. "I could not think of going to bed without telling you the news!"

Jane made a supreme effort. She sat up and lit the candle in the pewter lamp at her bedside. "What news?" she asked, trying to care.

"John—Mr. Fletcher—has spoken!" Caroline swirled to the bedside, then amended, "Well, not precisely, for he will have it that he cannot ask for my hand until my eighteenth birthday, even though that isn't until midsummer. He is *such* a dear with his quaint notions! But we have come to an understanding!"

The young girl glowed with her happiness and Jane roused herself to give her a tight hug. "That's the best news I could have had, Caro."

"Well, I wanted you to know. Helen should be up in a moment." She darted out. An instant later, she whisked back in to inquire solicitously, "Has your headache gone, Jane? I do hope you're feeling more the thing!"

"Thank you, yes," she replied mechanically, even as Caro was disappearing once again.

The following morning Jane reclined upon the padded sofa in the smaller of the sitting rooms, not trying very hard to keep her mind on the romantic novel lying in her lap. She had endured listening to breakfast talk consisting solely of the triumphant ball, which everyone had deemed an appalling crush and therefore an impressive success, until she felt she must surely give vent to a silent scream. When the Willoughby town carriage was called for, she pleaded exhaustion and was at last left to her solitude.

This she had not found to be much of an improvement, for Jane could not cease indulging in the bittersweet pain of remembering those brief, dizzying moments in Ruxart's arms. She was remembering them now, when a rapid footfall outside the door interrupted her reverie. The door flung open and Viscount Ruxart stood on the threshold.

With a start, Jane jumped to her feet, her unread volume dropping unnoticed to the floor. Ruxart's black eyes swept hungrily over her, driving all color from her cheeks. In two swift strides he was before her.

"Miss Somers—Jane—" he began, harshly.

"Helen is gone out," she said quickly.

One impatient shake of the head denied his desire to see Helen. "I've not slept for thinking of you, longing for you—"

"Don't! Please!" she cried, her hand raised as if to deflect a blow.

"I must speak with you!" He drew closer still.

She stood silent, gazing with pleading eyes. Ruxart reached quickly forward and pulled the ribbon of her mobcap loose. "Why the devil do you wear that damned thing?" he demanded. "To be acting as if you are old and dowdy instead of young and beautiful and desirable—"

"My lord! I cannot let you say these things," protested Jane in a flustered voice. She tried to straighten her cap and only succeeded in setting it more askew. She retreated two steps as the viscount's brows snapped together.

He began to pace in front of her, his expression dangerously set. Suddenly he stopped to face her. "Jane—what happened last night, can you deny you felt it, too?" he charged intently.

Her veridical nature would not allow her to speak the lie which sprang to her lips. "I must deny it," she said instead, her voice breaking a little.

"I think—my God, I think I've loved you from the first," Ruxart whispered in a tone of wonderment.

"Don't! Please don't torment me this way! It was hard enough to accept your betrothal when I thought you held me in dislike, but now . . ." Anguish rang clear in her fading voice.

Ruxart took a quick step toward her. "Oh, my love—"

"Kindly remember," she said shakily, "that you are betrothed to my sister!"

"Remember?" he echoed with a savage laugh. "How in God's name can I forget it?"

They stood speechless, their unspoken passion burning between them.

"Please, please go," she begged finally.

"Let me—just this once—declare my love, before I must set it aside. I love you, Jane Somers. Everything else is meaningless."

She knew she must force him to leave before she threw all propriety to the winds and surrendered to the love surging within her. "Lord Ruxart, I must ask you to go at once. Or I

158

must call for a servant."

His lordship remained a moment more, his eyes baring his love for her greedy inspection, before pivoting sharply on his heel and vanishing.

Two days later, withstanding all protestations to the contrary, Miss Jane Somers returned to her home in Norfolk.

Chapter Thirteen

As the month of May ran its course, the beau monde buzzed with tales of the Right Honorable the Viscount Ruxart. Half the *ton* believed it must be the love of his fiancée that brought about the startling change, while the other half wondered what fresh trick the devil's son could be at now. For Ruxart no longer passed the nights away at the tables of the gaming halls, nor roistered time in bacchanal fervor, while the only woman he was seen to dangle after was Miss Helen Somers. Lady Frances Fletcher began to be hopeful that the miracle had happened and Ruxart had indeed fallen in love with his fiancée.

Lady Frances was in error. But as each day passed, the pair came to easier terms. Ruxart set out to be as charming as only he could be, encouraging Helen to tell him all about her life at Sloley, her childhood and her family. If, in the course of these discussions, the name of Miss Jane Somers occurred rather more frequently than did, say, those of William or Clarence or Maria, it might be thought to result more from Helen's natural adoration of her eldest sister than from any skillful questioning of Ruxart's.

The object of these lengthy discourses found it difficult to return to her old life as it had been before a certain lord made her realize what happiness she had missed. Though her one sustaining gratification was the knowledge that she was loved as deeply, as totally, in return, Jane's pleasure in the little things no longer brought her the peace of previous years. The way Mrs. Beedle could fill the cottage with the warm aroma of fresh-baked bread or the way Georgie chased after kittens in the stable did no more than trace a faint smile upon her lips. Her mother's inventiveness with her continual illnesses no longer amused her. The ease with which she had once brushed aside the more acid comments of her sister-in-law deserted her. Her appetite dwindled and she lost weight.

"My dear, you're looking quite terrible!" exclaimed Dorothea one day late in the month. "I am certain you are unwell. I shall ask Dr. Newlyn to mix one of his restorative powders for you."

"It's not necessary, Mama," Jane replied listlessly. "I'm fine, truly."

"You do not look it! You are peaked and thin. I am reminded of when I was suffering from the stone. Does your stomach ache, dear? I have some medicinal potion here—"

"Mama, please!" protested her daughter.

"You cannot deny, Jane dear, that you have lost what looks you had," interjected Agnes stringently. "Perhaps, Mother Somers, it is Jane's lack of beaux that causes this decline. Mr. Bickford has ceased to call upon her, you know."

"Do not be snide, Agnes," chided Mama firmly. "I am certain Jane's diet is at fault and shall have Dr. Newlyn in to examine her. Perhaps she should be bled, though in general I am not in favor of it. It is not ladylike to be bled."

Jane made good her escape while her mother was rummaging through the vast selection of vials, bottles and pillboxes in her ornately carved medicine chest.

It may have been her mother's determination to have her

doctored or it may have been the earnestness of her sister's supplication, but whatever the reason, a day later Jane accepted a fervent appeal from Helen to return to London for the purpose of accompanying her to meet the Earl of Kerrington.

Agnes seemed to feel that she and William would provide better chaperonage for young Helen, but her husband unexpectedly put an end to this line of thinking, saying he had no wish to go careering off to some outlandish part of the country when he'd things of more import to do at home.

Thus, Jane once again stepped into Lord Ruxart's carriage (which had been thoughtfully sent for her) on her way to London. Dorothea sent her daughter off with numerous messages and packages, including a vial of Dr. Newlyn's powder. "For it is a great remedy, my love, as you will see!" she called out as the carriage began rumbling away.

Nothing, thought Jane, was likely to remedy what ailed her. Sitting on the luxurious cushions of the well-sprung coach, Jane had plenty of time to contemplate the nature of her sickness—and the folly of her action. The hours and scenery rolled by together as Jane told herself again and again she would treat Ruxart as she would treat a brother. Again and again, she pictured first with dread, and then with elation, their meeting.

In the event, she was not to meet his lordship upon her arrival in London, for Ruxart had already traveled on into Kent, desiring to prepare the earl for the party about to descend upon the Keep. In addition to the Somers sisters, Elizabeth Willoughby and her daughter were to go that the earl might meet Caroline, for the understanding between Caro and John, although not yet formal, was known to the family. Lady Frances and John very naturally rounded out the company. Ruxart had casually invited St. Juste, but Armand once again declined to journey with the viscount.

"But do not eat me again, Nick! I am to travel into Hampshire to call upon my mother," he explained with a lazy

163

smile, "and I am persuaded you'd not have me disappoint her."

"I would have no one disappoint Madame St. Juste, for she is a delightful creature! Present her with my compliments, will you?" returned Ruxart as the two parted on friendly terms.

Not on such easy terms, Jane noted soon after her arrival in town, were Caro and her intended. Jane wondered at this circumstance, for she was quite unaware that that veritable pink of the *ton*, Sir Osmund Pringle, had decided it was time to get him a wife.

Having decided thus, he cast about him for a likely chit and, from the moment of her appearance in the primrose gown at Helen's ball, had lighted upon Miss Caroline Willoughby to honor with his name. That she was, she told him, promised to another, only made Sir Osmund's quest the greater, for he was persuaded that the sight of him in his yellow pantaloons and dark green morning coat with spotted waistcoat would be the perfect foil for Caro's blond loveliness. He knew she would, in time, come to realize this and continued throughout the season to pursue her as if John Fletcher did not exist.

Each day brought Miss Willoughby some new bouquet, trinket or flowery outpouring from the depths of Sir Osmund's shallow soul. Fancying himself a poet as grand as Byron, he sent her sonnets bound up with colored silk which likened her to a golden goddess. As Caro was of a romantic nature, she could not remain impervious to his onslaught, though her love for the staid Mr. Fletcher never lessened one whit.

At last John was moved to remonstrate with his beloved on her inability to stem the tide of the baronet's passions. "You are not cool enough to his overtures, my dear," he chided gently. "In fact, it might be said that you have encouraged Sir Osmund's attentions."

"Oh, la! You are forever making a vast deal of noise over

nothing," Caro had returned airily. "It is too shabby of you to treat me as if I were chasing after him like the Lamb after Byron."

The opportune arrival of Mrs. Willoughby arrested Fletcher's retort to this vulgarity and ended what had threatened to become a heated exchange. But the doubts and jealousies were not forgotten and their subsequent meetings were tainted with an air of constraint. Caroline, though not enamored of Sir Osmund in the least, could not help wistfully wondering why it was that Mr. Fletcher never wrote her a sonnet or sent her flowers or sighed his devotion to her from across the room. For his part, John wondered how Miss Willoughby could claim to love one man to distraction while countenancing a coxcomb like Pringle to make calf's eyes at her. Both parties hoped the sojourn to Kerrington would set all to rights.

The cavalcade that proceeded to Kerrington Keep was impressive indeed. Three full coaches left London, the first bearing Lady Frances and her friend Elizabeth; the second, the younger ladies of the party with Fletcher as escort. The third was piled high with baggage and squeezed full with four ladies' maids (Helen and Jane having agreed to share the services of the redoubtable Betty) and Fletcher's impassive valet. The journey was concluded without incident; having stopped briefly for a luncheon along the way, they arrived at the Keep in midafternoon to be met with a fanfare of servants headed by the indomitable Leaming.

Ushered into the awesome Great Hall of the Keep, those who had never previously visited there stood in silent bemazement. Thick, lush carpets were scattered over the expanse of stone floor and various suits of armor stood silent sentry about the room, but little else intruded upon the centuries-old dignity of the hall. An enormous ancient fireplace in which six tall men might have stood abreast composed one entire wall. An old tapestry depicting a chivalrous knight rescuing a medieval maiden hung upon another and a wide, curved stairway of finely carved wood swept gracefully off a third. Numerous doors lead from the hall and it was to one of these that they were led.

The old earl's eyes were fixed upon his grandson when Leaming threw open the door to announce the arrival of their guests. He was startled, therefore, to see the sudden warm eagerness which passed over Ruxart and turned with heightened interest to meet Miss Helen. He was not disappointed. She was a brilliant sight in her stylish cherry traveling dress with the fringed gold epaulettes, yet he was aware of a question at the back of his mind. This bashful chit did not look to him to be the type of woman to set Nicky afire. He was even more bewildered when he beheld his grandson greeting his fiancée and her sister with a hint of unease behind his engaging manners.

Now what maggot could have got into the boy's head, wondered the old man, *that he must needs hesitate to present himself to his fiancée?*

He was not granted time to search out the answer to this puzzle before his daughter Frances was swooping down upon him.

"My dears," she said with a grand wave of her arm, "may I present to you the Earl of Kerrington?" As curtseys were correctly sketched, she made her father known in turn to Miss Helen, Miss Somers, Mrs. and Miss Willoughby. Kerrington wrote the young Willoughby chit down as a silly flibbertigibbet and just what you'd expect of that fool John, though her mother seemed a sensibly behaved woman. Passing over the elder Miss Somers, whom he knew for a dowdy spinster the instant he clapped eyes on her impossible maroon woolen gown, the earl set himself to studying the beautiful, graceful child who would one day be the next Countess of Kerrington.

In his turn, the Earl of Kerrington was closely examined. Jane had taken a seat a little removed from the rest of the party, from which she sat eyeing the old man. His white hair

166

was worn long in the style of the last century and was tied neatly back with a black velvet riband. His face, like his grandson's, was squared and marked with strength, but there were no lines of restless discontent to mar the earl's patrician features. She judged him to be an autocratic man, much used to bending people to his will.

As the company indulged in light chatter ranging from the journey to the September wedding, servants wafted into the room with seeming invisibility, bearing silver trays with crystal decanters and silver tea urns surrounded by plates heaped with sweetcakes, pastries and sugared breads. The earl and his daughter vied with one another to dominate the conversation and after a time, Ruxart drifted unnoticed to where Jane quietly sat sipping her tea and placidly observing them all.

With concern creasing his brow, he inquired in a low tone, "Have you been ill? You are much too thin."

"No, no, I have been . . . fine," she replied with reserve. Fearing to meet the intensity of his eyes, Jane kept her own firmly fixed on the claw-foot of the elaborate silver teapot standing regally on the table before her.

"It doesn't appear that you've been well," he said roughly. Ruxart signalled to a footman bearing a serving tray and after extracting a small dish from the platter, handed it to Jane. "I beg you will try one of these, Miss Somers."

"Thank you, but I am not hungry—"

"I'll not have you offending the kitchen staff, Miss Somers," cut in his lordship firmly. "The earl would be most grieved if the finest chef in England departed in rage at your refusal to eat his sweetcakes."

She wanted very much to kiss his teasing lips, but instead she meekly took the cake, casting a glance at Ruxart as she did so. Her glance was met squarely with a look that set her heart to racing.

Lady Frances was now holding the floor, enlightening them all as to her opinion of the shocking laxity of the modern society in which common baggage like the Wilson sisters could become fashionable. The eyes of the earl, sweeping the room in boredom, lit upon Miss Somers. As her teeth sank into the cake, he called out peevishly, "You! Why don't you speak?"

Miss Somers did not seem discomposed by this startling demand. She finished her cake, then tranquilly wiped her lips with her laced napkin. "I try, my lord," she answered at last, "to speak only when I have something to say."

"Humph!" snorted Kerrington, though he seemed mollified. His eyes narrowed as he looked more closely at her. Apparently there was more to this thin, calm creature than at first met the eye. His attention was recalled by a question from his daughter and the earl paid no further mind to Miss Somers.

"You've made a hit there, my dear," whispered his grandson irreverently before reluctantly moving from her side.

Shortly thereafter, the party dispersed to their rooms for a period of rest before dressing for dinner. Unlike Plumstead, country hours and informality were not practiced at the Keep and full evening dress was expected, no matter how large or how small the company.

Mounting the wide stairs, John touched Caroline's arm lightly. "I think you'd find the Gallery to be of interest, Caro. Have you a moment to view it?"

Understanding this to be a request for a private *tête-a-tête*, she assented rapidly and the two separated themselves from those following Leaming to their bedchambers. Turning first left, then right, they traversed what seemed to Caro to be a bewildering maze of passages before coming at last to an immense corridor with a gleaming polished wood floor that brilliantly reflected the light pouring in from the arched windows running its length along one side. The wall opposite was covered with paintings and portraits of centuries of Armytages staring haughtily down upon any who dared enter their realm. Here and there statues and chairs were scattered down the hallway, as well as a few low settees. It was to one of these that Fletcher guided Caroline.

Sitting beneath the likeness of the first earl with his perfumed peruke and ornately frogged blue-and-gold-skirted coat casting her own simple muslin into the shade, Caro gazed up at John with a question in her violet eyes. An underlying excitement seemed to give unusual vivacity to his serious face and she wondered at the reason for this.

More jealous than he would admit over the past month, John had suffered increasing doubts over his ability to hold Miss Willoughby's affections, for when compared to the dashing, romantic baronet, he felt himself to be a dull dog indeed. The constraint between them of late had added to his resolution to overcome his scruples and secure Caroline's hand now rather than waiting, as he had previously insisted, for her eighteenth birthday. Thus, he placed himself beside her and gathered her hand into his own.

"My dear," he said, "I find I cannot wait any longer—indeed, I see no necessity for us to wait the two months to your birthday when everyone already knows how we feel. In short, my love, I intend to speak with your mother tonight and if she agrees, I hope to make our betrothal announcement."

Throughout the whole of this disjointed but ardent speech, Caro's eyes had been growing ever wider, her mouth ever rounder. Now she returned the pressure of his hand fervently and exclaimed, "Oh, John! Dear John! I am so happy!"

He smiled tenderly at her animated face. "I also thought, sweeting, that you might accept this."

From his pocket he pulled a glittering diamond-and-pearl ring set in a band of filigreed gold. Caro sat with her mouth open, too stunned to speak as she stared at this unknown, sentimental John Fletcher. Then she sprang to action, flinging her arms about him, ignoring his protests as she cried out rapturously, "You dearest, sweetest, most wonderful thing!"

He managed at last to detach her arms from about his neck to ask in a calm tone if she should like to try the frippery on. Her assent was immediate and John slipped the ring on her eagerly outstretched hand. Within the instant, Caro spun from her seat to hold her hand against the windowpane, letting the westering sun add warmth to the ring's shimmering beauty. The skirt of her pink frock billowed as Caro twirled lightly in her excitement and a small square of paper fluttered to the floor. Behind her, John stooped to retrieve it; even as his hand closed upon the scented parchment, the happiness was fading from Caroline's suddenly whitened face.

"What's this?" he asked mildly as he straightened.

"N-nothing!" replied Caro in a suffocated voice. "G-give it to me, if you please."

His hand paused in the act of reaching toward her and a sudden streak of suspicion crossed his face. Caro's eyes widened in horror as his hand drew back.

"What could be of such import?" John queried slowly.

"It is nothing of import, I tell you," insisted the girl in a faltering tone. She stretched out a trembling hand.

Fletcher's hazel eyes traveled from parchment to hand to Caro's pale face, then back again to the paper in his hand. Against his will, he gradually unfolded it.

She treads the earth, A Golden Goddess, flowed the script which met his wrathful gaze. Through tight lips, he charged, "You've been wearing this against your heart!"

"It—it is not as you think. . . ." stammered Caro. Her voice trailed into nothingness as he turned upon her a look of such cold disbelief that her power of further speech was quite thoroughly extinguished. How could she explain to this frozen fury?

"What *I* think seems to be immaterial, miss," he clipped. "It is only too obvious that it is the thoughts of Sir Osmund Pringle which are an object with you."

"No—no!" she cried, recoiled from his vicious tone.

"Even so, Miss Willoughby," he continued harshly, ignoring her feverish protests, "I shall take leave to inform you of what I think. I think you have been playing a very pretty game—a game in which I am the unfortunate loser. But whatever you hope to gain by becoming Lady Pringle, there is one thing, at least, which you shall forfeit." He was livid with anger as the aggregation of centuries of Armytage pride seemed to spill into him from his ancestors lining the wall. His lips cracked into an ugly sneer. "That is the honest love of a good man."

By the end of this tirade, Caroline's shocked despair had given way to injured wrath. In glacial tones, she responded, "Love, Mr. Fletcher? What do you claim to know of love? You disavow your supposed love for me at the first opportunity and without awaiting my explanation!"

"You think you can explain away what my eyes have seen? I am not such a fool, miss!"

With a surge of fresh rage, Caro ripped the ring from her finger and icily begged Mr. Fletcher to remove the offensive reminder of her folly from her sight.

"Gladly! I'm only grateful to have discovered so quickly what a mistake I was making." With these last harsh words, John turned sharply and strode swiftly from her.

Caroline watched him go in rigid hauteur. As soon as his form disappeared around the corner, however, she sank back down onto the settee and wept bitterly. She looked with blurred eyes at the poem, the hateful, hateful poem. Then she tore it savagely to shreds. This afforded her little comfort. She would much rather, she decided, have shredded Sir Osmund and John Fletcher each by turns. Men were all, she now realized, abominable creatures and she was better off, much, much better, without them.

At length, her tears ceased to flow and she sat silently in dull misery, staring at her pink kid slipper. She did not know how long she had been sitting thus when she heard a steady footfall. She raised her head to dimly perceive Jane coming toward her.

"Caro! I've been searching for you this past hour! You must hurry to get dressed for dinner." As Jane drew near she saw the red-rimmed eyes, the woeful turn of Caro's usually smiling lips. "My dear, whatever has happened?" she asked in concern as she took the seat vacated some time since by Fletcher and enfolded the girl in her arms.

Fresh tears welled up in those violet eyes and as they spilled over onto the shoulder of Jane's best indigo kerseymere, Caro haltingly explained what had occurred.

"You see, the poem arrived just as we were leaving, so I—I stuck it in my dress to read later and when it fell out, John thought—John thought—" Caro finished with a dismal sniff.

"Do you . . . care . . . for Sir Osmund?"

"Oh, Jane, he is nothing but a *fop*!" disclaimed her cousin impatiently. "He wears his shirt collars so high he cannot even turn his head! And he does not even *know* what a figure he cuts! But he writes such pretty things about me . . . I just wanted to read it. . . ."

As the young voice died sadly away, Jane promised briskly to have speech with Mr. Fletcher and do what she could to set matters to rights.

"I do not think," said Caro mournfully, "that you will be able to repair the damage that I have done, dear Jane, but you are the best of good cousins to try."

Eventually, she allowed herself to be led to her bedchamber where she dressed with such an unusual lack of interest that her maid inquired solicitously if Miss was feeling quite the thing.

"Yes—no! It doesn't matter!" had snapped Miss in reply before descending to dismally partake in dinner.

Chapter Fourteen

Swan giblet soup and stewed eels were lavishly followed by a saddle of mutton, roasted guinea fowl and pigeon pie, which in turn, were removed to be replaced with the main course of oyster patties and fricassee chicken. Each succeeding course of the princely meal was served in the grandest of style and seemed interminable to more than one of the earl's guests. Conversation was as a result on the desultory side and as the meal wore on, Kerrington had turned more and more often to Miss Somers to sustain the discourse, which she did in her usual collected manner. The old man had been much impressed at the lady's cool observation that there had never yet been a minister to equal Sir Robert Walpole and from that moment on, the earl had begun to favor her with his opinions on the current outlandish policies of the Regent's ill-run government. As both Miss Somers on his left and Miss Helen on his right were good listeners, the earl was one of the few present to thoroughly enjoy his meal.

For her part, Jane had cause to be grateful to the golden French cherub who held aloft the candelabra, for he effectively blocked her view of the viscount. Since her brief but unsettling encounter with Ruxart that afternoon, she had humored herself for a time with wishing she had not come. But not being one to indulge in such fruitless conjecturings for long, Jane had soon put aside all fancies and reconciled herself to a trying visit. It was not as if she did not have anything to occupy her mind, she reflected facetiously, what with Mr. Fletcher and Caro rigidly exchanging commonplaces across the table and Helen returning Ruxart's pleasantries with a subdued abstraction. It was a matchmaker's nightmare and she was still puzzling over how she would disentangle the twisted affairs when Lady Frances finally stood to signal the removal of the dishes.

Neither of his grandsons appeared disposed to linger over the port so it was not long before Kerrington suggested they follow the ladies. When they entered the Keep's elegant Grand Salon, they found one member of the party already gone, for Miss Willoughby had retired immediately after supper, declaring herself to be excessively fatigued. This highly unusual circumstance was questioned by no one, though her mother had focused upon her a searching regard which Caro was unable to meet.

Fletcher seemed inclined to echo Miss Willoughby's sentiments and withdraw, but he was thwarted in his attempt to do so by his grandfather who thrust a glass of claret into his hand and demanded to know what it was he saw in the flighty young miss.

"I regret to inform you, sir," replied John as he stiffened, "that you are laboring under a misapprehension. Miss Willoughby and I have come to the conclusion that we should not suit."

"Eh? Well, 'tis like for the best, my boy. There's no denying that she's a taking little thing, but there's plenty more of her sort about and make no mistake," asserted the earl while shrewdly watching the young man from beneath half-closed lids. John colored, but made no reply and the old man soon shifted his eyes to the others in the room. As they came to rest upon Miss Somers seated on a remote sofa, he remarked in a less caustic tone, "Now there's a woman of sense."

Following the earl's gaze, Fletcher instantly agreed. "Miss Somers is most worthy, sir. I have the highest regard for her."

"To my way of thinking, it's a great pity a gel such as that ain't married," asserted the earl, stabbing a bony finger into the air. "That's a waste of a fine woman."

His grandson appeared much struck with this observation. "Yes, sir, I believe it is," he said in a thoughtful tone, but by then the earl had moved on to loudly demand of his daughter what she meant by foisting that mealy-faced schoolroom chit Emmeline onto the Farminghams, for if she thought to catch the young marquis with such a namby-pamby miss as that she would soon learn her mistake, and John's words were lost in the ensuing hostility as his mother rose to the defense of his young sister.

Crisis was avoided when Jane, seeing her sister turn white at the upraised voices of the earl and Lady Frances, pleasantly inquired if a servant might not be sent to her rooms to fetch her sewing. "It is most relaxing, you know, and after such a busy day I dare say my mind could benefit from the soothing qualities of taking a stitch or two."

Her request was immediately granted and Elizabeth Willoughby took the opportunity to suggest a game of whist, having heard the earl was one of the finest players to be met. It proved to be the perfect answer of how to occupy the remainder of the evening for both Kerrington and Lady Frances were avid card-players and all mention of Emmeline was forgotten as a table was made ready. Miss Somers firmly declined to play; her sewing was all she wanted of the evening. Miss Helen begged to be allowed to make her excuses, for though her stay in London had accustomed her to late hours, she wanted to be fresh for a promised early morning ride across the Keep's estates with Lord Ruxart. With a curtsey she was gone, leaving Fletcher to make the fourth, for Ruxart insisted piquet, not whist, was his game.

The party settled down to a quiet murmur over the card table while in her corner Jane began neatly stitching a monogram on a square of linen. The viscount paced the room several times, occasionally pausing to watch Miss Somers as her head bent over her nimble fingers. He was arrested in midstride by a curt command from his grandfather to make himself still or quit the room. Ruxart cast himself into a wingback chair which stood opposite Miss Somers. Stretching out his long legs and hunching his shoulders into the corner of the chair, he studied her from beneath his heavy lids. Each stitch went up and came down methodically and gradually the broad shoulders relaxed, the set of his lordship's jaw eased. Jane's eyes came up from her needlework to meet his. She smiled and the viscount was conscious of a rare feeling of contentment.

"You are a most . . . restful . . . woman, Miss Somers," he said before she could return to her work.

Her smile broadened. "Now that, at least, is a compliment I do not suspect you of practicing!"

"I cannot claim to have known many restful women," he admitted with a rueful smile. "Tell me, what is it you are sewing?"

"It is to be a gift for Helen—a wedding gift," she replied with only the ghost of her smile remaining. "I am working her new monogram upon it now."

The unhappiness which crossed his face tore at her, but she fought against showing any of this and said instead, "Do you know, back home in Sloley, I would have been abed an hour ago? I believe I must get my rest now or I shall not be a very restful woman any longer!"

Her attempt at raillery brought no response from Ruxart, though he stood and moved to open the door for her. As she retired to her room, Jane sighed a little at her inability to have spoken, as promised, with Mr. Fletcher on Caro's behalf, but she could not have borne the sweet torment of his lordship's company throughout the whole of the card game waiting to do so. As it was, her peace of mind had been quite thoroughly uprooted. She would, she vowed with determination, think only of catching Mr. Fletcher at the first opportunity on the morrow.

But it was of a pair of dark, downturned eyes that she dreamt.

In the event, Jane did not have to search out John Fletcher in the morning, for the gentleman appeared as she was leaving the breakfast room to beg a few moments of her time. With a quizzical lift of her brow, she went with him to a small but cheery sitting room the east windows of which afforded an excellent view of the Keep's well-manicured gardens. Turning her back upon this superb view, Jane sat on a bright green crocodile couch, folded her hands in her lap and calmly waited for him to begin.

He appeared to be having some difficulty collecting his thoughts, for twice his mouth opened and twice it closed before he nervously cleared his throat.

"Mr. Fletcher, if it is about your unfortunate misunderstanding with Caroline that you wish to speak, let me say that I am already fully informed of the circumstances," said Jane helpfully.

"No! That is to say, yesterday's occurrence only served to open my eyes to the folly I had committed in thinking Miss Willoughby a suitable wife for me," he responded forcibly.

"But she is! She loves you so very—"

"Madam, I've not come to speak of Miss Willoughby," cut in Fletcher firmly. "Let me make it clear to you that the association is finished."

"Oh, surely not! Such feelings as have passed between you—"

"Are now, gratefully, a thing of the past. Though I cannot deny certain . . . feelings still exist, they will no doubt diminish with time."

"Mr. Fletcher, you would do well to reconsider. Caro's indiscretion was not due to any lack of love for you, but to the natural flattery derived from Sir Osmund's poetry. Why, she does not even like the man!"

"Which makes her behavior in encouraging him all the worse. I am no flatterer, ma'am, and if Miss Willoughby will only sip from a honeyed cup, then we are much better parted."

His expression was closed and Jane saw that it would be useless at this point to protest further. Having two stubborn brothers had taught her a great deal about argumentation and she felt that if she waited, another opportunity to convince him otherwise would present itself. It was with a sense of shock that she realized he was speaking to her.

"But I still believe it's time I was married," he said, "and that is why I've requested a moment with you. Miss Somers, the more I have seen of you, the more impressed I've been with your dignity of manner and your calm good sense. In short, I am asking you to do me the honor of accepting my hand in marriage."

Her hand flew to her mouth as she leapt to her feet. "You cannot be serious!"

"I was never more so. Oh, do not be thinking I come to you with false fancies of love! I would not have you thinking me so fickle. Nor would I have you believing that I do not know my own mind. I assure you that I've given this matter great deliberation and am certain that we should be able to deal admirably well together. We are of much the same temperament and if I could not offer you any of the deeper feelings, I can and do offer you the home and hand of an honest man."

"My calm good sense, as you put it, sir, can only lead me to decline." She shook her head as he began to object. "It is true, we both admire and respect one another and I'm sure we could manage to rub along tolerably well together. But there, you see, I lack the desire to merely deal well with my husband. I want nothing less than a love match, Mr. Fletcher, and it is owing to this sad fault that I remain a spinster. I see you are shocked—you must even now be congratulating yourself on so narrowly escaping the union with one so filled with romantic notions as I."

"Indeed, you are funning, Miss Somers! I think the more of you for your frankness and can only say that if, after reflection, you should change your mind, I am your obedient servant."

With a bow he had gone from the room and Jane could only sink to the couch and wonder at the magnitude of her folly in ever agreeing to come to Kerrington at all. Much wiser, she saw in retrospect, to have stayed in Sloley taking Dr. Newlyn's restorative powders.

After a time, though not yet fully recovered from the shock of Mr. Fletcher's proposal, she removed to the library where she attempted to compose a duty letter to her mother. She was sitting staring at an empty sheet, nibbling on the end of her pen when Helen ran lightly into the room. Jane looked up with a start as the door opened, but upon seeing her sister, smiled widely and set the pen aside.

Her deep blue velvet riding habit swished as Helen rushed over to exchange a quick hug. "Jane, I've had the most famous notion!" she exclaimed happily.

"You have decided to elope to Gretna Green," teased Jane.

"No, this is much, much better!" Helen dropped gracefully onto the nearest chair and beamed at her sister as she pulled off her tan kid gloves. She was rosy and obviously bursting with some bit of thrilling news. "You shall never guess!"

Jane propped her elbows on the desk of the mahogany secretary and gazed at Helen over her laced fingers.

"You are to come live with us!"

Her hands parted. Jane sat upright. "What?"

"You mustn't think you would be intruding for I have asked Ruxart and he was very, very kind. He thought it an excellent notion—in fact, he insisted upon it!" she explained proudly. When her sister did not respond with the enthusiasm she had expected, her pretty face fell. "What's wrong, Jane? Is it not what you should like?"

"Of course, dearest, but there is Mama, you know, and the boys—"

"Is that all?" interrupted Helen with relief. "You know Mama is quite content with Agnes and the boys will be going off to school soon. And we'll go home for visits as often as we like, for my lord has said we might. It must be better, surely, to live with *me* than to remain under Agnes' charity!"

"But I cannot wish to impose upon newlyweds," she protested dully.

"Don't be a ninny! I shall *need* you, especially if—if there are babies soon. So no more argufying with me! It is as good as settled!" She jumped up and with a quick kiss on Jane's cap, ran from the room.

Jane sat stunned. She could not make her home with the Viscount and Viscountess Ruxart. The daily torment of seeing Ruxart, yet never having him—and oh, the temptation!—made such an action clearly unthinkable. She wanted as she had never wanted before to cast away every scruple and fall in with Helen's scheme. But if she did, how long could she resist her desires? She was weak, too weak. Eventually, she would give in and become Ruxart's mistress. Such a course could only end with them loathing what they had done, despising themselves and one another.

The idea of returning to Sloley to live out the rest of her days in her brother's home was equally depressing. And even, thought Jane slowly, were she to return home, there would be no refuge. Family gatherings would throw them together perilously often. Not that Ruxart would ever countenance her return. What had Helen said? *He thought it an excellent notion—in fact, he insisted upon it!* No, he would not easily let her retreat to the nebulous comfort of Plumstead Cottage.

There could be but one way to remove the danger of her vulnerable love for Ruxart—marriage. Jane had ever scoffed at those who denied love as the sole basis for marriage, but she knew her own love match could never be. It did not matter whom she wed, only that she do so quickly.

Through the dull ache of her heart crept the realization that she must accept John Fletcher's proposal. Though she tried to argue against it, it was a futile battle. Jane saw only the need to place herself beyond the menace of her yearnings.

She sat rubbing her fingertips against her temple, then rose and crossed purposefully to where a finely worked tapestry bell-pull hung invitingly on the wall. Jane reached, hesitated, then grabbed the pull and yanked with a strength that sent the bell in the servants' hall dancing wildly. She was still standing motionless by the pull when a young footman appeared. In a voice void of emotion she requested him to inform Mr. Fletcher that she desired to see him, if he pleased.

Before the footman returned with the gentleman, she had ample time to compose herself. When Mr. Fletcher bowed over her hand and murmured, "Servant, ma'am," with a questioning look in his hazel eyes, she was able to meet that look without the least appearance of the great agitation she had been experiencing.

"I trust you'll not think me flighty, Mr. Fletcher, or given to frequent changes of mind, for in general I assure you, it is not my way," she said by way of introduction as he seated himself opposite her.

"Do you lead me to hope, Miss Somers, that you will accept my suit?"

"I—I wish to know if you still desire to make me your wife."

"Yes, I do."

"Then, sir," she said, taking a deep breath, "I am grateful to accept the honor you are bestowing upon me."

A solemn, yet pleased, smile spread over his face. "It's I

who am grateful, Miss Somers. And though we do not start this match based on the more sentimental feelings considered natural to the married state, I am certain those feelings will not be long in forthcoming. I respect and admire you greatly and shall endeavor to make you a worthy husband."

"I—I am sure you shall, Mr. Fletcher," responded Jane, slightly overcome with this sober speech. "Do you wish for us to be . . . married soon?"

"There is little reason to suffer a long engagement," he replied, stretching his smile into a grim line. "What say you to a double wedding with your sister and Ruxart?"

Jane's face paled, but she assented readily with a nod. The September date having been agreed upon, it only remained for the families to be notified. Miss Somers seemed strangely reluctant in this regard, but Mr. Fletcher won out in the decision to announce their betrothal without delay. The interview was concluded soon after and Jane was left to contemplate in solitude the result of her decision to marry a man she did not love in order to avoid living with one she did.

Seeking to escape the turmoil of her thoughts, Jane stepped briskly out from the double glassed doors leading to the terrace which overlooked the Keep's meticulously groomed grounds. She wandered through an exquisite arbor, trying not to think of anything beyond the fragrant beauty of the blossoming flowers, at last sinking to the ground. As she argued with herself over the step she had impulsively taken, her long fingers plucked blades of grass, playing absently with a handful before discarding it upon the lap of her gown to take up another.

She was thus employed when she caught sight of a commanding figure striding toward her. Ruxart was still dressed for riding and as the wind caught at his long coattails, emphasis was given to the slim hips and long legs encased in the doeskin breeches and dark topboots. Her first wild thought was to hide somewhere, but it was obvious he had seen her, so Jane resigned herself to the meeting and came to her feet.

"The last time I saw you wear that frock," said his lordship in greeting, "it was covered, I believe, with straw. I see you have switched to the more seasonable grass."

Jane flushed deeply, though whether it was from the embarrassment of discovering her brown dress to be flecked with bits of green, or from the warmth of the teasing note in the viscount's voice, it could not have been said. "You must think me quite a hoyden, Lord Ruxart," she said as she vigorously brushed the blades from her gown.

"I believe you know what I think of you, Jane," he rejoined on a husky note.

She looked up from her task, startled to hear him speak so. "What you think of me, my lord, is quite immaterial," she stated, striving for a neutral tone.

"I do wish, my dear, that you would bring yourself to use my name instead of my title. Try it. Say Nicholas. I long to know the sound of it upon your lips."

"Do not be absurd, Lord Ruxart," she said tersely, returning her attention to her gown.

"I love you," whispered Ruxart.

Her head whipped up again at that. "Do not say so! Indeed, how can you?"

"I can because . . ." He stopped abruptly, seeing the distress in her eyes. It pained him to know he caused her pain and he labored to keep his voice level as he went on to ask, "Has Helen spoken to you about coming to live with us?"

"Yes, but you must realize that it would be impossible for me to take up residence with you," she replied earnestly.

"I—we—Helen and I both wish for it. Helen fears the running of a large establishment and relies upon having your help. And if you would but only consider the advantages, my dear, I'm persuaded you'd agree that it's for the best. There would be no more drudgery, no stinting, no old-fashioned woolen gowns! You could have a life of fashion and leisure, such as you deserve."

"Such an arrangement would be a disaster!"

"I know what you are thinking," he said quickly. "You are thinking I should importune upon you, but my love, I swear it shall not be so! I shall treat you only as the beloved sister you shall be—"

"Oh, my lord, my lord," interrupted Jane with a shaky laugh, "you would only remember I was your sister until it suited you to forget it!"

With one step forward, Ruxart swept her into his arms. Their heartbeats met in a fierce pounding as his lips pressed warmly against her temple. He strung a trail of heated kisses to the ruffled edge of her cap where he moaned hoarsely into her ear. "Jane, my love, my life—we'll explain to Helen, tell her of our love—"

He got no further for Jane tensed within his hold, her eyes widening at something beyond his shoulder. The viscount turned his head to see his cousin bearing grimly down upon them. His soft curse was severed by John's harsh words as he approached.

"You will kindly unhand my fiancée, Ruxart," bit out John.

He did not loose his hold upon Jane, but stared at his cousin as if seeing a headless ghost. "Your fiancée?" he repeated, stunned.

"Miss Somers just this very morning honored me with an acceptance."

His lordship's hands tightened about her arms, causing her to wince. "Is this true?" he demanded.

"Yes," she whispered, refusing to meet his angry eyes.

Ruxart released her so abruptly, she staggered and might have fallen had not John reached out to support her. Fletcher pulled her back a step, as if out of further harm, and said furiously, "I realize, of course, it is a habit of yours to make love to other men's wives, but I trust you will refrain from the custom within the family."

To Jane's great surprise, the viscount made no reply to this insult, but asked John coldly, "what prompted you to this?"

"Thank you!" cut in Jane with a choke.

"Jane—Miss Somers—do not be a fool! I didn't mean anything of that sort!" Ruxart snapped. His visage was so thunderous that Jane at once subsided, but John seemed ripe for hostilities and inquired icily precisely what my lord had meant.

"What the devil do you think I'd meant?" he returned fiercely. "Be grateful, cousin, that the earl does not tolerate brawling on the estate—whatever the provocation." On that threatening note, he pivoted and swiftly left them.

Chapter Fifteen

The announcement of the betrothal of John Fletcher and Jane Somers was not without effect. Although the audience receiving the news was small, the reactions were many and ranged from delight to disgust.

Shocked indignation and utter anguish fought to be uppermost on Caro's face as she stared accusingly at her cousin. Jane, who in the emotional upheaval following her interview with Helen had forgotten Caro, forgotten her promise, forgotten everything except her need to escape her future, realized with sudden dismay the enormity of what she had done in stealing Caroline's beau. Anger won out as Miss Willoughby flounced from the room in what can only be termed high dudgeon.

Her mother watched her go, but did nothing to restrain her. Elizabeth's warm pleasure for her niece's happiness was tempered by a wave of consternation for her daughter, but knowing Caro was young enough to have plenty more opportunities for falling in love, the smile she directed at the happy couple was sincere.

Sitting beside Mrs. Willoughby, her mouth open but for once soundless, Lady Frances was clearly displeased. She had been perfectly willing, and indeed happy, to accept the daughter of her closest friend as the wife for her son, but the niece was another matter altogether. In her view, John could do far better than to waste himself on this virtual nobody who had been sitting on the shelf for *years*!

The bright blue eyes of Helen Somers shimmered with surprise, joy and doubt as they intently searched her sister's face. Helen noted, too, the taut line of Ruxart's lips and the heat of his dark eyes before he turned to stand staring into the cold cavern of the unlit fireplace, one booted foot upon the grate, one hand gripping the mantel. She began to wonder why he should be so extremely vexed, but had no chance to examine this notion as the earl raised a toast to the couple.

Kerrington was as delighted as his daughter was not. He clapped John on the back and embraced Jane as he presented her with a dry kiss on her cheek. As a servant bestowed a glass of his lordship's finest sherry to each of those present, the earl called out in a voice crackling with cheer, "To the health! to the happiness! of the betrothed couple!"

Ruxart's head snapped up at this. Though his hand held the wineglass, he did not raise it to his lips. His eyes seemed to bore through Jane until she felt she could not bear it any longer. She turned away to accept the felicitations with a wan smile, her face ghostly pale against the dark brown of her gown.

"You sly thing!" chided Helen gently, hugging her. "You never said a word this morning! But when is the happy day to be?"

"W-we rather thought—that is, if you do not mind—" stumbled her sister, for once visibly disconcerted.

"We thought a double wedding with you and Ruxart would be charming," supplied Fletcher.

The viscount's glass came down onto the mantel with a thump, freely baptizing the ledge with sherry. "If you will excuse me," he said curtly. His abrupt departure spurred the dispersion of the company. They did not all meet again until gathering around the dining table that night.

If talk the evening before had been desultory, tonight it was dismal. Little was said beyond the commonplace and more than one member of the small party showed an alarming tendency toward silence altogether. Miss Willoughby was among the latter, having been induced to come down for dinner only by her mother's tart observation that if she wished to remain in her room and appear the jilt then by all means she must do so. Beyond casting one venomous glare at Jane, Caroline had not removed her eyes from her plate, though little of the offerings she saw there appealed and course after course was taken away untouched.

Her lack of appetite was shared by the object of her animosity and when the earl demanded to know why Miss Somers was not eating, she lamely offered the excitement of the day as an excuse. This earned her a fulminating stare from her future mother-in-law. Having her eldest son refuse to answer her demands for an explanation to his incredible behavior had only served to exacerbate Lady Frances' already foul temper. Helen and Elizabeth strove vainly to stimulate conversation, but when they found themselves remarking for the fifth time how lovely the weather had been today, they, too, fell silent. At last the seemingly endless meal wound mutely to a close.

When the ladies stood to leave, Lord Ruxart moved quickly to the door. "I find I am obliged to return to London in the morning. I therefore bid you all goodnight." With a brusque bow and without waiting for his grandfather's response, he retired.

Ruxart left the Keep long before breakfast was served on the following day and though he had not said goodbye, he left a note for Helen telling her crisply that he would see her on her return to town. His early departure saw him in London long before noon. After a brief visit to his lodgings

189

in Half Moon Street, where he changed into fresh morning wear and flipped through the number of invitations, notes and other correspondence awaiting him, he paid a call at St. Juste's. There, however, he was informed by Dobbs that Mr. St. Juste had not returned from his journey, though he was expected later that day or the next.

In Hampshire, St. Juste had just entered his mother's böudoir to bid her farewell.

They stood in a room as delicate and airy as the woman who occupied it. Silk-covered chairs were daintily arranged over a fringed, willow-green carpet and matched the straw-colored draperies ornamenting the fanlight windows. A quartet of gilt angels carried the flaxen silk hangings as they guarded the enormous poster bed lining one wall, while a fifth angel hovered coyly over the carved mirror of the vanity opposite the bed.

It was beneath this angel that Simone St. Juste had positioned herself, occasionally running a tortoise comb through the hair that had once been likened to a sunbeam reflected on still water. As she conversed with her son, she thought he looked superbly handsome in his tight, dark riding coat, though she wished he were not so very pale. Her full lower lip pushed forward, a sign of her determination to discover the cause of Armand's somber spirits before he left her this day. Her delicate heart-shaped face was filled with unaccustomed gravity as Simone dropped the comb onto the table and turned to interrupt her son's amusing description of Lord Petersham's refusal to use a light snuffbox in an east wind for fear of catching a cold.

"*Vraiment*! I do not wish to hear of this Petersham. I wish to hear of *you*, Armand! Will you not tell me what brings the sadness to your eyes, *mon petit*?"

There was a perceptible pause. "I rather fear, my dear *maman*, that you would laugh to hear it," he drawled as he leaned his shoulders against the white marble mantelpiece.

"But, *non!*" she denied with a vivid flutter of her hand. Simone gazed shrewdly at her son. "It is *une femme, non?*"

His rare, blinding smile rewarded her percipience. "How very like you, *Maman*, to be so perceptive," he said lazily.

"But, tell me! Is she pretty, this one?"

"Like an exquisite porcelain figurine come to life."

"Ah . . . you love this woman, *n'est-ce pas?*"

"Love?" he echoed. "How can I say? I am not . . . well acquainted with love. Indeed, I had begun to accept that such emotions were not for me." He left his stance by the unlit fireplace and wandered to stand looking out one window. "I only know that when Helen is in the room, I am . . . satisfied. And when she is gone, I miss her."

Madame St. Juste drew in her breath. Keenly watching him, she demanded, "But what then is wrong? Does she not return your regard? *Tiens!* That is *stupide!*"

"I believe—indeed, I am nearly certain—that she does . . . care . . . for me. But as she is betrothed to the Viscount Ruxart, it does not much matter what she or I feel." The indifferent tone, the bare shrug as he turned to face her, did not deceive Simone.

Adroitly, she drew the tale from her reluctant son. He made light of the wager and of his own loss of heart and at the end of it, returned to stand before the fireplace while his mother stared thoughtfully into her mirror.

"Ah, *mon fils*, it is not right that you should be unhappy. *Non!*" she said on a sigh when she at last twirled to face him with a swirl of her lacy peignoir.

"I dare say, *Maman*, that I shall live through it," he answered with a rueful smile.

"But you love this girl, *non? Eh bien!* You should have her. You tell me she is not yet married, *et bien plus*, that you do not think she loves her fiancé. It is very plain to me, *mon cheri*, that you must marry this Hélène, *mais oui!* even if she is not at all what I should like," she finished in a burst of

191

sacrificial generosity. She rose and floated to her son's side.

"I cannot marry another man's fiancée, *Maman!* Most especially not Ruxart's," protested St. Juste dryly.

"Vraiment!" she exclaimed, nearly stamping one petite foot. "That is the *anglais* way! But me, I am not *anglaise*, and you, you Armand, should remember that you are not also. Listen to me, *mon fils*, if you wait until she is married, it will be too late and everyone will be unhappy, especially your Hélène and that boy *remarquable*, Nicolas, who is sometimes more *le français* than you." She gently ran her hand along his cheek as she spoke. St. Juste took the hand in his own and kissed it.

"You are, as always, *ma chere maman*, the wisest and loveliest of women," he whispered softly before releasing her hand. In the doorway he turned to add, "It is perhaps a pity, my dear, that Helen is indeed everything you should like."

Simone watched her son disappear, then heaved a sigh. She earnestly hoped she would like this Hélène Somers for, *bien entendu*, Armand must marry her. Her son was another such as her husband—there would be no other love for him. Armand gave his affection sparingly, she knew. To herself, to that wild, *charmant* Nicolas and now, it seemed, to this Hélène, whom she hoped would be tolerable. But whether she was or not did not matter to Simone, for she knew she must somehow erase the unhappiness from Armand's eyes. She began to pace the room with feathery steps, forming her plans.

Blissfully ignorant of his mother's schemings, St. Juste journeyed back to London, arriving late in the day to learn that the Viscount Ruxart had called earlier. By the time St. Juste ran his friend down in the wee hours of the morning, mingling with all manner of people and drinking vast quantities of Blue Ruin in the back room of a dingy shop in the slums of Tothill Fields, Ruxart was well on his way to scandalizing the *ton* with a week of unmitigated dissipation.

Old men shook their heads and women whispered behind their fans wherever Ruxart appeared, as the *haut monde* fairly hissed with the daily doings of the hellbent viscount. It was generally agreed that poor Miss Helen Somers did not know what a rakehell she was getting for a husband, though some more charitable souls felt it was a pity she had returned to Norfolk with her sister, for it was plain to see that her presence was needed to keep his lordship in line.

For once, not even St. Juste could tame his friend and when at last Ruxart was seen in the Manderleys' private box at the Covent Garden theater taking snuff from the wrist of the passionate Pen, Armand gave up hope of discovering what had gone awry at Kerrington. With the slightest lift of one thin brow he gave the viscount to understand he disapproved. It was not to be wondered at that within a short period of time Ruxart was seen leaving the box with Mrs. Manderley on his arm. The hum of gossip arose like a wave crashing on rocks to die away and swell again as St. Juste was noted turning his back when the viscount and his companion passed by.

When Ruxart returned to his town house late the following morning, it was obvious he was in an ugly mood. From his having found violent fault with three of his servants' habits, dress and abilities in as many minutes, the downstairs staff was given to understand that his lordship's temper was as rumpled as his clothes. Thus it was somewhat reluctantly that Goswick approached him in the study bearing a small silver salver.

"What is it?" asked Ruxart acidly as the door opened. He was seated at his desk, a glass and half-empty bottle standing at his elbow.

"A message, my lord," replied the butler tonelessly. He proffered the tray. "I was asked to give it to your lordship immediately upon your return."

With a scowl, Ruxart took up the folded note from the

tray and waved his man brusquely away. He did not read the missive immediately, but set it aside to stare instead at the sheet which lay on the desk before him. *My dearest Jane* was written in an unsteady hand across the top, with nothing thereafter. In sudden rage, his lordship's hand crumpled the sheet and he sat with the paper trapped in his clenched fist before dropping it to cradle his head in his hands.

Ruxart was roused sometime later by the sound of a tradesman calling out his wares in the street outside. He poured himself the remains of the bottle with a hand that shook, sloshing wine upon his desk. He apparently did not care, being more concerned with emptying his glass. But his eye was caught by the note Goswick had delivered—how long ago? He stood weaving beside his desk and held the paper to the light of the window.

I beg your earliest attendance to discuss a Matter of Importance, read Ruxart. He did not recognize the elaborately embellished script and was startled to see the name of Simone St. Juste with her London address at the bottom of the page. Armand had not mentioned the arrival of his mother in town, but then Ruxart remembered that he was not confiding in his friend of late. He stood a moment longer, gazing unseeing at the note, before tossing it into the crimson puddle of spilled wine. As he left the room, he was calling for Oundle in a voice that left little doubt that his lordship's frame of mind had not improved with his brief rest.

Some hours later, refreshed by a bath, a change of clothes and a breakfast of cold ham and ale, Ruxart presented himself before Madame St. Juste. There was little to be seen of his all-night debauch beyond the dark circle beneath his heavy-lidded eyes when Simone received him in her morning room. To her polite inquiry as to how he did, the viscount replied that he was well and she did not question this. During the pause which followed, his lordship thought again how much Armand favored his mother, for both were extremely fair with silvery blond hair and stunning green eyes. Madame St. Juste, however, could never be so motionless as her son, for every inch of her petite frame vibrated with expression as she spoke. Her hands darted over the decorated front panel of her muslin day dress even now as she considered how to begin.

"*Eh bien*! You are wondering for what I have asked you here, *n'est-ce pas*?" she asked, coyly wagging one slim finger. With the air of one confiding a great secret, she continued, "I wish to ask of you, Nicolas, a very *grande faveur*."

"I should be honored to oblige, Madame," responded Ruxart with a slight inclination of his head. He was wondering what favor she could possibly want of him and was totally unprepared for the words which followed her quick smile.

"*Très bien*! I ask of you not to marry this Hélène Somers. It is not so *très difficile*, eh? You do not love this Hélène?" Simone examined Nicholas carefully as she asked this last, for she was not certain her son could be right. She knew the viscount was a man of passion and she thought perhaps he would not marry without love.

His lordship appeared speechless. "I beg your pardon?"

"Your fiancée—you do not love her?"

A dangerous flash crossed through Ruxart's dark eyes. "I do not see, Madame St. Juste, what concern it is of yours—"

"*Voyons*!" she cried. "It is of all things very simple. I do not want you to marry this Hélène Somers. If you do not love her, then it is simple, *non*?"

"May I inquire, ma'am, just why you do not wish for me to marry Miss Helen?" queried her visitor stiffly.

"But for Armand, *bien entendu*! He has the *grand passion* for this Hélène, but he will not tell you because he has the *anglais* notion of honor. But me, I have no such notions and so I ask of you to give up this one." She watched as Ruxart digested this. The muscles of his jaw flexed while he appeared engrossed in the design of her plush, patterned rug.

195

"You did not know?"

"No, I did not know," he confirmed tightly. He raised his eyes to hers and Simone gasped at the naked torment visible in their depths.

"So you do love the *petite* Hélène," she said sadly.

"My God, had I known!" he exclaimed harshly as he jumped up to pace a restless line before her. "Love Helen? I've never loved Helen! I shall never love Helen!" He stopped at her side, captured one of her hands and said in a voice charged with emotion, "I would give anything to be able to grant you this favor! But I cannot. I can't cry off from my obligation to marry Helen—it would be a despicable action."

"Bah! It is ever the same with you *anglais*!" declared Simone, withdrawing her hand. "To sacrifice the happiness of all for the honor of one! It is what I cannot understand!" A heavy frown tugged at her pretty lips, a scowl overlaid her brow. "*Mon dieu*, can you do nothing, Nicolas?"

The sorrow she had detected in her son's face could not nearly match the misery so deeply etched into the square face before her. Ruxart stared directly into her fiery eyes, his soul for one instant bared within his own. Then he straightened and with his lids lowered over those black pools of desolation, said solemnly, "I give you my word, Madame St. Juste, that Armand shall have her."

"You will break off this betrothal?"

"Helen shall be free to marry your son," he said in answer.

Simone St. Juste clapped her hands together. "*Très bien*! You are *magnifique*! But do not, I beg of you, tell Armand that I have spoken with you, for he would have the great displeasure. And I hope, *mon cheri* Nicolas, that you will find your own happiness," she added earnestly as Ruxart turned to leave.

"Is there happiness in hell?" wondered the viscount under his breath.

196

Chapter Sixteen

Despite the hundreds of brightly burning candles, the chamber seemed dimly lit. Dark, heavy drapes were pulled tightly across the windows and only the soberest colors had been chosen for the room's furnishings. Tables, large and small, were positioned at angles beneath the glowing candelabras; surrounding each table, men of all descriptions kept conversation to a low murmur. For this was Crockford's, the supremest of the gaming halls, where play was ruinously deep, each night, throughout the night. Here, bloods chanced enormous sums upon the turn of a card, the roll of a die or the spin of a wheel, and all with a nonchalance that belied the significance of a fortune won or lost at a sitting. Though such games of hazard were illegal, officialdom appeared conveniently unaware of such establishments, and even the great Duke of Wellington was at one time a member of Crockford's managing committee.

On this particular night, play at one of the larger oval tables was obviously considerable, for scattered around the table men sat in shirt sleeves, lines of concentration furrowing brows as attention was claimed by a pair of dice tumbling in a box. Sprawling easily in their midst, a cynical cast resting hard upon his handsome face, Viscount Ruxart tapped idly upon a crystal glass while casually placing his wager. He did not generally consider faro his game, preferring play of skill to that of chance, but his lordship had readily joined this table, for sitting opposite him, cool and elegantly bored, was Armand St. Juste.

They had not yet spoken, but it was enough for them to convey with a tilt of the head, a lift of the lips, their agreement over the absurdity of Lord Elwinson's spotted waistcoat and the certainty that the foppish young fool would tuck himself up before the night's end and thereby finish what had been a respectable fortune when he had succeeded to the title. Elwinson's unsteady hand wavered, unable to decide upon his wager, and Ruxart removed his eyes from the tedium of the table.

Of a sudden, his hand ceased its nervous play upon the crystal. St. Juste's back was to the door, but he had heard the opening and he recognized from the hard glint which flashed through Ruxart's eye that something of moment was about to occur.

"I did not realize," remarked Ruxart loudly, "that Crockford's now opened its doors to the rabble. The very air in here grows foul."

Within the threshold of the double doors, two men halted abruptly, and a pair of hard hazel eyes whipped to the viscount's face. Robert Manderley's body went rigid as the impact of the insult penetrated.

"I fear, St. Juste, that we must become more selective in our choice of haunts," continued Ruxart colorlessly. "It is apparently becoming a distressing habit of mine to be pursued by Manderleys."

A sharp hiss reverberated as all interest in the game ceased. Only the hand of his companion upon his arm restrained Manderley from storming forward, while throughout the room men dropped their cards to stare at the impending drama.

At the head of the faro table, a thin, gray-faced gentleman cleared his throat. "Had we not best get on with the game? I ask you, gentlemen, to place your wagers now, if you please."

They apparently did not please. Ruxart did not so much as glance his way, but exchanged a deadly smile with St. Juste which had the effect of halting activity along the table altogether. The message of that smile was clear. St. Juste put up his quizzing glass and studied his friend for a hushed moment.

"How often have I told you to be more circumspect in your choice of companions?" he complained on a soft sigh. He leaned forward and lazily tipped his beribboned glass to Ruxart's arm. "Just look at your sleeve! Now where, I ask you dear boy, did you get hair of that color on your arm?"

Puzzled faces riveted on the viscount as his lordship made a great show of removing a strand of hair from his full, snowy white shirt sleeve. Various gentlemen later claimed that there was no hair to be seen, but others asserted quite emphatically that the strand was indeed clinging where it ought not to have been. No one at the time, however, disclaimed its existence as Ruxart stated into the uneasy silence, "Ah—I must, I really must, stop associating with persons who have copper curls. It does tend to look . . . untidy, shall we say?"

Manderley's face matched the maroon of his jacket; his knuckles turned whiter than the frill of his shirt as they wrapped tightly round his gold-topped walking stick. He roughly brushed his friend's restraining hand away and surged forward in fury.

"Tell me, St. Juste," the viscount drawled coldly, "do you think something should be done to clear the air?"

"That would depend, my friend," responded St. Juste as he examined his nails.

"On what?"

"On how willing you are to sully your hands, of course."

199

The gold head of the cane crashed across the table top. While others jumped, Ruxart merely raised his eyes in a look of mild inquiry at the man who stood breathing harshly, their hatred separated only by the table's width.

"You cur! You dog! You shall pay for your insults!" seethed Manderley, his face mottled with rage.

The languid shrug with which his lordship received his angry words served to enrage Manderley further still. His jaw worked as he strove to overcome his speechless wrath. "You shall name your friends, Ruxart!" he rasped at last.

"Gentlemen, please! Let's be sensible," interjected the shaking man at the table's head. His words were utterly disregarded as all eyes focused on the viscount.

Ruxart leisurely unfolded himself from his chair, a grimace of gratification on his lips. "St. Juste will act for me."

"Lowell?" tossed Manderley over his shoulder.

"Of course," agreed that man morosely. "I will call upon you in the morning, St. Juste."

Candlelight spun off the golden hair as St. Juste tipped his head in acquiescence. Ruxart and Manderley stood motionless, eyes locked, in the feral stillness. Then with frightening calm, the viscount retrieved the fancy stick from where it lay as a testament to Manderley's moment of madness and held it out to the other gentleman, an unpleasant smile playing upon his lips. Tense with animosity, Manderley stared fixedly a few seconds more before whisking the stick from Ruxart's hand and sweeping furiously from the room.

The viscount resumed his seat, though everyone else remained immobile. Holding his glass to his lips, he paused to lament in a gentle tone, "Have you made no decision yet, Elwinson?"

There was a great deal of scraping of chairs, calling for wine, buzz and hum as gentlemen returned to their games with the appearance of normality. Even as they did so, bets were being laid as to the outcome of the meeting, with odds heavily favoring Lord Ruxart. He had, after all, twice bloodied his man and though it had been some years since his lordship had dueled, it was acknowledged that he had both skill and experience behind him.

The faintest tinge of dawn streaked across the sky when Viscount Ruxart and Armand St. Juste finally stepped out into the night. They strolled wordlessly, refreshed by the cool air after the stuffiness of the closed gaming rooms. After a time, St. Juste halted beneath a lit streetlamp and busied his hands with the readjusting of his hat. He angled it to the left. "You've begun a fine scandal tonight, Nick," he commented casually, moving his hat to the right.

"Someone must keep the *ton* entertained, don't you think?" said Ruxart lightly.

"You have, as always, fulfilled the role to admiration," observed St. Juste dryly. When his friend made no answer, he returned his hat precisely to where it had originally been and set forth. "The choice of weapons lies with you."

"Yes. Pistols, I think."

"Manderley is accounted a fine shot. On the other hand, his fencing skill is but fair."

"Precisely. I must have *some* sport! Pistols it must be."

Armand acknowledged the truth of this with a laugh and the pair began to speak of other matters, including the news of Madame St. Juste's first sojourn to town in a score of years. Ruxart accepted St. Juste's invitation to call upon his mother, but not, he rather thought, until after the matter of the duel had been settled, which he urged St. Juste to arrange as quickly as possible. The two parted in a companionable mood just as the sunlight touched the streets in earnest.

It was the first duty of a second to seek a reconciliation. This, however, St. Juste did not do. He was not the man to expend energy in futile occupation. Instead, he made certain his man had a choice of evenly matched weapons and a favorable position in the duel. He left it to Nick to determine how badly Manderley should be hit and did not bother him with the question of apologies.

Between them, St. Juste and Lowell concluded the arrangements quickly. Lowell met the viscount's choice of pistols with relief and agreed readily to Putney Heath as the site. The Heath's reputation as a haunt of highwaymen and vagabonds would assure them of the privacy necessary for the illegal proceeding, which they set for the following morning, both principals seeming anxious to have the matter over and done with. Lowell appeared disinclined to remain in St. Juste's company a moment longer than was essential, and as soon as Armand engaged himself to bring a doctor along, the lachrymose Lowell departed.

All of this was related to Ruxart within the hour as he stood before his bedroom mirror, loosely knotting the unstarched muslin à la Byron. Achieving the desired effect, he waved Oundle away and, as his valet disappeared with the armful of untried cravats, turned to St. Juste, who sat on the edge of a nearby table, lazily swinging one booted foot.

"I'm glad you've taken care of the arrangements so speedily. I dislike having these little affairs drawn out."

"Speaking of drawing, how much of Manderley's blood do you intend to spill?" questioned St. Juste, coming to his feet.

"Come, come, Armand! Do I look so bloodthirsty?" the viscount rejoined with a crooked smile.

"It has been my misfortune, Nick, to discover that you are ever what is least expected of you," his friend pointed out in an apologetic tone.

They repaired to the viscount's breakfast parlor to share a cup of coffee and were sitting there discussing minor details of the duel when the door swung wide and Penelope Manderley dashed dramatically into the room. Behind her, a white-faced Goswick stammered an apology, "I beg your lordship's pardon—the lady—"

"You may go, Goswick," cut in Ruxart, all the while watching the woman standing before him. It was plain at a glance that she was suffering from the effects of great agitation, for her bosom was heaving and her narrow face was suffused with an unbecoming crimson. "Well, Mrs. Manderley, as honored as I am to receive you, may I inquire as to what brings you so . . . forcibly . . . to my side?"

The gentle sarcasm quite removed all the nasty color from her cheeks, leaving her whiter than the plain gown she wore. "Inquire as to . . ." she repeated dully.

"Yes, my dear. Surely you did not call merely to stand staring whilst I drink my morning coffee?"

This time the sting of his words galvanized her. "You know perfectly well why I have come! How could you? I was like to swoon when I'd heard what you had done! You must stop this now!" Her wild green eyes swept the room, stopping at St. Juste. "You! Tell him he cannot go through with this."

"My good woman," said Ruxart with a calmness belied by the lines settling on the sides of his mouth, "your ravings make little sense. If you refer, as I collect, to the impending duel with your husband, I take leave to inform you that it was he who issued the challenge to me."

"But you provoked him to it! And there was no cause! You have not been near me since—since that night at Covent Garden and then you did not so much as touch me! But Robert would not listen to me! I tried to tell him, to explain . . ." She sounded almost mournful and the viscount set down the cup he had pressed to his lips.

"My God! Never tell me you have formed a *tendre* for your own husband at this late date!"

"Robert has ever been kind to me. I know *you* could never understand, but I have always cherished a fondness for him."

"My God!" repeated Ruxart.

Penelope leaned forward, bracing her arms against the tabletop. "Please, Ruxart, I beg of you to cry off from this

203

meeting! He is so much older—people would call it a charitable act. As a favor to me, I beg of you."

"It is . . . impossible."

"If not for me, then perhaps for your precious Helen," she grated with an angry sneer. "Do you think she'd enjoy a *tête-a-tête* with me? I'm sure I could tell her things she's heard from no one else!"

"You think to threaten me?" he inquird softly.

"I can do more than threaten, my lord!" Her hand lashed out, grasping the wedgewood cup. Ruxart shot out a hand to stop her, but she managed to throw the cup, spraying coffee through the air, until it smashed into the wall behind the viscount.

His lordship sighed. "When are you going to learn that your dramatics merely bore me?"

"And when are you going to learn that I hate you! I hate you!" cried Penelope with a stamp of her foot.

"Ah, then I see no reason to detain you any longer, my dear," said Ruxart coolly. He rose and moved to hold open the door.

With a violent shake of her coppery curls, she hissed, "You will regret this!"

"Undoubtedly. But not so much as I regret ever having involved myself with you, my pet," he asserted before she flung out of the room. Ruxart firmly closed the door behind her. "To think it shall be said that I'm dueling over such as she!"

"And, er, aren't you?" inquired St. Juste with interest.

A guarded expression came over Nicholas. "Not a bit of it!" he laughed. "I am dueling, as ever, for my own pleasure. Though the thought that all London shall be convinced otherwise very nearly leads me to cry off after all."

"But not quite."

"But not quite, my dear Armand, not quite," agreed Ruxart.

*   *   *

St. Juste eyed with approval the viscount's dark, tight pantaloons and black riding jacket, for he did not want his man to present more of a target than was necessary. With a nod of satisfaction, he stepped behind Nick into his lordship's coach. Still doubtful of Ruxart's intent, Armand had decreed they travel in this vehicle, prepared to fly should Manderley be mortally wounded. But reassured by that dark garb, he now relaxed on the seat.

On the box, Jem sat beside the viscount's taciturn coachman, his thin, freckled face alive with excitement. He had not been in his lordship's service on those previous occasions of honor and the young lad beamed with pride as the coach lumbered on its way.

Inside, Ruxart lounged into the corner, extending his long legs and closing his eyes. They traversed the short distance to the house of the attending physician in complete silence. Studying his lordship's casual pose, doubts returned to haunt St. Juste and a faint mark creased his brow. As the coach pulled to a stop, he leaned toward his friend.

"Promise me, Nick, that you'll not kill him today."

The viscount lifted open an eye. The unusual solemnity of St. Juste's tone, the gravity of his countenance, brought a crooked smile to Ruxart's lips. "You think me such a fool, Armand?" he asked gently. "I assure you, I'll not kill Manderley today or any other day."

St. Juste fell back in his seat, but the sense of dissatisfaction remained. He continued to search Ruxart's face even after the stout doctor had climbed heavily in. Displaying his tall, tapered instrument case with pride, the medical gentleman hastened to assure his patron that he was well prepared for the event.

"You needn't fear, my lord, that I've not had experience in these matters, for as I told Mr. St. Juste, many's the time Cyrus Barnett's been called upon to render service for such affairs. I trust I'm the man to meet your needs on this occasion." Dr. Barnett then embarked on a detailed explanation of his previous outings; Ruxart did not bother to stifle his yawn before again closing his eyes.

Theirs was the sole carriage disturbing the quietude of Putney Heath. The three fell silent as they stepped down to tread the field that was soon to be the tableau of drama. Even the loquacious doctor found he had no comment with which to interrupt the dawn's peaceful beauty.

The sky was a bright gray flecked with pink and the morning air smelled freshly clean following the night's gentle rain. Birds sang merrily out to one another, piercing the stillness as the men crossed the damp green carpet of the heath. Of all these things was Ruxart keenly aware.

St. Juste's green eyes narrowed as he watched his friend. Never had he seen Ruxart so calm. The air of tranquillity which sat about him was so foreign to his lordship's nature that St. Juste knew a stab of anxiety he was unable to dispel.

"Ruxart, about this meeting," he began with a note of worry he could not fully conceal.

"Have you bespoken breakfast anywhere?" Nick interrupted to inquire.

"But of course," replied Armand, relieved. "Is that not the most important duty of a second? We shall soon grace the Boar's Head with our patronage."

"A fine choice," remarked the viscount absently. His attention was captured by the rumbling sounds of a fast-approaching carriage.

The instant he disembarked from his vehicle, Manderley, pale and tight-lipped, indicated with a curt nod of his head his readiness to begin. Carrying a low, flat case, Lowell signalled to St. Juste who joined him at a point midway between their principals to closely examine the contents of that velvet-lined case.

Breathing heavily, the portly physician planted himself at a spot atop a sloping knoll from which he hoped to procure the best view of the duel. Not that he expected much action, for having, as he had told his patrons, attended many such affairs, he had ceased to expect the fatal ending usually ascribed to duels by the misinformed. Not once had he seen a man killed and only rarely had he been called upon to tend any but the most superficial wounds. But, he thought with a sigh, he meant to enjoy himself nonetheless and he fell to considering just what he should order for his breakfast as he watched the seconds pace out the proper distance.

Ruxart and Manderley selected their weapons and stepped to stand facing one another sideways across an expanse of greenway. Both men pointed their slender pistols downwards; both cocked their weapons upon the command to do so.

"Gentlemen," said Lowell loudly, pulling a large white handkerchief from his pocket, "as I drop this, it shall be your signal to fire." He stood to the side, centered from either man, with his hand extended. The linen danced in the breeze; a moment later, it fluttered on its way to the ground.

On the instant, Ruxart's hand jerked upward, directly upward, as he discharged his shot into the air. Too late did Manderley realize that the viscount was deloping. His finger had already pushed against the pistol's mechanism and though his hand pulled to the left, Manderley's aim had been well taken. When the smoke cleared, he saw with horror the form of the Viscount Ruxart prostrate upon the ground. He ran forward and though he was pushed roughly back by his friend Lowell, he managed to see the blood seeping through Ruxart's clothes to vividly stain the grass beneath him.

Chapter Seventeen

St. Juste knelt over Ruxart's still form and set grimly to work. He wrenched the floppy cravat free from the viscount's neck and tore open his clothes, then pressed the wad of muslin against the gaping wound in an attempt to staunch the flow of blood. The doctor ran clumsily across the grass to bend awkwardly over Ruxart's other side.

"Oh my. Oh my," he mumbled as he pulled his case from his pocket. He continued to cluck under his breath while his hands probed the area of the wound, setting St. Juste's teeth on edge.

"Is he—will he?" whispered Manderley in fearful hesitation.

"I do not know," replied St. Juste flatly. "You should be off. I will contrive to get word to you if there should be need for you to leave England."

The older man paled at this. "Had I but known he meant to delope! But I was certain—I did not mean—"

"For God's sake, man, be off before you are discovered!" cut in Armand sharply. With a quelling stare upon the shaking man, he added brusquely, "There is nothing for you to do here."

With Lowell tugging persistently at his sleeve, Manderley allowed himself to be dragged over to his carriage, but still he did not mount the step, seeming unable to tear his eyes from the critical activity surrounding the man lying motionless upon the grass. He had not expected to be the one to deal death this dawn.

Searching for the bullet, the doctor's fingers continued to tentatively stab at the viscount's bloodied shoulder. He was none too gentle about the business and he soon drew a moan from his lordship.

"The devil take you! Can't you be more careful?" snapped St. Juste. With a sudden restless movement, Ruxart's eyes flew open to gaze unseeing into his own. Armand thought his heart would stop in the moments it took the cloud to lift from those dark eyes, but at last the light of intelligence flickered as Nicholas struggled to rise up.

"I want . . . to go . . . to the Keep," he said with effort.

"Impossible," said Dr. Barnett instantly. "The bullet must be removed and the wound dressed as quickly as possible. He cannot travel in this condition."

"I am going. . . ." persisted Ruxart, trying again to sit up.

"Don't be a fool, Nick!" St. Juste pushed him firmly back into the grass. "You are going to lie still and have your shoulder attended to."

"Take me to the Keep, damn you!" rasped Nicholas through lips whitened with pain.

"I tell you, he cannot make such a journey!" objected the doctor.

Ignoring him, St. Juste stared down at the lines of discomfort cut into Ruxart's face, at the eyes once again dulled with pain. His own eyes shadowed as he came to a decision. "All right, Nick. I'll take you to the Keep. Just lie still a moment more."

"Sir! I must object," began Barnett in anger.

"Then do so by all means, but some other time, if you please!" interrupted St. Juste hotly. "For the moment, all I

210

ask is that you help me properly bind this wound."

With a deep grunt, the doctor set about padding a square of heavy cloth over Ruxart's shoulder and tying it securely into place. "I tell you plainly, Mr. St. Juste," he said as he finished binding the bandage, "I'll wash my hands of the case if you persist in moving his lordship."

"Very well." St. Juste wrenched a small velvet bag from his pocket and tossed it across to the portly man. "I'm certain I need not caution you to keep your own counsel over this." Without waiting to see the physician's indignant reaction, Armand turned his attention to the two servants behind him. "Jem, take one of the wheelers and ride on ahead. See that fresh cattle await us at every post-stop and warn the earl that we are coming."

The lad accepted this order with a doleful nod and turned to run to the carriage. His way was blocked as Manderley stepped out of the shadows. "Take one of mine! You'll need a full team."

Jem hesitated, betraying his distress with trembling lips and clenched fists, but St. Juste called out impatiently, "Do as he says!" As the groom scrambled to unharness one of the bays from Manderley's trappings, his master's friend and foe scrutinized each other for a pungent moment. With his eyes still riveted on the man for whom, oddly enough, he felt a great pity, St. Juste abruptly addressed the doctor. "I suggest, Barnett, that you beg a journey home with Mr. Manderley. I fear we shall be unable to take you up."

At that, Robert Manderley pivoted and climbed at last into his carriage. St. Juste did not watch to see the doctor enter behind him, but signalled to the viscount's coachman, who appeared at his side on the instant. Between them, they lifted Ruxart to his feet, but his lordship pushed their supporting arms away. "I can . . . walk," he gasped. He staggered a few steps, then leaned heavily against St. Juste. Weaving drunkenly, they crossed the grass to the coach where Ruxart sagged against the crest on the door. As

Armand caught him, he whispered hoarsely, "Manderley?"

"Has gone, Nick," answered St. Juste. Together with Harry, he lifted the viscount onto the cushioned seat and the viscount mercifully lost all consciousness.

As they traveled the long miles to Kerrington, St. Juste cradled Ruxart's limp form in his arms, cursing each rut they hit, yet urging Harry to spring the horses as fast as possible. He felt as if he were in a death vigil, watching the life drain out of his friend as the continued loss of blood washed all color from Ruxart's face. Nick appeared all too much like the corpse Armand feared he soon would be.

The first stop was accomplished in record time. A pair of waiting ostlers ran forward as the carriage rolled into the courtyard to quickly undo the horses' trappings, bearing evidence that Jem had been before them. Since Ruxart kept his own animals stabled along this oft-traveled road, the fresh team led to the coach consisted of only the best blood, regular sixteen-mile-an-hour tits, Harry informed St. Juste as they pressed onward. They covered mile after mile, with the sun climbing ever higher. The bright beauty of the summer morning jarred with the nightmare of the journey as Armand tried to make sense from a senseless act.

"Why? In God's name, Nick, why did you delope?" he asked again and again, with no answer beyond an occasional low moan.

By the time they drew into the cobbled yard of a small Kentish inn, the sun was nearly overhead and St. Juste's clothes clung damply to him where Ruxart had lain pressed against him. His neck was stiff and he had long ago lost feeling in his right arm. As he was considering shifting his burden, a tall, broad man emerged at the small window of the coach to proffer a tray.

"'Tis brandy, sir," explained the innkeeper, rubbing his free hand on his rough apron. "I thought as how Master Nick, his lordship that is, might stand in need of reviving spirits."

Altering his position in order to accept one of the glasses, St. Juste disturbed the viscount slightly and the innkeeper gazed in with every appearance of interest. "I've always said as how his lordship would go his length one day, but 'tis certain I never thought 'twould end like this, him being such a fine shot and all."

The look directed at him sent the tall man scurrying back to his door. St. Juste had no further time to remonstrate with the man, for Ruxart once again stirred. Gently cupping the glass to the viscount's ashen lips, Armand said rather briskly, "Here, Nicky, just swallow a sip or two of this."

His lordship did so and instantly choked, then lay back weakly. He appeared to be struggling and St. Juste bent closer. "Just lie still, Nick," he said gently. "We're nearly there."

"You may . . . tell John . . ."

"Save your strength, man!"

"Tell him . . . he can tell me . . . I told you so . . . now," finished Ruxart, a shade of a smile upon his lips.

The coach lurched forward once more and the only sound to disturb the silence within was the labored breathing of the viscount, unconscious yet again.

When at last Harry pulled the horses to a halt in the graveled court of the Keep, it was apparent they were expected, for a swarm of servants descended upon them. The earl appeared at the top of the marbled steps as Ruxart was carried from the coach. The old man, shaking and sallow, but still erect, watched the procession in silence, only inhaling sharply when he saw the deathlike mask of his grandson's face. Together, St. Juste and Kerrington followed the small cortege up the sweeping staircase, neither needing to give voice to the grief so vividly felt.

Upon his arrival, Dr. Mallory was led directly to his lordship's bedchamber. Having attended the viscount since birth, the doctor had fully expected to find that the frantic young groom sent to fetch him had exaggerated the seriousness of Master Nick's latest scrape. But one look at the white face disappearing into the crisp linen told him otherwise.

Without pausing to greet the earl, Dr. Mallory rapped out a sharp series of orders, sending servants scrambling for water and fresh linens, while stripping off his jacket. "I suggest, my lord," he said to the earl when he had finished setting his instruments on a stand by the bed, "that you await us downstairs."

It was not in Kerrington's nature to accept a dismissal meekly, but for once he did not demur. At the door, however, he stood with one fist braced against the wood. "Damn the boy!" he muttered heavily. "Damn the boy!" His step seemed slower as he left the room and St. Juste would have gone to give him an arm had not Mallory commanded him to shed his coat, wash his hands and prepare to extract the ball lodged in Ruxart's shoulder.

This was accomplished with relative ease, his lordship remaining, for the most part, unconscious throughout. But as he dressed the wound with basilicum powder, Mallory gravely inquired if it were not true that the viscount had been planning to marry shortly.

"It is," answered St. Juste abruptly.

"It would, perhaps, be as well to inform the young lady of the viscount's condition," said the doctor, shrugging himself into his coat. "The sooner, the better."

"What are you saying? Is he dying?" demanded St. Juste.

"Well, as to that, only God can say," was the evasive reply. "But he has lost a great deal of blood, a great deal of blood," he added with a look that sent shivers down the other's back.

St. Juste stayed only long enough to eat a small luncheon before again setting forth, this time on the road north. He told the earl to expect his return, with Miss Helen, in two days' time, but he doubted if the old lord had understood or cared. Since being closeted briefly with Mallory, the earl had subsided to a chair, to sit in stooped and silent anguish.

The long miles were tedium personified, leaving St. Juste

weary emotionally as well as physically. The afternoon gave way to night and still they surged on, making only the briefest of stops. St. Juste was unsuccessful in his efforts to sleep, as he was in his attempts to drum out the thought that Ruxart might already be gone. Again and again, the vision of Miss Helen rose before his tired eyes, but the realization that she might soon be free brought only bereavement into his narrowed eyes. Finally, just as the sky began to lighten with the coming of dawn, St. Juste dozed fitfully, the demands of his body overcoming the torments of his soul.

Noon had barely gone, the sun was dazzling in a sky of gloriously bright blue when Freddy Somers dashed into the sitting parlor of Plumstead to echo his springtime announcement that a carriage was coming. "And it's my lord's, it is!" he finished happily before darting out, while his audience displayed various degrees of astonishment. Wonderment was heightened when Mrs. Beedle followed Freddy's words with the disclosure that a Mr. St. Juste was calling.

St. Juste halted in the frame of the door, stiffening at the sight before him. Helen stood perched on a small stool, resplendent in a wedding dress of white tulle embroidered with tiny pearls and graced with a long train which fell from her shoulders to dust the floor. The high waist, square bodice and puffed and laced bretelle sleeves set off her petite figure to perfection. Armand's heart constricted and he stood transfixed.

He was himself the recipient of a round of stares. His usually flawless appearance was quite sadly rumpled, the hours cramped in the carriage having creased his dark pantaloons and jacket beyond, his valet would insist, repair. The starch had long ago wilted out of his knotted cravat, which hung limply against his wrinkled and stained shirt.

Jane was the first to recover, saying as she set down the scissors and pins she had been holding, "Forgive us! Freddy

215

quite led us to believe for an awful moment that it was Lord Ruxart come to call, and you must know it would be fatal for his lordship to see Helen in her wedding dress before the day!"

St. Juste winced at her words, but collected himself sufficiently to enter and bow over Miss Somers' hand.

"Allow me, Mr. St. Juste, to present my mother and my sister-in-law."

The elder, delicate-looking lady reclining on the settee received his brief nod with a flutter of the hand, but the spare woman standing beside Helen merely inclined her head slightly, a curtsey seemed unsuitable, in her view, for a mere "mister." St. Juste's attention had already, however, fixed on Helen.

"I am afraid," he stated flatly, "this is not a call of pleasure."

Stepping down from the stool, consternation crossing through her vivid blue eyes, Helen asked quietly, "Whatever is wrong, Mr. St. Juste?"

"Is it . . . Viscount Ruxart?" questioned Jane sharply.

"Forgive me, I bring bad news," he replied grimly. "Lord Ruxart has been badly wounded."

Amidst the loud shrieks of the older women, Helen's hand flew to her cheek, her eyes widened in shock. But Jane had seemingly encountered Medusa, remaining utterly motionless throughout St. Juste's terse explanations. She was suddenly galvanized to action, however, when Helen cried softly, "What shall I do?"

"Do? We must go to him—at once! If there is the least chance we may yet arrive on time, we cannot hesitate!" She pulled her unresisting sister from the room, ignoring Agnes' plea to pick up the train and brusquely begging Mr. St. Juste to wait.

For twenty minutes Armand endured the incessant barrage of questions, interspersed with mournful exclamations from both the Mrs. Somerses. He sustained himself with port, but even this was inadequate when Agnes ventured to suggest a deathbed wedding, should they arrive in time. It was perhaps fortunate that at this moment Jane reappeared with Helen in tow. Each wore a simple traveling dress, poke bonnet and gloves; in addition, Jane carried a single portmanteau.

"We are ready, Mr. St. Juste," she said woodenly.

"Oh, my dear, sweet child!" wailed Dorothea, clinging to Helen. "That you should suffer the misery of widowhood so soon, so young!"

"She is not a widow yet, Mama," put in Jane dampingly, "as she has neither married Lord Ruxart nor as yet confirmed his death."

"So much the worse!" insisted her mother on a sob, an opinion with which Agnes seemed heartily inclined to agree.

In time, they managed to detach mother from daughter and joined young Freddy as he stood talking with Harry and the viscount's postillions. For once the boy did not wear his merry smile and he knuckled his eyes, determined not to shed any unmanly tears. Jane gave her mother and Agnes a swift kiss each, then entered the coach without another word. Helen climbed in beside her, bewildered and not a little concerned at this sister who suddenly seemed drained of all emotion.

As the vehicle jerked forward, it was Helen who leaned out the window with promises to write as soon as may be. Jane asked no questions, offered no comments. She sat, erect, immobile, as hour chased hour upon the road. St. Juste and Helen spoke in the hushed tones of the bereaved, and though the sharing of the grief brought them both consolation, it only increased Jane's own dull misery.

Their progress slowed considerably after the sun passed into night. The full moon was covered by a haze while dark streaks of clouds skimmed across its face. The golden reflections bespoke a mysterious world of beauty in which Jane could take no interest. For her each mile was sounded out by the horses' hoofs repeating, *Let me be on time—on time* over and over again until her head fairly pounded with the refrain and the hands in her lap clenched in frustration.

When next the coach rolled to a halt in a posting yard, St. Juste descended and passed into the inn. He soon returned to extend a hand to Helen, and after seeing her to the ground, to Jane. She did not take it.

"Come, Miss Somers, you will accomplish little by arriving at the Keep weak as well as tired. An hour's stop and a good meal will do us all good." He again put out his hand, which she reluctantly accepted.

The warm aroma of the meal being set upon the table by a sleepy-eyed male and the comfort of the chair to which she was ushered were more welcome than Jane would have admitted. The large brim of her poke bonnet had effectively shadowed her face all day and as she now removed it, Helen was shocked at the drawn look of her sister's wan face, at the deep circles beneath the sorrowing eyes. Throughout the short meal, Helen made small conversation with St. Juste, in which Jane took no part, but as the plates were cleared away, she asked him to procure them some scented water that they might freshen up. He glanced knowingly from sister to sister, then excused himself from the private room.

"How long has it been?" asked Helen after a brief silence.

"Has what been?" responded Jane in a tired tone.

"That you have been in love with Lord Ruxart."

Jane's head bobbed up. She saw a sad understanding in her sister's gaze, but none of the distress she had feared would be there. "It seems . . . forever," she finally said, sadly. "I—I am sorry, dearest."

"Oh, Jane, 'tis I who am sorry!" cried Helen, rushing to embrace Jane tightly. "I've been so blind! So stupid!" They were still clasping each other when St. Juste discreetly coughed from the door.

They slept, after a fashion, in the darkness of the closed

218

coach, each to dream of the restless young man with the moody eyes and the charming smile. Helen and Jane held hands and by morning had achieved a new dimension of their love. It was not, however, until well into the afternoon that the wheels of the carriage at last stopped spinning and the three disembarked to enter a house as still as death itself.

Chapter Eighteen

Despite the Keep's air of sepulchral gloom, Nicholas Armytage still clung to life. He had been in a state of fevered delirium, Leaming informed them, and the doctor was again due to call at any time. The earl was at Nick's bedside when the three entered the room, having aged shockingly in the space of two days. Each line on his ancient face stood out with startling clarity; his figure bent with the weight of his woe. He glanced once at the visitors, then turned his eyes back to the still form lying beneath the satin coverlet.

Jane's eyes swept the room and anger brought some color back to her pallid face. None of the summer day had been allowed into the chamber as heavy drapes covered each window; a few candles cut into the darkness, but most of the room was encased in funereal shadows. Her ringing voice cut through the muted mood. "It is little wonder he is near death when you have shut out all signs of life!"

Shocked faces turned upon her as she ran to rip open curtains, flooding the room with brilliant sunlight. "Open these windows, if you please!" she commanded. "Fresh air is what is needed, not the stifled air of death!"

The footmen standing in attendance looked to the earl,

who was staring intently at Jane. "Do as she says, you fools!" he ordered harshly.

She paid him no mind, but moved through the room snuffing candles. When she had thrown off her bonnet and stripped off her gloves, she moved at last to the bed where she bent to lightly touch Ruxart's brow. The dry heat caused her fingers to tremble, but her voice was steady as she remarked, "We need to bring his fever down. I shall require towels and lavender water." She looked to the group of people surrounding her in wide-eyed wonderment. "Well?" she inquired in a tone of icy hauteur that sent the servants scurrying to do her bidding.

The earl's eyes met hers across the vast bed. "Do you think to save him?"

"I do not know," she answered, "but I do not intend to sit idly back to watch him die."

The old man flinched from the sting of the words. Helen came to his side. "Come, sir, there is nothing worse than a crowd in a sick room, you know. And Jane is a marvelous hand at nursing." For a moment, it appeared he would resist her coaxing, but he glanced at his grandson stirring restlessly and rose with an air of decision.

"Please inform me when the doctor arrives," said Jane as they left. "I wish to speak with him."

For the next hour she was undisturbed, for once the servants had deposited a stack of fresh towels and a silver bowl filled with lavender water, she had dismissed them. One last tap upon the door had brought her a tray with ratafia and macaroons, sent by the earl.

The refreshments lay untouched, for she was fully occupied in trying to place a towel damped in lavender water upon the viscount's brow. Each time she laid it gently upon his forehead, Ruxart tossed his head. "Lord Ruxart, please do not fight me," she requested with gentle urgency.

His eyes flickered open, but there was no recognition in the glassy stare. Jane's heart seemed to stop in the seconds they rested, unseeing, upon her. It was with relief that she was interrupted with the message that Dr. Mallory awaited her downstairs.

He watched her enter with an air of interest, for he had by now discovered that she was not, as he had at first supposed, the viscount's fiancée, but his future sister-in-law. He was wondering just what to say without bringing on any womanish hysteria when Miss Somers addressed him firmly.

"Thank you for seeing me, Dr. Mallory. I desire to know precisely what your consideration of Lord Ruxart's condition is."

"Well, Miss, it is a physician's frailty that he can never be too precise," he answered in a fatherly tone. "The viscount's progress is not, perhaps, as rapid as we should like, but—"

"Excuse me, Doctor," cut in Jane, "but as I have been thrust into the role of nurse, I have a need to know what Lord Ruxart's chances of recovery are. I can scarcely place my sensibilities above his needs, and I beg that you will not do so either."

Mallory seemed taken aback by her frank speech, but after a few moments he cleared his throat and said more matter-of-factly, "Very well, Miss Somers. Though I could wish this had been a good, clean sword wound and not the messy, tearing—humph!—well, the short of it is that though his lordship has lost a great deal of blood and sustained a very high fever, there has been no injury from which he could not recover had he the will to do so. But I very much fear that Lord Ruxart does not wish to recover. In short, Miss, there is very little that I can do to save the viscount."

As the doctor paused for breath, Jane thanked him in her usual calm manner and promptly returned to Ruxart's room where she stood holding her sides and swaying against the door for a full half-minute. Then she droppd her hands and, drawing a deep breath, took her place by his bedside once more.

"Lord Ruxart—Nicholas," she whispered fervently, "you

223

must listen to me. This is Jane, dearest, and I want you to stop this nonsense now, do you hear me? You can get better, you must! Oh, Nicky, please!" she cried softly, burying her head into the covers at his side.

The hand lying beside her bent head moved. She saw this dimly through her tears; when it moved again, she raised her head and stared into Ruxart's eyes. They were focused on her and this time a lucid light shone behind the feverish gloss.

"Jane?" he hoarsely wondered.

"Yes, Nick, yes! I am here, dearest, and I shall not leave, I promise you."

The light had already faded and Ruxart was again tossing, but his hand rested in hers and Jane felt insensibly cheered.

Through the long hours which followed, Jane refused to be spelled from her vigil at the viscount's side, and as she waited and watched, she had plenty of time to once again review the utter stupidity of her unhappy decision to wed John Fletcher. That he still loved Caroline had been patently obvious to Jane during his brief visit to Sloley. Mama and Agnes had, of course, been vastly surprised, but expressed themselves thrilled with the news of her betrothal (Agnes even admiting that she'd never thought such good fortune would come to pass). But with each fresh summer day, Jane had regretted more intensely her impulsive action—she had been mad, there was no other explanation—and yet she felt trapped into continuing with her madness.

Now, looking at the beloved figure lying so unnaturally still, Jane knew she could never go through with such a match. Far better, instead, to return home to remain a spinster as soon as the present crisis passed.

If it passed.

Her first elation upon learning she had, indeed, arrived in time had turned to despair upon seeing the fevered glaze of Ruxart's eyes and now had subsided to a numbness touched by an occasional surge of hope or sting of dread.

She eventually nibbled at the supper sent up to her and

drank at last a glass of ratafia, but her attention remained fixed upon his lordship. She was rewarded when his breathing no longer sounded like a shallow rattle and his body no longer threshed beneath the covers. Twice he actually took a sip of water and Jane finally began to relax her first fears that he would not live through the night. At last, she fell asleep curled up in her chair, her head laid against her outstretched arm, her hand still clasping his.

A faint pressure upon her hand roused her. She opened her eyes to see Ruxart, his lank hair sticking to his damp forehead, staring in amazement.

"My God, I thought I'd dreamed you here," he rasped weakly.

Her breath was drawn audibly, then released slowly. "Nicholas," she murmured shakily, "thank God, thank God."

His eyes followed her as she rose, covering her joy with a series of nursely ministrations. She put her hand to his brow, which, though clammy, was wonderfully cool. "It appears, my lord, that you have broken your fever," she said happily.

He attempted to catch her hand when she removed it, but she was faster than he. "My dear—" he began.

"I'll swear you are ready for some food," she broke in briskly.

"The sight of you is food enough," he whispered.

A slow smile lit up her pinched face. "I believe, however, that gruel would be more sustaining. For now, my lord, I prescribe a bit more sleep. And later, you will wish to see the earl and Helen."

"Helen is here?"

"Yes, and Mr. St. Juste as well, little though you deserve it. You silly boy," she scolded gently, "you frightened us all with your schoolboy tricks!" She paused, lowering her gaze to where his hands lay still upon the satin coverlet. "Promise me, Lord Ruxart, that you shall never again do such a foolish thing."

She raised her eyes to see his head turned into the pillow, a heavy frown pulling at his lips. Picking up his hand, she said in her nursely tones, "There! I mustn't be worrying you just yet, but I warn you, sir, I shan't be leaving without your promise."

At that, he looked directly at her. "Then you shall never have it. I should much rather keep you here."

She answered him with a shake of her head, which loosened two of the pins in her hair and sent one lock cascading over her ear. She left the room and he closed his eyes to picture again the delight of that captivating vision.

The news that the viscount had overcome his fever at last and was quite lucid, if still weak, worked like a restorative upon the household. Servants no longer tiptoed through rooms, laughter replaced whispering and everyone down to the least scullery maid pronounced himself certain all along that Master Nick would pull through. The old earl seemed inclined to credit Miss Somers with having saved his grandson and remarked acidly that she could show that old fool Mallory a thing or two, but the lady shook her head and begged he would not be so foolish.

"I only used common sense, sir, nothing more. It was Lord Ruxart's strong constitution that did the trick." She then retired to her room for the first real rest she had been granted in the last forty-eight hours.

The only member of the house who still seemed distressed was, perhaps, the one thought most likely to be joyous. Helen sat on a rosewood and satin settee in one of the lesser drawing rooms, her elbows propped on her knees and her chin cupped in her hands, frowning at an ornately worked pole-screen standing across the room. She did not stir from her deep brown study when the door opened behind her and only raised her head with a start upon hearing herself addressed in a cool tone.

"My dear Miss Helen," said St. Juste, coming forward, "I was about to give up hope of finding you." He broke off as he saw her woebegone expression and was before her, holding her hands in the instant. "My dear! No one can have told you! Ruxart is quite past danger!"

"I know, I know and I'm grateful, truly I am!" she burst out in distress. "But oh, Mr. St. Juste, was there ever such a dreadful coil? Here am I betrothed to Lord Ruxart whilst Jane is to be wed Mr. Fletcher. It only remains for you to solicit Caro's hand to make the farce complete!"

He placed himself on the sofa beside her, studying the way her dark curls brushed tantalizingly against her neck. "I had wondered," he mused tonelessly, "just when you would discover what a tangle we are in."

"You knew?" she asked with a blaze in her eye.

"I . . . suspected. I only learned for a certainty that Ruxart loves Jane after the duel."

"He loves Jane? Oh, that makes it even worse!" cried Helen, rising to her feet. "You see, I've only learned—it's been plain to see—that Jane feels . . . deeply about him. But that *he* should love *her*! Oh, whatever can we do?"

"For a start, my pet, you can sit calmly down." His air of tranquil authority had its effect. Helen returned to her seat and summoned up a tremulous smile for him. St. Juste tilted her head up with his fingertips and lightly brought his lips to hers. "Now Helen . . . my sweet . . . beautiful . . . child," he murmured as he punctuated his words with a series of light kisses, "you are going to tell Ruxart you are releasing him of his obligation to you, because, quite frankly, my little love—" here he set a kiss upon the tip of her nose—"I am quite bored with being patient and honorable. I fully intend, dearheart, to marry you myself."

His kisses were now returned with a fervor which would have astonished the viscount, who had begun to fear his bride-to-be was of a frigid nature. St. Juste found Helen far from lacking in passion and it was quite some time before the original object of their discussion reasserted itself.

"But, Armand, even so," said Helen, a little breathlessly, "it will not do Jane or Ruxart the least good, for there is Mr. Fletcher to be thought of! And poor, poor Caro!"

"Ah, as to that, my love, I begin to perceive that I must bestir myself on the behalf of my future relations. Am I to understand that Miss Willoughby has a *tendre* for John Fletcher?"

"Yes. And he was to have married her, but there was some misunderstanding whilst we were here before and—and Jane ended up betrothed to him. I thought at the time it was most odd, but only now do I understand it had nothing to do with love."

"Ah . . . I confess, I had wondered what had set Nick on," admitted St. Juste to his bewildered love. "Well, you are to leave this problem to me, Helen. Do not, as yet, broach the subject with your sister, however."

"You do not wish to have her hopes raised? Oh, Armand, if you could only set the matter to rights! Then my happiness would be utterly complete!"

Women who knew of Mr. St. Juste's antipathy to having his clothes disarranged the slightest degree would have been astounded at how meekly he accepted the crushing embrace which quite thoroughly destroyed the intricate folds of his cravat.

It was not until two days later when Dr. Mallory pronounced his patient was fit to receive brief visits that anyone other than Jane and the earl was allowed into Ruxart's room. But at the first opportunity, Helen, with her hair pulled into a charming Grecian knot and tied with a ribbon as yellow as her buttercup gown, entered the room with her chin held high.

The viscount was supported by a vast pile of monogrammed pillows, his dark hair gleaming against the whiteness. His burgundy brocade dressing gown accented the pallor of his face, but his black eyes were alert and he appeared transformed from the deathly ill person of three days ago. Upon seeing her, he smiled crookedly, looking much like the schoolboy Jane had termed him, and held out his hand. As she came to take it, he spoke with a seldom-heard solemnity.

"I've been anxious to see you, Helen. I very much wish to make you my apologies—again! It must seem to you that I'm forever bringing some fresh scandal down upon us—"

"No, indeed!" she interrupted quickly. "There is no need for you to apologize to me, my lord! I'm just thankful you are on the way to mending. It—it was a frightful scare."

"But I am sorry, Helen, for the gossip you will have to bear," he persisted. His eyes swept the room, then finally came back to rest upon her face. "I shall not put you through such straits again."

"My lord, please! There is something I must say, and then I think it shall be I who have to beg your pardon!" He looked quizzical; she found she could not meet his eyes. Removing her hand from his, she played nervously with the lace ends of her sleeves. "I find that I must do what I ought to have done months ago. My lord, I must release you of your obligation to me. Wait, please! Let me finish! There are two reasons—"

"There is no need to explain, Helen," he interjected.

"Why we cannot marry," she continued, forcing herself to stare squarely at him. "Armand and Jane."

A myriad of emotions crossed his face. Gradually, an understanding smile touched his lips. "Has Armand spoken?"

"Yes. I—I've loved him from the first, you know." She bent her head rather shyly. "I am afraid that between the two of us we very nearly made a rare muddle of it."

Ruxart recaptured the nervous hand. "May I offer you my sincere congratulations, Helen? Armand is . . . unique."

"Yes," she agreed simply. "He is."

They were interrupted by a knock, followed instantly by the entrance of Jane. She saw her sister sitting on the edge of his lordship's bed, their hands resting comfortably together. She stopped and said in some confusion, "Oh! Pardon me! I did not know—"

"Miss Somers, don't leave! You may be the first to felicitate us," said Ruxart lightly.

"Felicitate you?"

"Miss Helen has had the rare good sense to throw me over."

As Helen giggled, Jane's bewilderment grew. "Throw you over?"

"Yes, my dear. I am a jilted man!" He laughed, which led to a fit of coughing. Jane carried a glass of water and thrust it rather ungently at him. "Serves you right, my lord, for making very unpleasant jest."

"But he's not!" exclaimed Helen through her own laughter.

"You are not—marrying?" inquired Jane in a hollow voice.

"No! We have just unbetrothed ourselves," replied Helen happily. "Or should I say, unplighted our troth?"

"Whichever," answered Ruxart with an airy wave of his hand. "Furthermore, Miss Somers, I believe you've good cause to congratulate your sister. She is about to contract a brilliant match."

Understanding dawned. "It is to be Mr. St. Juste?"

"It is!" assented her sister brightly. "And though in general I would dislike dueling extremely, I find I've good cause to be grateful to Robert Manderley—for otherwise I'd not have discovered that Armand loves me!"

"Anything to oblige, my dear. After all, it was but a small hole in my shoulder. . . ."

Helen blushed at this, but Jane said quite firmly, "If you two are quite through funning, I believe Lord Ruxart should take a nap. Yes, my lord, a *nap*!" She shooed Helen out and followed rapidly behind.

Retreating to the haven of her room, Jane tried to sort

through the chaos of her emotions. She sat on the curved window seat and leaned against the leaded panes. The excellent view of rolling hills carpeted in emerald held no interest; her attention was given wholly over to the astounding news that Ruxart was not, after all, to wed Helen.

Thoroughly shaken from her usual equanimity, Jane's heart raced wildly as her initial disbelief gave way to a rush of absolute happiness. Having Ruxart so suddenly free of his obligation brought an upsurge of hope that fulfillment of their love was no longer beyond reach.

As it had almost from its inception, the folly of her betrothal to John Fletcher taunted her moment of happiness and she chastised herself even more bitterly than before for her impulsive acceptance. Jane's growing conviction that she would never be able to marry Fletcher now crystallized into a determination to end the mockery of a betrothal as quickly as possible. She would, she decided, inform Nicholas of her intention the first moment he declared his love.

But when, over the next few days, Ruxart made no such declaration, Jane began to suffer the heartache of doubt. There had been no lack of opportunity. Though the viscount's natural good health asserted itself and he began to mend with astonishing speed, Jane still came to his room on numerous occasions each day. Not trusting her own emotions, she kept her distance from his bed and spoke to him of only the most unexceptional topics. She felt more often than saw as his eyes followed her movement and waited for him to speak. As each day passed without so much as a hint of what she so desperately needed to hear, Jane came less and less frequently to tend her patient.

For Ruxart, those few occasions were the highlights of his very dull days. No matter how foul his mood, she had only to walk into the room to restore him to good humor. When she was gone, he occupied himself with devising methods to end his cousin Fletcher's engagement. End it he would, but

231

Ruxart meant to take the greatest care of both Miss Somers' reputation and her feelings. Thus, with unaccustomed self-control, he refrained from speaking the words of love he longed to shower upon Jane.

On the viscount's first venture from the sick room, the small party ranged themselves on the outside terrace to play a rubber of whist with an air of festivity. Ruxart stretched easily over a chaise longue, propped up by a bank of plump cushions. Owing to the bulk of the bandage padded over his left shoulder, the viscount sat in his shirt sleeves to a devastatingly handsome effect. Everyone else had dressed as for a party, since the arrival from Norfolk of the sisters' trunk and from London of St. Juste's outraged valet had occasioned almost as much excitement as the viscount's first day up.

His lordship was paying little mind to the game. He stared with a frown at Jane's indigo kerseymere, wondering how many times more he was to have that drab frock inflicted upon his sight before he could get the chit to accept the gift of a decent gown or two, when his attention was claimed.

"I do wonder," drawled St. Juste, "what the talk will be when I insert the notice announcing the ending of your betrothal, Ruxart."

"London will undoubtedly say they are relieved to find Miss Helen Somers came to her senses in time."

"And when they read the accompanying notice of my betrothal to Armand?" inquired Helen with a coy laugh.

"Ah, then they will say the poor girl is beyond hope!" replied Ruxart with promptitude.

"Should you care to wager which of the two excites the most comment?" asked St. Juste.

"I think . . . not," said the viscount, gazing directly into Jane's gray eyes. "I rather fear my wagering days are over, St. Juste. At least until the stakes are irresistible."

"For you, my lord," said Jane repressively, "any stake is irresistible."

"Now there, my dear, you wrong me. It may have been so at one time, but now I find only one thing irresistible."

Jane flushed deeply and bent her head over her cards to hide her embarrassment, offering them only the view of the top of her best lace cap. While Ruxart's eyes appeared to bore through her card hand, Helen took pity on her and changed the subject, asking his lordship if there was anything St. Juste might bring back from London.

"God, yes! Bring Oundle, will you? I'd have sent for him days ago, but the poor man cannot stand the sight of a wrinkle or a wound and I seem to have been abundantly possessed of them both. But by the time you return—when? in two or three days?—I should be sufficiently mended for my valet's sensibilities."

Laughter eased the situation and Jane was able to finish the game credibly. But she realized she would soon have to leave the Keep. It had gradually become painfully apparent to her that what she had mistaken for love had merely been a lustful passion. Ruxart wanted her, but not as a wife, and the realization bruised her more surely than any blow. She hid the anguish of her despair well and resolved never to give in to her own yearnings.

The danger was only too real. She saw it in the way his eyes ran over every inch of her, in the way his full lips lazily smiled, and most of all, she feared, in the way her own body trembled in response.

Chapter Nineteen

Caroline Willoughby could not have been said to be in spirits. Over the weeks since the disastrous visit to Kerrington Keep, she had evidenced only the most lackluster interest in all the plans advanced for her amusement. Her mother began to realize that Caro's affections had been more deeply engaged by Mr. Fletcher than she had at first supposed. She was even wondering, as she sat watching her daughter listlessly flip the pages of the latest issue of *The Lady's Magazine*, whether she ought not, perhaps, let Caroline attend the ridotto at Vauxhall after all. It was not the sort of affair she would normally have considered as suitable for a moment, but quite anything was seemingly preferable to the continuation of Caro's doldrums.

Caro heaved a sigh and turned another page. Elizabeth decided to let her go to the ridotto, but got no further than taking a breath to speak when the opening door interrupted her. Caroline scarcely raised her head when their caller was announced, but when Mr. St. Juste explained that he carried a message from Miss Helen, she at last showed a spark of interest.

"You've been to Sloley, Mr. St. Juste?" she asked, putting

aside the magazine.

"I have come, Miss Willoughby, directly from Kerrington Keep."

"Oh! So it is true, then!" Caro's violet eyes rounded. "Was Ruxart very badly shot?"

"Caroline," chided Elizabeth quietly.

"But, Mama! It's been the most famous *on dit* in years!" protested her daughter indignantly.

"Lord Ruxart sustained a severe wound," St. Juste said with one of his rare smiles, "but he is happily recovering. I believe Miss Helen writes to request your company at the Keep during the convalescence."

The young girl eagerly took the paper he extended toward her and broke open the seal. "Oh!" she exclaimed after reading a bit. "She writes that she and Ruxart have decided they would not suit!" Her eyes ran the length of the thin sheet. "Oh!" she again shrieked loudly.

"Caroline, could you not at least strive for a ladylike tone?" inquired her mother in a damping tone.

"But, Mama, Helen is to marry Mr. St. Juste!"

The gentleman in question received the pair of inquiring stares with a short bow. "I have the honor to be betrothed to Miss Helen."

"But—but what about the viscount? Was he not outraged? Did Helen jilt him for you?" demanded Caro.

"Such curiosity, my dear, shows a vulgarity of mind that cannot be liked," scolded Elizabeth. "Mr. St. Juste, may I offer you my sincere wishes for your future happiness?"

"Thank you, ma'am. Miss Willoughby, will you be joining Miss Helen for the length of her stay at the Keep?"

"Yes, that is, I should like to. . . ." She looked anxiously at her mother and when that lady nodded her head, she jumped up. "I must see to packing instantly, for Helen writes I am to come as soon as may be!" She skipped from the room, to leave her mother shaking her head.

"She's a sad romp, but it's been such a time since I've seen

236

her look so happy, I could not scold her. I must thank you for the invitation."

"As to that, Miss Willoughby will be doing Helen a kind service and, I believe, may find her own interests served." The lazy tone was noncommittal, but Elizabeth's brows raised.

"Whatever can you mean, sir?"

St. Juste's shoulder lifted slightly. "Only that a visit could serve to divert her mind. Pray see that she leaves no later than tomorrow morning, if you please," he said as he rose.

"You haven't some nonsensical notion of fixing her with Ruxart, have you? For you must know that I would not—"

"My dear woman, do not think to cast me in the role of Cupid, I beg you. It should not do at all." With his brilliant, slow smile, St. Juste was gone.

Elizabeth was still envisioning the memory of that smile on the following morning when she saw Caroline off. She had not been able to decipher the puzzle of St. Juste's purpose, but a great deal would have been made clear to her had she been standing in Curzon Street somewhat later that day. From such a vantage point Mrs. Willoughby would have met with the highly edifying view of St. Juste entering the lodgings of John Fletcher.

Her surprise, had she been able to witness it, could not have matched that of Fletcher himself, for upon the identity of his morning caller being made known to him, John had perfectly imitated a fish at feeding time. His servant having taken his reaction in a positive light, St. Juste soon joined his host. Fletcher recovered himself sufficiently to beg his guest to be seated, and as St. Juste languidly placed himself in an oval-backed armchair, inquired in a constricted tone if this call concerned the Viscount Ruxart.

"In a manner of speaking, yes," replied St. Juste easily. "Being Ruxart, he is once again doing that which is least expected by making an astounding recovery."

A breath was audibly released. "I am glad to hear it." Fletcher nervously drilled his fingers upon the thin arm of his chair, then added self-consciously, "Despite all our differences, it would give me great pain to lose him."

"We are not to lose him this time. A fact which brings relief to a great many and outrage to a great many more," remarked Armand in his mocking tone.

"Yes. Well, what brings you here?" demanded his host somewhat less than graciously.

"I come to apprise you that I have this morning inserted a notice in the *Gazette* announcing the termination of Ruxart's betrothal."

"What?"

"The recent, er, accident brought Miss Helen and Ruxart to the realization that they should not suit." St. Juste studied his well-kept nails. "I thought it might interest you to learn that I also inserted the notice of my own betrothal."

"Oh? May I offer you my felicitations?" This was received with an inclination of St. Juste's fair head; after a pause, Fletcher felt something more was needed. "May I inquire who is to be the future Mrs. St. Juste?"

"I have been honored with an acceptance from Miss Helen Somers," replied Armand, amusement glinting in his lazy eyes.

If it is possible to reel whilst sitting upright in a mahogany armchair, Fletcher did so then. His mouth worked, but he said nothing. At last he achieved, "Oh."

Feeling that the time was now ripe to thoroughly catch his host's attention, St. Juste commented in a musing tone, "Do you know, Fletcher, that Ruxart is still determined to wed as soon as possible? He insists that he owes it to the earl, particularly after this contretemps involving Manderley. I cannot say that I believe he is making the best decision, but you know what it is to try to reason with Ruxart." An emphatic nod assured him that John did indeed know. With a bland

238

smile, Armand went on, "Yes, to Nick, one chit is as another, and this one, he insists, will do as well as Helen would have done."

"This one?"

"Did I not tell you? How stupid of me! Ruxart has settled upon Caroline Willoughby."

Fletcher staggered from his chair, blanching. "Caro!" he exclaimed in a strangled voice. "But he will encourage her high spirits into every form of wildness!"

"Oh, I quite agree. But to Ruxart, you know, wildness in a woman is not altogether a fault."

"I must talk with her! Excuse me, St. Juste, but I must call in Brook Street without delay!"

"It will do you no good, you know," he yawned.

"You think to stop me?" flared Fletcher.

"My good man, I haven't the least desire to stop you," his guest protested truthfully. "But I think you might wish to know that Miss Willoughby is from home."

This quiet statement had the effect of halting Fletcher at the door. "From home?" he repeated in a hollow tone.

"Ah, yes. She is this very minute on her way to the Keep."

Color now rushed back in full force into Fletcher's face. He stood, undecided, by the door, while St. Juste made a great show of rising from his chair. "Your own fiancée is there now, bearing Helen company. Should you care to visit Miss Somers, I would welcome your escort. I leave tomorrow morning."

"To—to see Miss Somers. Yes. I—I should do so by all means," stammered the unfortunate Fletcher.

"Splendid. I shall call for you early tomorrow then," said St. Juste, leaving Fletcher looking very much as he had found him, only for a far different reason.

The object of John Fletcher's concern spun from her carriage the instant it came to a standstill and danced into her

239

cousin's waiting arms. "Helen! You sly thing! You positively must tell me absolutely everything! Was it because of Penelope Manderley or Armand St. Juste that you jilted the viscount?"

The sound of her chatter echoed to silence when Caroline entered the Grand Salon. The sight of Jane Somers placidly reading aloud from a chair angled to that of Viscount Ruxart's drove all words from her lips. She threw a fulminating look of accusation at Helen and pivoted sharply. A tone of lazy command halted her.

"Miss Willoughby! You arrive just in time. Come rescue me from the mad prophecies of William Blake."

Slowly Caro turned to see Lord Ruxart stretching out a hand. His lips were spread in a smile, but the glint in his eye brooked no defiance. Caro moved reluctantly toward him, her lower lip pushing forward, but as he took her hand he flashed her a truly warm, gratified smile and the pout disappeared before it had properly developed.

No one could withstand the viscount when he chose to be charming and for this day he was very charming indeed. Caro was soon restored to her natural good humor, even going so far as to coolly address Jane during the course of the evening. Her frank questions regarding the infamous duel caused an awkward moment over the dinner table, with Kerrington snorting in disgust and Ruxart nearly choking over his wine, but it was soon smoothed over and the meal passed in tolerable ease.

The motivation for his lordship's calculated display of captivating manners lay in his certain knowledge that Miss Somers would have removed herself from the Keep to avoid causing Caroline Willoughby distress. His efforts were rewarded when, strolling onto the terrace the following morning, he came upon the two women seated on a stone bench where Caro's bright blond head was buried into Jane's muslin shoulder. His eyes met Jane's over the golden curls and he knew that the foolish, loving child, incapable of hate,

240

had finally been reconciled with her cousin.

"Good morning, ladies," he said as he walked forward.

With a hiccough, Caro's head jerked up and she appeared poised for flight. But as Ruxart seemed not to notice anything out of the ordinary, her shoulders relaxed and she remained seated.

"Since that old fool Mallory does not allow me to ride," stated his lordship with a sigh, "there is little to occupy me of a morning. I am persuaded a stroll over the grounds would suit the purpose, but—" with another sigh—"I fear walking alone would be most dreadfully dull."

"Oh, but I'd walk with you!" declared Caro promptly.

"How very kind," murmured Ruxart smoothly. He shot a look full of meaning at Jane. "And would Miss Somers care to join us?"

"I—I am sorry, my lord, but I engaged myself to—to accompany the earl on a round of morning calls." Jane stood as she spoke. Before she could effect her retreat, however, the viscount possessed himself of her hand.

"Present my compliments to the old bear, will you?" he drawled lazily. With a dangerous smile, he bent his head and lightly grazed her fingers with his lips before they were snatched from his hold.

Departing in search of Kerrington, Jane hoped she was not blushing, for it was certain that her fingers were tingling. She found the earl in the Long Gallery with Helen, showing the young miss all the rascals and rogues that he claimed kept the name of Armytage to the forefront of every generation. Miss Somers supplied the information that should his lordship be making any calls this morning, she would be most happy to accompany him, a notion which pleased the old man greatly.

Kerrington had accepted the severing of his grandson's betrothal with equanimity. He had believed from the first that Miss Helen was not the woman to keep his young fire-eater from continually providing the polite world with all its

241

most scandalous gossip, and could not but be relieved that she had realized it, too. But the devil of it was, mused the earl, that the one woman he was quite certain *could* tame that rakehell Ruxart was now engaged to the stuffy, prosing son of Fanny's!

Fanny's prosing son was shortly to be seen making his descent from St. Juste's elegant equipage to the Keep's courtyard. As so often happens, fortune seemed determined to back an established winner, for as they entered the Great Hall, St. Juste was gratified to see the viscount and Miss Willoughby crossing together to the staircase. Gratification was not to be found among the emotions galloping through Fletcher as his horrified eyes took in the damning sight of the pair before him.

Each bore evidence of their recent outdoor excursion. The colorful bouquet of wildflowers carried by Caroline could not hide the rumpled state of her pale cambric gown, which bore condemning marks of having been in contact with the lawn. The outrage felt by John at viewing the blossom perched gaily over Caro's ear was only exceeded by that which he felt upon seeing a twin nestled into the dark locks above Ruxart's. John further found fault with his lordship's too romantic appearance: the deep blue jacket flung round his shoulders, the open neck of his linen shirt and most of all, the cynical smile dancing over his lips. The smile, however, disappeared on the instant of espying his cousin.

"John!" exclaimed Caro, her nosegay spilling unnoticed to the floor.

Fletcher bowed stiffly. "I have come to see Miss Somers," he announced rigidly.

"She—she is gone out," Caroline whispered dully.

"And Miss Helen?" inquired St. Juste, lowering the quizzing glass through which he had been surveying them.

"I do not know. . . ." she replied leadenly.

The ever-present but invisible Leaming discreetly coughed. As all eyes turned upon him, he disclosed in an expressionless voice that Miss Helen had departed with Miss Somers and the earl.

"Ah, well, I would be grateful for some refreshment while I await their return, Leaming," said St. Juste. "Come, Ruxart, join us in the salon."

Ruxart remained immobile, staring at his cousin with narrowed eyes a moment more, then, putting out his arm to Caro, prepared to follow his friend into the salon.

"I would think," announced John on a scathing note, "that Miss Willoughby would prefer to change her gown."

Immediately, Caro plucked her hand from the viscount's sleeve and fled up the stairs without a backward look.

"I would remind you, Fletcher, that Miss Willoughby is *my* guest!" flared Ruxart.

"That is only too apparent!" returned John through clenched teeth.

How matters would have proceeded cannot be known, for just then Kerrington entered the hall, regaling the Somers sisters with a mildly exaggerated exploit of his youth. Upon seeing Fletcher, he abruptly halted and interrupted his own commentary to exclaim, "What! You here!"

John's flushed face and Ruxart's equally pale one spoke volumes, but as the earl's views on argumentation within the Keep were well known, the two greeted him civilly, if with restraint.

Restraint figured largely in the atmosphere surrounding luncheon. While St. Juste and Kerrington exchanged commonplaces, the earl's grandsons exchanged a series of smoldering looks. Helen and Jane were left to entertain one another for Caro had subsided into a morose silence, occasionally reviving enough to send Mr. Fletcher what she hoped were glances of withering scorn. While mute, but meaningful, looks passed often between Helen and her new fiancé, nothing at all passed between Jane and either of the other two men present. Knowing herself a coward, she none-theless avoided them both. It seemed an agonizing length of time before St. Juste expressed the desire to see Kerrington's newest racehorse, an Arab mare the earl was certain would rival Vandyke's successes and the luncheon party dispersed.

At Armand's gentle suggestion, Fletcher followed the other two to the stables, leaving Ruxart to entertain the ladies. As he followed the women from the dining room, Helen hung back to beg a favor.

"Do, please, show Caro how you manage the trick of snapping open a snuffbox with one hand. Caro has admired the trick forever and Armand tells me no one can do it to match the way you can. I'm certain she would find it diverting to learn how it's done."

"You think she needs diverting?" he asked in the same hard tone he had used for his sparing comments throughout lunch.

"Of course! The sight of Mr. Fletcher with Jane has affected her most deeply, you know."

The viscount did know, for he himself had been profoundly affected upon seeing the two of them enter the dining room together. Thus, he was soon seated beside Caro instructing her in the art of opening a snuffbox with the flick of one thumb. She was listening attentively, her red lips pursed together, her violet eyes narrowed in concentration, when Fletcher entered the room with St. Juste behind him.

John checked on the threshold, a scowl marring his features as he took in the way Caro's fair curls contrasted against the dark locks bent so near, and the way her hand curved lightly in his lordship's as together they clasped a jeweled snuffbox.

"This is handsome behavior toward a *guest* indeed," he declared cuttingly.

The hand cupping Caro's tightened, defeating that lady's efforts to extract it. With great deliberation, Ruxart brought his eyes to meet Fletcher's. It had been said of the viscount that he had a stare more sharply pointed than the finest rapier. He aimed the full thrust of that stare at Fletcher now and remarked on a dangerous drawl, "I was not aware, cousin, that my behavior was any of your concern."

"It is the unfortunate concern of every member of this family!" snapped John, his fury fully pricked by the piercing gaze directed at him. "You can scarce let a week pass by without finding some fresh source of mud to drag our name through!"

"Does a Fletcher dare to dictate rules of conduct to an *Armytage*?"

This was asked with such savage softness that Jane felt it time she intervene. She moved quickly to stand beside her fiancé, saying as she did so, "John, I'm sure you realized Lord Ruxart was merely showing Caroline a trick of opening a snuffbox."

"Oh, I see quite well what trick he is demonstrating."

"And I see, cousin," rejoined Ruxart, at last releasing Caro's hand to stand, "that you are spoiling for an altercation. As I have the greater cause, I am only too eager to oblige you."

"Be sensible, the pair of you!" put in Jane. "You cannot come to fisticuffs in the salon. And at any rate, the viscount's shoulder is not yet sufficiently healed."

Her words went unheeded. Fletcher clenched his fists and issued a mirthless bark of laughter. "*You* have cause? Your notions of honor are strange indeed, Ruxart, but as soon as you are able, I shall be happy to instruct you in the true meaning of the word!"

"No, no!" cried Caro, jumping up to pull on Ruxart's full shirt sleeve. "My lord, he did not mean—"

"I damn well did!" broke in Fletcher furiously. The sight of Caro's gesture had darkened the angry flush staining his face.

"I am very certain, Miss Willoughby, that Mr. Fletcher meant precisely what he said," his lordship agreed. He shook free of her grasp as if shaking free of a bothersome puppy. "I shall, of course, meet you whenever and wherever you care to name, Fletcher."

Caro ran sobbing to Helen, who stood white with fright behind the viscount. Only the reassuring glance from St. Juste kept her from adding her protests to those of her trembling cousin. It was Jane who again moved to stand between the two angry young men, Jane who quietly admonished them not to be so foolish.

"I suggest, cousin, that you learn to control your future bride's tendencies to interfere where she has no business!" offered Ruxart with an ugly curl of his lip.

"I'll thank you not to concern yourself in my relationship with Miss Somers. My fiancée's behavior is, thankfully, not your affair, but mine!"

"My behavior, Mr. Fletcher, is strictly my own business," contradicted Jane in chilling accents.

"My dear, you must allow that I know best," he informed her just as Ruxart was asking St. Juste if he would again second him. Overhearing this, John addressed Armand with a grim laugh, "See that he doesn't delope this time, will you?"

Ruxart lunged forward and Fletcher stepped eagerly to meet him. Jane strode to the mantel and calmly plucked a Sèvres figurine from its resting place. She poised it in the palm of her hand, then deliberately threw it to the floor, where it landed with a resounding crash. The effect was instantaneous. Ruxart and Fletcher halted in their tracks while Caro's screeches abruptly died. Helen ran to the safety of St. Juste's arms and gawked from the cushion in his shoulder at her sister.

"Do not be thinking that I care a button what happens to either of you," Jane said with deadly calm. "I am, in fact, extremely hopeful that you will quite put an end to one another. But I will *not* tolerate your doing so in front of me!"

Admiration mixed with amusement to replace anger in the viscount's droopy eyes. "I tell you, John, you'll have to learn better how to handle this fiancée of yours."

"And I tell you, Nick—" began Fletcher in hot reply.

"I take leave to tell you both, gentlemen," interrupted Jane icily, "that I am no one's fiancée any longer! What I do now, is, as it has always been, my own concern!"

With that, the ever-composed Miss Somers shocked them all by suddenly bursting into tears and running from the room.

Chapter Twenty

She had stopped running and stood leaning against a tree, pressing her cheek into the roughness of the bark. Her cap rested crookedly atop her hair while brown curls spilled in enchanting disarray over her cheeks. She heard him halt behind her, breathing hard. An instant later his hands gripped her shoulders, forcing her to face him.

"Jane—my dear—why?" Ruxart asked lovingly.

Tears stained his hand as she bent her head to the side, trying to avoid his dark eyes. With fingers and thumb, he compelled her head upwards. She heard his breath stop, then start again. "Oh, my little love! That you should shed tears— a single tear!—because of aught I have done!"

"Please, Lord Ruxart," she whispered, vainly attempting to turn her head away.

"Nicholas," he commanded. He bent close and tenderly traced the track of her tears with his forefinger. "From now on, my dearest, my only love, you will call me by name."

"You cannot want me," she protested.

"I can and I do—terribly," he answered in a husky tone.

"When we first met you stared right through me."

"My God! You can't hold that against me! I was a green

249

youth, puffed up in my own conceit—"

"Your treatment of my sister—"

"Has been unforgivable, I know full well. And yet, Helen has forgiven me. Can you not bring yourself to do the same?"

She caught her breath on a small sob. "Oh, my lord, what *would* people say?"

The viscount very sensibly put an effective end to any further protestations by pulling her firmly into his arms and molding his mouth warmly to hers. Jane's lips parted beneath the insistence of his and tremors raced from one to the other. They swayed together as passion spiraled. Abruptly, Nick pulled away on a low groan. His hold on her constricted, then he nuzzled the tip of her ear visible beneath the ruffle of her cap.

"My grandfather will tell you, m'dear," he murmured unsteadily, "that an Armytage need not pay the least attention to what people may say."

"But I am not an Armytage," she responded shakily.

"You soon will be. And when you are, my sweet, you will oblige me by giving over this ridiculous penchant of yours for wearing ugly mobcaps." As he spoke, his fingers busily untied the ribbons of her cap. Soon, he removed the offensive article from her soft brown hair.

Jane decided she must raise no further objections to any of his lordship's notions, for she had always been told one should humor the mad. Ruxart was undoubtedly mad, for he seemed disposed to while away the remainder of the day kissing every feature of her bemused face, from the brow over each eye to the tip of her chin. When he had satisfied himself that no particular had been missed, he returned his lips to hers, where they seemed quite content to stay.

At length, however, Jane persuaded the viscount it was time they returned to the house. Since he was perfectly willing to do so upon the receipt of her promise to marry him as soon as might be, the pair was shortly to be seen passing through the Keep's terrace entrance. One step into the hall, they encountered the earl who began exclaiming the instant he clapped eyes on them.

"What the devil's come over everyone, Nick? The salon is filled with Bedlamites! There's Miss Helen resting in St. Juste's arms and that flighty young cousin of hers is dancing about insisting she's to have Fletcher after all—"

"Oh, I do hope so!" broke in Jane.

Kerrington's eyes narrowed as he suddenly absorbed the ruffled appearance of the two before him. Devoid of her cap, Miss Somers' pretty brown hair fell in disordered charm about her shoulders, while the state of his grandson's cravat could only be termed disheveled.

"Oho! So 'tis to be a match with you, eh?" he asked on a gleeful chuckle.

"Yes, sir, it most definitely is," replied Nick, smiling.

A pair of leathery lips were pressed to Jane's cheek, her hands tightly clasped in the old lord's. He set up a shout for Leaming and when the ancient servant appeared, bade him to unlock the best champagne to be found in the cellars. "And, Leaming, crack a bottle belowstairs as well! This is a celebration, indeed!"

They were fairly thrust into the salon, the earl proclaiming continuously that he had hoped for just such a match and if Jane were not treated well by his scapegrace of a grandson, he, the Earl of Kerrington, would have something to say to the subject.

The scene in the salon was much as the earl had described it, although Caro had calmed sufficiently to take a seat beside her John. Upon the trio's entrance, Fletcher glanced up to meet his cousin's eye with a sheepish grin.

"Nick, I—I did not mean any of those things I said—"

"Good God, John, do we ever mean any of the angry words we hurl at one another?" Ruxart's smile widened as he turned to Caro. "Am I to wish you happy, m'dear? Ah—but the shine in your eyes answers for you! Once we are wed, Jane and I hope that you and John will often be guests of ours."

Amid the hum of congratulations that met this statement, Helen skimmed across the room to tightly embrace her sister. "We can still have our double wedding!"

"I am not waiting two months to claim my bride," inserted Ruxart firmly. "I'd be riding off for a special license now, in fact, if your sister would but agree."

"Not until Dr. Mallory approves your mounting a horse, my love," said Jane.

Her matter-of-fact tone did not diminish the effect of her endearment. Nicholas might have been so far moved as to have passionately embraced her on the spot had not Caro startled them all with a reverberating squeak.

"But how famous! It's quite simply the best tale in years and years and to think I know of it before anyone else!"

"My dear, such a want of manners," started John.

"Tell me, if you please," Jane quickly requested, "just what made you come to your senses, Mr. Fletcher? I've known from the start how wickedly wrong it was in me to accept your proposal—you have loved no one but Caro and I . . ." She let her voice trail away while her eyes rested upon Ruxart.

It was St. Juste who replied in his sleepy drawl. "I am of the opinion that Fletcher would have failed to do so, but for the fact that as he attempted to follow the viscount out after you, Miss Willoughby had the great presence of mind to fling herself about his neck and beg him not to endanger himself further."

"And when he demanded to know why I should care, I told him it was because I love him!" the young lady put in happily.

"So I very naturally stayed to argue the point," finished John with an embarrassed, but pleased, smile.

The room was still ringing with laughter when the champagne arrived. The earl capered with delight behind each servant as glasses were passed to them all. Full glasses were raised. "To the future Viscountess Ruxart!" he declared.

It felt like some enraptured dream for Jane as everyone hoisted a toast to her, as Nick gazed steadily at her over the rim of his glass, his eyes glittering with love. As the toasts were lowered, Kerrington signalled impatiently for them to be refilled.

"I should like, if you don't mind, sir, to propose a toast," said St. Juste. With his glass held high, he pledged, "To the winning of a wager!"

A series of blank faces greeted this. "But what the deuce?" wondered Ruxart.

Studying the amber bubbles clinging to the side of the crystal, St. Juste offered a lazy explanation. "My dear Nick, had you not won our wager, or pursued Helen, neither you nor I would be celebrating our winnings now."

"What wager?" asked Caro, but no one seemed disposed to answer. The viscount threw back his head, his laughter unrestrained, while John made a great study of his finger-nails.

"Well, *I* think the money you wagered over Helen should be given back," said Jane dampingly.

"But what wager over Helen?" vainly begged a wide-eyed Caro.

"Impossible, my sweet! You must know that to return the money would be an insult. But," added the viscount with a mischievous smile, "St. Juste may have the chance to regain his guineas with a wager on whether our first is a son or a daughter!"

"A toast to the future heir of Kerrington!" cried the earl.

This prompted a round of toasts ranging from "To wedding bells!" to "To friends and relatives!" which resulted in quite the most jovial mood witnessed in the Keep in a score of years, as Leaming informed those celebrating, as instructed, belowstairs. A thoroughly musical, but definitely silly, giggle from Helen led St. Juste to suggest it was time they retired to dress for dinner. From the amount of hugging and kissing exchanged before they did so, a stranger would have been led to believe they were parting for destinations further afield than the stately bedchambers upstairs. Eventually, however, the party filed out, Caroline making one last entreaty as they did so.

"Will no one tell me about this wager?"

His lordship's hand upon her arm detained Jane from following the rest. "One moment, love. I need a word more with you." He guided her to the settee, where she released a happy sigh as she calmly folded her hands across her lap. Her head felt brilliantly buzzy and the tingling of her nose kept her pleasantly entertained while she awaited Ruxart's speech.

Ruxart, meanwhile, had begun to stride agitatedly before her. Eyeing the long, narrow hands lying peacefully together in the folds of her gown, he abruptly took his place beside her.

"You are so restful, my love."

"So you have often told me."

"I am determined to have you—life without you would be intolerable!" he said harshly.

"But, Nicky dearest, you are to have me," she reminded him. "If you think I shall let you cry off from this betrothal—"

"I must warn you, Jane, that life with me will not always be . . . comfortable."

"You cannot think I want comfort! Oh, my dear, darling Nick, with you I feel so alive! After twenty-six years of comfortable, dull, reasonable living, you are all that I could ask for!"

As if to prove her words, Jane captured his head between her hands and kissed him repeatedly, lightly at first, then with increased fervor. Nick pulled free to fold her into his arms and possess her lips with inflaming ardor. He proceeded to kiss her giddy and caress her until her body hummed with warm response.

In time, Ruxart leaned back and softly grazed her cheek with his fingertip. "I'll not make you many promises, my love," he said intensely, "But you have my word that there will be no Penelope Manderleys in our life."

"If you mean to speak nothing but nonsense, Nicky," she responded on a breathless whisper, "then I shall go change for dinner."

"Into that damned blue woolen thing, I suppose. When we are married, it shall be my great delight to deck you out in proper gowns," he murmured into the tendrils curling above her left ear. "Or perhaps," he added huskily, "I shall not deck you in any gowns at all."

Decidedly, thought Jane, the Viscount Ruxart was quite utterly mad and must be humored. She promptly did so by turning her face obediently up to meet his kiss.

MORE RAPTUROUS READING